RUFFLED FEATHERS

GRACE McGINTY

Sticks and Stone/Break My Bones

Omega Lottery:

Tryst In The Dark

Hanging By A Thread Duet:

Tangled Threads Of Fate/A Single Thread of Hope

For Duckie The Chicken and the rest of the farm. Thanks for all the inspiration.

RUFFLED FEATHERS

Prologue
Truett

Ottillie-James Baler. What a completely ridiculous moniker to be saddled with for life. The name was sweet and demure, like she should be a shy, quiet little Omega who'd just stepped off the prairie. The girl was anything but.

She was naive; that was true. She'd lived basically off the grid with her father for her entire life, but it hadn't made her shy. If anything, I was pretty sure she'd punch a grizzly bear in the nose if it looked at her wrong.

She was still undesignated, and at nearly seventeen, that meant she'd probably end up a Beta or remain Unshown, the name for anyone who didn't present with a designation before their seventeenth birthday.

She was wildly out of place here in Rock Hill, South Carolina, amongst the Southern belles and debutantes, the sweet little Omegas with soft smiles and fluttering eyelashes. It had been made glaringly obvious by the way she'd wobbled down the aisle in her three-inch, periwinkle-blue satin heels, and was further supported by the fact they were no longer periwinkle blue or attached to her feet. They were haphazardly strewn across the expansive grass lawns of the Chalmers Estate.

It had been the shoes that alerted me to the fact something might be wrong. I'd looked all around the reception for Otillie-James, but no matter how hard I looked, or what polite enquiries I made, no one had seen the runaway bridesmaid.

The idea that she had indeed run away crossed my mind. She'd been shipped down here from the wilds of Montana to the steaminess of a late Southern spring. She was always mumbling under her breath about the heat. Maybe she'd decided to hitchhike her way home.

If I had to hazard a guess, though, the weather would've been the easiest thing for Otillie-James to overcome. She stuck out like a fly in the soup here—at least according to Edison Chalmers, her new stepbrother and my best friend. She didn't know the unspoken rules, the etiquette of Alphas and Omegas, and exactly where on the social ladder everyone stood.

It had just been her and her father in the wild for too long. Despite the fact that he was an Alpha, they'd basically spent their lives out there, like they were Unshown.

I was going to need help to find the girl.

Edison was easy enough to find in the crowd; you just had to look for the group of fawning mothers and their pretty, yet entirely vapid Omega daughters. Sonny was a society catch—a strong Alpha, with a bank balance that'd make grown women get an attack of the vapors. He hated it. He was also too polite to tell them all to fuck off.

I had no such qualms. Deciding to save him, I wandered over to the group, the scowl on my face telling them all that I had zero interest in listening to their pandering drivel. "Edison, your stepfather would like a word."

Utter bullshit, but it wasn't like the old biddies could protest a request from the groom of the wedding they were attending. Sonny did a great job of keeping the relief from his face, instead smiling at them all charmingly as he excused himself.

Sonny and his mother Citrine were rich-rich. Among Southern society, they were shiny diamonds in a sea of glass jewels. But it wasn't just their fortune that made them stand out. No, it was the fact that all that money hadn't corrupted them completely.

Citrine gave away a gross amount of money every year to various charities and foundations, and it barely dented her fortune. She was sweet and kind, the epitome of a Southern Omega, and had been utterly loyal to the memory of her former Alpha, Victor. However, Sonny had once told me that she kept up the mourning widow facade to keep the fortune hunters and unscrupulous Alphas at bay. She was savvy like that, and after a few years, the opportunistic Alphas had stopped sniffing around.

You only had to look at her to know she missed

Victor, though; it was in the sadness around her eyes, the way she'd sometimes stare off into the distance. I noticed it, even back when I was barely a teen and didn't know anything but rage and mischief.

Honestly, Citrine was the reason Sonny had become the man he was. Good-natured and gentle, despite the fact he was an Alpha, and a strong one at that. Citrine had bucked the expectations of her designation, and that trickled down to her son.

For instance, Citrine had continued to work after she was mated, which baffled the Rock Hill society scene, but I understood. Behind the rich, classically beautiful Omega image, there was a kind heart and a knife-sharp mind. She'd been in college to become a geophysicist when she first met Victor Chalmers, and had refused to quit just to become someone's Omega.

Victor, by all accounts, had been a hundred percent enamored by her drive, and together, they'd been a powerhouse couple until his death when Sonny was six. Since then, it had just been Citrine and Sonny.

Until now.

I looked over at Sonny's new stepfather. Like his daughter, Buck Baler stuck out in polite society like a sore thumb. However, unlike his daughter, his gruff manner was seen as admirable, rather than something to be ridiculed by tittering teens in overly ruffled pastel dresses.

He was a tall, broad Alpha, with a neatly trimmed salt-and-pepper beard and heart eyes that shone at

Citrine every time he saw her. They'd met at some conference about rock formations in the Montana mountains, and by all accounts, it had been love at first sight. An instant scent match.

It helped that he hadn't known or cared how much money Citrine had. It also helped that Citrine didn't care he had a wild daughter in tow. Single parenthood had been something they'd bonded over, apparently.

Sonny threw me an appreciative look as we moved quickly across the lawn. "Does Buck really need to talk to me?"

I shook my head. "No, but you looked like you needed saving, and we might have a small problem."

He raised his eyebrows, loosening his tie around his neck as we walked. "What kind of problem?"

I pointed to the shoes across the lawn. "I can't find your new stepsister. Just her shoes. Very Cinderella."

Sonny's face scrunched as he stared at the shoes, before looking around, like the girl in question would just appear. "Maybe she's eating cake, or with her dad or something?"

I shook my head. "I checked. She's not anywhere in the gardens or in the house. Although, perhaps she's just very good at hide and seek."

Sonny was still frowning. "So we're... worried?"

Was that what I was? I guess, maybe a little. I didn't want Citrine's day to be ruined, just because her new undesignated stepdaughter was a flaky little drama queen.

Not that she struck me as one of those—and trust me, I'd met many—but weddings were different. Also, I kind of felt sorry for the girl. Her whole life had been uprooted. In her position, maybe I'd run away too.

"I think so. Seems unusual that her shoes are here, but she's nowhere to be found."

His face smoothed into another expression I knew all too well: calm determination. It was why he'd been both valedictorian and prom king in our senior year. In fact, it was why he'd been everything from hall monitor to class marshall all throughout our school years. Because when there was a crisis, Edison Chalmers was an unflappable leader everyone could get behind.

He chewed his lip as he thought. "I don't think we should disturb Mom and Buck with this yet. Not until we've searched at least once more. I'll check with the staff under the guise that the photographer wants some family photos, and they can search the house and grounds." He continued laying out a plan that involved everyone short of the National Guard, but I'd kind of tuned him out. Sonny would get it done. I'd played my part as dutiful almost-son to Citrine.

A flash of blue in the treeline suddenly caught my eye. A soft blue amidst the verdant green of the spring growth in the sycamore tree.

It couldn't be, right?

Grabbing Sonny and the shoes, I towed him along to the tree, kind of hoping it was a bird and not his new stepsibling up the fucking tree. Though he'd been very adamant *not* to refer to her as his sister. As he liked to point out, he'd known her for only two months and had spent a total of six hours in her presence before the wedding.

I snorted at his insistence. It had nothing to do with how long he'd known her, and far more to do with the fact that while Otillie-James Baler was wild, she was also beautiful. Or maybe she was beautiful *because* she was wild. Either way, Sonny had probably had a few impure thoughts about the girl, and no one wanted to think like that about someone who's meant to be their sibling. Talk about awkward as fuck.

Any hope I had about the flash of blue in the tree being a bird disappeared, though, because from the base of the trunk, there was no doubting that it was indeed Otillie-James up the damn tree.

"Uh, what the fuck?" I called up to her, looking around to make sure no one else was watching. I dragged Sonny to the other side of the trunk, so we were at least a little obscured by the tree.

Silence.

"Otillie?" Sonny yelled. "Are you okay?"

The aggravated huff answered that question more than words ever could. "I'm stuck. This stupid frou-frou dress is caught, and I can't get it out without dropping them."

So many questions. I raised an eyebrow at Sonny, who looked as confused as I did.

"Dropping what?" he called, a little more quietly.

More huffing, followed by the unmistakable sound of fabric ripping. She gave a tiny screech of rage. "The squirrels."

I glanced at Sonny. "Maybe someone spiked the punch?" I looked back up the tree. I really couldn't see much of her, just her stockinged feet and swaths of fabric. "What color are the squirrels, and are they talking to you?"

"Shut up, dickcheese."

A laugh burst from my lips, unbidden. Fucking hell, this was how she spoke to an Alpha? She really was going to be eaten alive by society.

Completely ignoring me, she continued to tug, her grunting getting more pronounced. "They're babies. They fell out of their nest, and I wanted to put them back. They're too young to climb back up themselves, but they'll die if they're down there for too long." The branches bounced, and now I was a little worried she'd fall out and break her stupid little neck. "But this *fucking dress* isn't made for climbing. Now I'm stuck."

Unsurprisingly, Sonny was already slipping off his jacket and loosening his tie. *For fuck's sake.*

"Look, maybe you should just leave them up there and hope their parents come back?" I suggested. "You know, the circle of life? Besides, I thought if they smelled humans on the babies, they'd reject them anyway?"

"That's not *true*," she yelled down, as if *I* was the idiot, rather than the person who was currently stuck fifteen feet in the air. "It's a lie parents tell stupid kids to stop them plucking baby birds out of their nests."

Sonny jumped and dragged himself up onto the lowest branch, while I ran a hand down my face. I was going to have to tell both Buck and Citrine that their children had ended up with broken spines on their wedding day.

Though, Sonny and I had spent our fair share of time in these trees as kids. He was already scaling it like a damn monkey. "Otillie, I'm going to come up and untangle you, and then I'll put the babies back in their nest," he called up to her, ever the shining Alpha hero.

"I don't need your help, Light Bulb!" Her strangled tone suggested otherwise.

"Light Bulb?" I asked him.

"I made the mistake of calling her Juice. You know, because her initials are OJ," Sonny called down. "I know you don't need my help, Juice, but I'm still going to come and give you a hand, because a dead child is the last thing Buck needs on his wedding day," he responded to her. His words were sharp, but his tone was cajoling, like he was trying to corral a pitbull into a tutu.

Rolling my eyes, I watched him nimbly climb the tree, like he was born to it. Maybe he was; he'd never had much fear, so he was pretty well equipped for highwire rescues.

Not me. I'd provide ground support.

I strained to see what was going on, and the soft sound of them bickering echoed back down, too quietly for me to hear the words, but the tone was enough. He was trying to herd her somewhere, and she was being stubborn. It would've been amusing, if it wasn't so dangerous.

"Stop tugging on your dress before you overbalance!" Sonny snapped, and I could hear his calming inhale from here. "At least give me the basket so you can unhook the fabric, Otillie-James."

"Don't bark at me, asshole. That shit doesn't work on me yet. I'm not designated." But I could see the flash of a baby-blue and white wicker basket being passed over. "Don't drop them," she warned, and I had no doubt she'd exact revenge for the lives of those tiny little rodents from my friend's very flesh if anything happened to them. Hell, maybe she'd designate as an Alpha. She had the balls for it.

She didn't need to worry about their furry little lives, though. Sonny was a textbook sufferer of white knight syndrome. If he dropped that basket, he'd probably dive out of the tree after it, irrespective of his own personal safety. It was one of his more annoying traits, if I was honest.

There was more huffing and puffing, which I hoped meant that she was about to climb down and I could go back to the open bar.

"Be careful," Sonny warned.

"Don't tell me what to do," she snapped back.

The rest happened in slow motion. The cracking of a branch, a scream, the sound of tearing fabric.

"Otillie!" Sonny shouted down, and then she was hurtling toward the ground, hitting branch after branch as gravity dragged her back to earth.

I watched, moving like I was in quicksand, as her dress caught on a branch and tore, suspending her ten feet in the air by the barest scrap of fabric. Racing around, I stood under her.

"OJ, are you okay?" I shouted up, catching a glimpse of Sonny's pale face above her. Her eyes were wild, and her face was white as a ghost, contorted with fear. "I'll catch you," I told her calmly. "We're family now. I'll always catch you. You can trust us, Otillie-James."

She shook her head, then screamed as the fabric continued to tear slowly.

My heart was pounding in my chest as I stood beneath her, grabbing her gaze and holding it. "Just watch my face. I won't drop you. I've got you. You have *nothing* to worry about—do you hear me?" I put every ounce of my budding Alpha power into that promise. Another tearing sound, and another squeak of fear. "Look at me, OJ. I've *got* you."

With that, the thin chiffon gave way completely, and she fell the rest of the way, her shoulder hitting a branch before she landed in my arms. Her weight crashed against me, knocking me onto my ass, but she was safely in my grip.

Whimpering and crying, she clung tightly to my shirt, like she wasn't convinced she was done falling. I wasn't sure why the sounds of her tears made my heart hurt. Maybe because her bravery was something I admired so much?

"See? Told you I've got you."

That seemed to snap her out of her terror. She scowled at me and tried to wiggle out of my arms, then hissed with pain. *Fuck.* She was hurt. Of course she was goddamn hurt—she'd just fallen out of a damn tree and hit every branch on the way down.

Shifting her in my arms, I moved her to my lap so I could get a better look at her. "What hurts? Is it your head?" I searched for blood and bumps in her honey-blonde hair, but couldn't find anything, and breathed a sigh of relief.

She dragged her head away from my probing fingers, her jaw gritted. "My arm." Still so fierce, like a little hissing feral cat.

Pulling back to look, I winced. Yep, that was broken, or at least dislocated, because it was sitting at an unnatural angle. *Fuck.*

"Is she okay?" Sonny sounded frantic. "I'm coming down."

"No!" she shouted. "Put the babies back first."

I couldn't believe this girl. "For fuck's sakes, Otillie-James. Forget the fucking squirrels. You're hurt."

She pulled away from me, her hiss turning into a moan of pain, and I wasn't prepared for the clenching in my gut at the sound. *Fucking fuck. Fine.*

"Put the damn squirrels back in their nest so we can get the princess to a damn hospital," I yelled up to Sonny.

She glared at me, and I glared back, but I was all too aware of the fact that she was basically naked in my arms, with a pinch of pain around her eyes.

Grunting a noise of annoyance, I stood with her still cradled against my chest. Honestly, I used every core muscle I had to make it seem effortless. "Did you hurt your legs? Ankles?"

When she shook her head, I put her gently on her feet, holding her steady as I grabbed Sonny's jacket from the ground at our feet and wrapped it around her shoulders. She was such a slight little thing, like a strong wind would blow her over; I probably could've wrapped Sonny's jacket around her twice. She winced as it hit her shoulder, and I wanted to beat myself up for causing her pain. I didn't let it show, though.

"Leave the nuts in the nest for the mama too," she called up, though her voice was strained. "To tempt her back, despite the fact you've been there."

This girl...

But Sonny didn't complain, following her orders quickly until he was climbing back down, wicker basket in hand. I realized it was one of the flower girl's baskets. Damn, the girl was resourceful.

"What nuts?" I asked her, trying to distract her from the pain.

"The bombo-things that Citrine picked as wedding favors."

I snorted. "You're feeding them the sugared almonds from the bomboniere? They're going to start life with diabetes." She just glared, and then Sonny landed in front of us like a fucking superhero, and I saw her eyes go wide.

Yeah, yeah, he's impressive.

"She's got a broken arm, maybe a dislocated shoulder. You need to get Buck, and she needs to go to a hospital."

She began to protest, but a stern look from Sonny made her quit. Hell, maybe I needed to cultivate that look. Sonny ran off to find Buck and Citrine, while I gently led Otillie-James around the back of the buildings toward the estate's garages. It was a little farther, but if I dragged her through the reception with only Sonny's suit jacket on and not much else, this accident would follow her for years, with the rumors getting further and further from the truth, and far more salacious.

Leading her into the garage and over to Citrine's Range Rover, I propped her gently against the car. Her face was now even more pale, and her teeth were gritted through the pain.

I slipped off my dress shirt, my undershirt still covering my torso. "Here. This will cover more than Sonny's jacket." Holding it out, I gently maneuvered it over her good arm, then buttoned it up. My fingers were shaky, and I could feel the warmth of her skin against my knuckles. I gave myself a stern talking-to about the fact she was my best friend's stepsister as I fastened the buttons over her chest, then right up to her neck. The shirt went down to her knees, and while she was seventy percent covered, there was something... appealing about her in my shirt.

Fuck. I'm going to hell.

As if he could sense the fact that I was lusting inappropriately over his daughter, Buck burst into the garage, Citrine and Sonny behind him. As they took in the scene, it took everything in me to not leap away from Otillie-James like I'd been doing something wrong.

But like the father I'd never have, Buck only had eyes for his child. I doubted her outfit even registered in his brain.

Citrine, however, looked the girl over, then looked between Sonny and I, the question—and the disapproval —silently evident on her face.

"Mom, don't even. We found her up that damn tree. The dress is still there, if you need proof. We were perfect gentlemen," Sonny whisper-yelled as Buck gently helped his daughter into the back of his SUV.

Citrine gave us the stink-eye. "And it better *stay* that way." *Or else.*

"I promise," I said, crossing my heart. It would be an easy promise to keep, because in a few months, we'd be off to college. Otillie-James would be a funny anecdote we'd tell at frat parties, and nothing more.

But as I met her eyes in the back of the car and watched her lips mouth the words *thank you,* I wondered if I'd already fallen a little in love with the wildcard that was Otillie-James Baler.

ONE

Otillie-James

Tonight, I was going out. I was dressed in black. I had my make-up on. I was feeling *fierce*. Granted, the black I was wearing was a pair of skin-tight cargo pants with a thick, hooded sweatshirt, and my makeup was just boot polish smeared across my cheeks, so I could blend in with the darkness. At least, I was pretty sure that's why they used it in all those action movies. My hair was tightly braided and pushed up into a knitted cap.

As I climbed the chain-link fence, I kept one eye on the road and the other on the junkyard in front of me. The steady thump of music from the mechanic's garage could've been because the workers were tearing down cars late into the night, but I knew it wasn't some hard-working employee.

When I'd heard about this place, it had sat heavily on my mind for weeks, until I couldn't stop myself, despite the fact this was a terrible damn decision. My parents would have my skin if they knew what I was doing. They'd have me packed up and shipped off to Nebraska to Great-Aunt Trudie's before the week was out.

Fortunately for me, Dad and Citrine were in Alaska on an assignment, doing research on the effects of drilling on the surrounding geo-something or other, and ecological landscape. They'd be there for at least a year, which meant I was down here without a safety net.

Lancelot had made me promise not to do anything rash, but this wasn't rash. I'd thought this out. I'd planned. I'd surveilled from my Fiat. I *knew* what I was doing. It wasn't rash, though it could be argued that it was stupid.

There was a burst of cheering from a hidden crowd, and I knew I had to hurry. Wiggling my way over the fence, I dropped down the other side and hoped there wasn't a junk-yard dog in here waiting to tear me to pieces. It wouldn't be its fault, but I'd still rather keep all my arms and legs intact.

Bending closer to the ground, I moved swiftly through the shadows. Luckily, there were lots of places to hide amidst the banged-up, crumbled car bodies. I was Unshown, so the Alphas inside the garage shouldn't really be able to scent me, but just in case, I'd sprayed a liberal amount of scent blocker all over myself. Even if I'd eaten an entire garlic clove for lunch and rolled in a puddle of essential oils, they shouldn't be able to smell me over the rest of the scents here.

A cat scurried away, and I watched it go. Hopefully, it was safe from the people inside these fences, but I doubted it. One thing at a time, though.

Sprinting the open distance between the last car and the dilapidated building, I aimed for the tiny half-door on the side. Slipping in slowly, I let out a small sigh of relief. Step one was done.

Inside the garage, people were packed almost wall to wall, standing around the pit. I knew what was happening in there; I just couldn't look. I tried to tune out the sounds of people cheering, the smell of cigarettes, weed, and cheap whiskey.

And blood.

Moving slowly, I hung back in the shadows. I knew exactly what I needed, and I knew where I'd find them. I just hoped I wasn't too late.

Spotting the cages on the other side of the pit, I worked my way around slowly. Slow and steady, that's what dad had taught me. He'd been talking about escaping mountain lions, but it probably worked for these kinds of predators too.

There was another roar from the crowd, followed by some people muttering curses and others boasting their achievements as two men climbed into the pit and returned with two roosters—one alive and one dead.

My stomach turned. Cockfighting. Barbaric and

cruel. I wanted to cry over being too late for those poor creatures.

I'd done the responsible thing. I'd called the cops and told them what was happening. They'd thanked me for the report and then done *nothing*. Another cockfight had happened the following weekend—still nothing.

Now, I was taking it into my own hands. I couldn't save them all, but I could save a couple. Maybe more. I had five sacks tucked into the pocket of my cargo pants. Five lives I could potentially save tonight.

They kept most of the cocks drugged, then strapped long knives to their feet, so they'd inflict maximum damage. Despite what people would argue, most roosters didn't want to fight; they just wanted to wander around a farm, pecking at worms and living their best life.

As people collected their winnings, or placed new bets, two more birds were plucked from their cages and carried to the pit. I silently apologized to those birds, that their lives would be the distraction I needed to save their competitors.

Silently, I waited until everyone was hovering over the pit, watching the current fight, before I made a break for it. Most of the birds were banging against the bars of the tiny cages, or moving their heads up and down, trying to find a way out. All except the dead bird that lay beside its empty cage like discarded trash, and the victor of the last fight, who didn't look much better. He was bleeding from all sorts of places, and looked dazed. He definitely needed medical attention.

Opening the cage, he didn't even struggle as I picked him up. I slipped the barbed gauntlets from his feet, his claws still bloody.

"Poor baby," I whispered. "You didn't want to fight, did you?" Carefully, I tucked him inside one of the sacks I'd pulled from the pocket of my cargo pants.

That's when the front doors of the garage flew open, and the night turned to chaos.

"FREEZE! POLICE! NOBODY MOVE!"

Oh, so now they decide to do something?

I threw an apologetic look to the still-caged birds, knowing they'd be okay now. Animal control would take them to some kind of rescue for fighting birds. They had them for dogs rescued from dogfights, so surely there'd be one for fighting birds? But I knew the bird in my arms would just be put down, his wounds too severe.

So I tied a knot in the bag, stuffed it up my hoodie, and crept to the back of the garage. I *couldn't* go back to jail again; Dad would murder me. Hiding behind a beat-up car, I waited until they started cuffing people before I edged around the back, toward the manhole-sized door I'd originally come through. The rooster I was holding hadn't even stirred, and I started to worry this had all been for nothing. That he was already dead.

I made it three steps before a torch illuminated my face. "FREEZE! Rock Hill PD!"

Fuck. I reached under my hoodie to grab the rooster in the bag, and shit escalated quickly.

"*Do not move.* Put your hands up!" the cop shouted,

clearly not caring that his request was impossible. I couldn't not move *and* put my hands up.

"There's a chicken in my sweatshirt. If I put my hands up, it'll fall and get hurt. I promise I'm not reaching for a weapon."

"Do not *move!*" he repeated, edging closer.

I had one hand in the air, with the other cupping the bottom of my hoodie, and as the cop drew closer, I groaned internally.

"Juice?" Francis Gunner exclaimed.

Fuck me. Of course it had to be Francis.

"Hey, Frankie. I heard you became a cop. Congrats." My voice was a little wobbly, but at least he wouldn't shoot me. "I also heard you and Sarah got married. Well done." That one, I meant a little less. Sarah Copeland—now Gunner, I guess—was a beautiful, picture-perfect Omega, who'd bullied the absolute hell out of me for the final two years of my education.

Frankie was okay, though, for an Alpha. He'd been on the varsity football team with my stepbrother Edison, and Truett, his best friend. Those two had been the ones to give me the dumb nickname of Juice, which had stuck all through my school years.

"Do you really have a cock in your sweatshirt?" he asked, and I nodded.

"Yep. I'd appreciate it if I could get it out, though, before your partner shoots me." The older man beside him looked like he was searching for a reason to stun me with his taser, and I didn't relish the idea.

Frankie laughed. "Sure thing. It's fine, Heff. I know Juice and her brother." He holstered his weapon, and I frowned.

"*Step*brother," I gritted out, but pulled the sack containing the rooster from beneath my shirt. Untying the top, I looked in, and the rooster looked up at me dazedly. *Shit, he doesn't look too good.* Tucking him back into the bag, I smiled pleasantly at Frankie. "Well, it's been great to see you, Frankie, but I have to go."

He reached around and rubbed the back of his neck. "Yeah, about that, Juice... Unfortunately, you're at the scene of a crime, holding incriminating evidence. You're going to have to come down to the station with us."

I blinked at him. "You can't honestly think I had anything to do with a cockfighting ring, right? I'm the one who nailed Oliver Petra in the balls when he kicked that dog." I'd shown him that a little kick could cause serious injury, no matter how much he'd argued that it couldn't.

Frankie shrugged. "That's between you and the detectives. For now, you better come down to the station and explain why the hell you're in a junkyard at midnight with a banged-up cock."

I ran a hand down my face. "Fine. On two conditions."

"Juice, I'm not sure you get to make condit—"

I held up a finger. "One, you swing by my place and drop the rooster off to my housemate, so it can get some medical attention. I don't want it to die." I held up a second finger. "Two, you don't call my dad." I paused. "Actually, three. You stop making cock puns, like ASAP."

Snorting a laugh, Frankie nodded. "Sure thing. Otillie-James Baler, you'll need to come with us down to the station." He held out his hand, and I carefully passed over the chicken. With a sigh, I followed him and his beefy partner out to their patrol car and climbed into the back.

This definitely didn't go to plan.

"So, you decided what? To rescue a bunch of fighting cocks?" the detective asked me again, incredulously.

"Yes."

"And you intended to steal them out from under the noses of the organizers, then leave with five fighting roosters in bags in the dead of night, on the bad side of town?"

"Yes."

"And then do what with them?"

In truth, I hadn't gotten that far into my plan. I'd figured once they were at my house, we could come up with a stage two. "Uh, maybe send them to rehab—"

The door burst open. "Otillie-James, *be quiet.*" I groaned as the Alpha in the doorway stepped fully into the room. I was going to kill Frankie. "I'd like a moment to talk with my client."

The detective rolled his eyes. "No need. We've heard

enough. Otillie-James Baler, you're currently being charged with participating in disorderly conduct, and conduct against public decency. You are also charged with trespass and theft of an animal, as well as being in possession of cockfighting instruments, i.e. the cock."

Truett Heathstone turned his disbelieving gaze my way, then back toward the detectives. "This isn't going to stand up in court; we both know it. She's a law-abiding citizen with—"

"With a previous assault charge," the detective finished. "Take it up with the DA at her bail hearing."

"I'd like a moment to speak to my client before she's taken back."

The detective shrugged and left. Truett turned his gaze on me, his disapproval a physical thing. I struggled to hold his gaze and looked down at the shiny metal table. I hated when he Alpha-d me.

"Otillie-James, what the fuck were you *thinking?*"

I lifted my chin, stubbornly meeting his gaze, even if it was only briefly. "That someone had to do something."

"And you thought the best course of action was to break and enter on private property, steal a bunch of vicious birds and… what?"

"None of your fucking business, Truett. How did you know I was even here? At no point have I ever wanted or needed your help." I already knew how, but I kind of wanted to be stubborn.

He gave me that droll Truett expression I'd seen more than a few times over the last six years. The one that made it no secret he thought I was an airhead. "Frankie called me. And it *is* my business, because you're about to get a criminal record for being an idiot."

Frankie, that traitor. I guess he'd technically followed my conditions, but had called Satan here instead.

"Fine. I'm sorry. Is that what you need to hear? I didn't think it through." That was a lie, but it was what he wanted to hear, and I could do without the ten-minute lecture. I'd rather be in the holding cell with Babette, who farted so loudly it echoed off the walls, as she slept off her drunk and disorderly arrest.

Shaking his head, Truett stood. "I'll post your bail and then pick you up. Do not leave without me, Otillie-James. I mean it."

Sure, sure. Haughty ass. Just because he was an Alpha and I was Unshown, it didn't mean he could just boss me around and I'd say, *"Yes, Sir."* I was going to lose this jerkwad as soon as humanly possible and go back to my life.

I gave him my most innocent look. "I promise."

Two
Truett

In the six years since the day I first met Otillie-James, I'd learned a few things about my best friend's stepsister.

One, she had a heart that was way too big and full of empathy, and it got her into more trouble than any single undesignated girl should be able to achieve.

Two, that empathy didn't often extend to the human species, and especially not to me. Otillie-James and I butted heads more often than not, so Sonny was always between us, playing mediator.

Three, she was stubborn as hell. So I knew with absolute certainty that when I told her to wait for me, she'd do the exact opposite.

I would bet my license to practice law in the state of South Carolina that she'd be out the door of the station any minute now, just to spite me. It was why I just sat in the parking lot, leaning against my Maserati—which she'd once called a giant cock on wheels—and waited for her to come to me.

Satisfaction hummed along my veins when the doors opened, and out came one Otillie-James Baler in wrinkled clothes, a plastic bag of her possessions clutched in her hand. When she looked out and saw me, her eyes narrowed.

Stepping back, I opened the passenger door. "Get in the car, Otillie-James."

She lifted her chin, and I could see the argument brewing in her pretty mind. I gave her my stony Alpha expression that said I would not be swayed, and that she was either getting in this car herself, or I was picking her up and stuffing her in.

Sighing heavily, she stomped over. "I can make my own way home, Truett."

Shaking my head, I herded her toward the open door and waited there until she'd buckled herself in. She glared at me like a petulant child, and I shut the door with a little more oomph than I normally would. Moving around the hood, I briefly wondered if she'd make a break for it. However, she showed a little bit of maturity and stayed in the car as I slid behind the wheel.

When her father and stepmother had gone off to Alaska, they'd made Sonny promise to keep an eye on her, which he had. Of course, that meant *we* had to keep an eye on her. She was twenty-two, for Christ's sake, not an infant. Though I guess if last night had proved anything, it was that she might actually *need* a babysitter.

Finally, the silence became too much. "Remind me again what the *fuck* you were thinking?" She just turned to stare out the window. "This is serious, Otillie-James."

"Stop calling me that," she snapped, her eyes flashing in my direction. "Tillie, or OJ. Hell, even Juice, if you have to. But stop full-naming me like you're my dad."

"Fine, OJ." My sarcasm was in full swing. "If they send this to trial, and you get found guilty, you're looking at jail time, at worst. At best, community service and a criminal record."

She shook her head stubbornly. "I didn't do anything wrong."

"You were busted with a fucking chicken at a cock-fight, OJ. That's like being busted with a suitcase full of drugs and telling the cops you were just holding it for a friend. It's hard to prove that you weren't there for the wrong reasons, and your pretty little face and innocent eyes aren't going to sway a judge."

She was seething. "I'll get a good lawyer. A lawyer who doesn't think I'm some stupid kid who doesn't think through her actions. A lawyer who'll bring up the fact that I tried to get those damn fights shut down for *weeks* before I took matters into my own hands."

I growled as I pulled off into the gated community that held the Chalmers Estate. It was always like this with her. "You'll do no such fucking thing. If I let another lawyer handle your case, they'll fuck it up, and you'll end up in jail. Then I'll have to explain to Buck why his daughter is the fresh meat at the Women's Correctional!"

As I pulled up to their gate, OJ almost launched herself out the door. "Here's fine. I can walk up the driveway without getting into trouble." I had anecdotal evidence that wasn't true at all.

I narrowed my eyes at her. She sounded a little too eager to get rid of me, which set my lawyer—and general OJ-wrangling—instincts onto high alert. So I relocked the doors and pressed the gate open button. "I'll drive you to the door. I insist."

She ground her teeth so loudly, I could hear it. "*Fine.*"

I tried to keep my amusement locked down as I pulled up the driveway, and the first sign that maybe something was amiss was a goat eating Citrine's azaleas. OJ's eyes went frantically wide, but I pretended not to notice all the goats as we drove past, and she relaxed a little.

As we pulled up in front of the house, and I unlocked the doors, OJ was out like her ass was on fire. "Thanks for the ride. I'll message you about the court case. Thanks again." She slammed the door, and I couldn't help but chuckle. As if I was just about to drive away now.

For as long as I'd known her, Otillie-James's emotions had played out across her face like a children's picture book. She sucked at poker, but would have been an incredible mime.

I lazily climbed from the driver's seat and followed her up to the door. She whirled around on her toes, looking guilty as hell. "What are you doing?"

I happened to be a great poker player, so I just looked at her blankly. "I thought I'd come in, so we could discuss your case, and how things are going to progress from here."

Screwing up her nose, she stood in front of the door. "Can't we video call or something?"

Finally at the end of my patience, I gave her a hard look. "Cut the crap, OJ. You look more guilty than a priest in a whorehouse. You know I'm getting inside, whether you come up with a million lame excuses or not, so better to just get it over with now." She looked like she was going to protest. "Or you know, maybe I could just drop by and visit some other time. I still have a key. I can just let myself in."

She looked both furious and frustrated. It was an attractive look on her pretty features. "Whatever happened to the right to privacy, Mr. Lawyer?"

I grinned. "Went out the window when you got caught at a cockfight. I've messaged Sonny too. He should be over after his shift."

She sighed heavily, her shoulders sinking. "Fine. Don't freak out." As with every time we verbally sparred, I felt both elated at winning our little tussle, and achingly guilty at her look of defeat.

Pushing open the door, the first thing I noticed was a three-legged dog with its tongue sticking out the side of its mouth unnaturally. It had bulging eyes and fur that was dishwater brown and wiry. It looked like it had died at some point, been buried in a pet cemetery, then someone had dug up its corpse and reanimated it.

"Doodles!" OJ cooed, scooping up the ugly beast. "Let me get your medicine."

Another dog bounded in, though bounding might have been an exaggeration. It hobbled in, too round to do more than waddle and wag its tail enthusiastically. Its wagging tail had tiny fat rolls around the base.

The more I looked, the more animals I saw. A small bird with no feathers that looked like something served up at a Michelin star restaurant. A cat with one ear, one eye, and a tail that jutted out at a weird angle.

And is that a fucking pig?

"What on earth..."

A man strolled into the room, holding a bandaged-up rooster, his eyes running over the full length of OJ's body. "I was worried. I was going to call the 'Whoopsie' number."

My senses tingled. A Beta.

I stepped in front of OJ defensively. "Who the fuck are you?"

The sound of OJ's sigh as she stepped around me pissed me off. "No need, Lancelot. Someone ratted me out and called it on my behalf."

I was mildly amused that I was the person she had

this... man call, if she was in trouble. "I repeat, who the fuck are you?"

He might be a Beta, but he was as big as an Alpha. His clothes were stained and had holes, and he had facial hair that wasn't even a little bit tamed. The beard made it hard to guess his age; he could've been anywhere from twenty to fifty, but I'd seen enough unhoused people on the streets to know that this guy had come from there, and recently.

OJ turned and scowled at me. "Watch your tone, Truett. This is Lancelot. My temporary housemate."

I ground my back teeth together. "Lancelot looks like he lives under Wildcat Creek Bridge."

The guy in question stared me down, no embarrassment or anything else in his expression. Stone cold. It took some serious balls—or something seriously broken inside a brain—to be able to hold an Alpha stare like that as a Beta.

The same couldn't be said for Otillie-James. Her cheeks were flushed with outraged anger. "And what if he did, you self-righteous asshat? Lancelot needed a safe place to sleep, a good shower, and access to food. This house has ten bedrooms, Truett. I had space, and he needed a hand."

I hissed a frustrated noise. "You know nothing about this guy. He could be a serial killer." I looked over at him. "No offense." His expression didn't change, but he did raise an eyebrow. "He could have raped and murdered you in your sleep. People aren't all good. In fact, I'd argue that most people are opportunistic animals, who are one unchecked, impulsive thought away from being the worst humanity has to offer. You can't just invite people to come and live with you, OJ. The world isn't a damn Disney movie."

"Don't patronize me." She whirled away and strode over to Lancelot, grabbing the chicken from his arms. "How's he doing?"

Lancelot looked down at OJ, his face softening from its cold mask. "I thought he was too far gone. I patched him up, kept him somewhere safe and warm, and this morning, he was alert and hungry. If you have any antibiotics lying about, it might be worth trying to sneak some medicine into his food. Some of those wounds were deep."

The chicken didn't look like a killer. It didn't look like a justifiable reason to end up in prison, either.

OJ nodded. "We'll keep him isolated for a few more days, and then we might try introducing him to Gert. She won't take his shit, and I'm hoping with some food and safety, he'll integrate easily. Sometimes creatures just need a chance."

At that, the girl, the man, and the rooster turned to stare at me, like I was the one being unreasonable here. Sonny needed to hurry the fuck up so I wasn't outnumbered.

Sighing like I was the most disappointing creature on earth, OJ turned and moved toward the kitchen. "Is everything okay? The kittens?"

"When it was clear you wouldn't be back, I did their night feeds," the Beta told her, and I followed along behind them, my eyes narrowed. I didn't know who the fuck this guy was, but I was going to find out.

And what kittens?

THREE

OTILLIE-JAMES

It had been a long-ass night, and I was tired. Emotionally, physically, and I was more than tired of Truett being here, judging me with his all-seeing eyes. *Asshole.* Lancelot gave me a questioning look, one that said he'd happily make Truett leave if I wanted, and I shook my head minutely.

I knew Truett's heart was in the right place, even if he was high-handed and pompous about it. He was worried about me, and granted, if I was in his position, maybe I would be too. But they'd always underestimated me—as if just because I was raised in the wilds, I was some naive little kitten they needed to protect.

I wasn't an Omega who needed to be coddled and protected from the outside world. Eventually, those two would find the perfect little Omega to finish their pack, and I'd have to rely on myself. I wasn't going to readjust my life to make sure I was kowtowing to theirs.

Despite Truett's belief that my upbringing had made me some innocent fool about to wander into a criminal trafficking ring around every corner, growing up the way that I had taught me it was that humans couldn't be trusted, and I was always on guard. Animals, to a degree, were predictable. They wanted to protect their territory, their young, and their food source. All simple desires, and if you weren't an idiot with no awareness, you'd be fine.

Humans were not predictable. Their needs and desires were varied and erratic. What one person wanted, another abhorred. Add in the different impulses of the designations, and there was no rhyme or reason to people's behavior, which meant that I tended to treat them all like they were rabid until proven otherwise.

Lancelot had gotten me out of a scrape. More than a scrape, really. I'd call it a *situation*. One I wasn't ready to tell Truett about, because he'd just use it as further evidence that I was some airhead who had no idea what was going on most of the time. Lancelot had done it selflessly, without promise of reward, and that told me what kind of heart he had.

So I owed him a lot. More than I could ever repay. I'd had to almost pressure him to return here with me, and he hadn't even given me a moment of worry since he'd arrived. He was polite and helpful, and I wouldn't admit this to anyone else, but I'd desperately needed the help. I was one more animal away from being wildly out of my depth. But whatever Lancelot had done before he became unhoused, it had been something where he'd had to think with a clear head, and he was handy with a Betadine swab and butterfly bandages.

I looked down at the rooster, eyeing his injuries, but Lancelot had done a great job. I put him back into the kennel in my parents garage, and he clucked around, but didn't look stressed. He'd come out of his night much better than I had, that's for sure.

"Let's call him Spartacus."

Lancelot snorted, but didn't disagree. Truett made a choking noise, and I turned to glare at him, but I realized he wasn't laughing at the rooster's name. He was just shocked by the garage.

I sighed. There was no way this wasn't getting back to my parents.

"Holy shit, OJ. *What the hell?*"

It probably was a little shocking. The walls of the garage were lined with kennels, many with injured or quarantined animals in them. The kittens were in a tall cat incubator, though most of them were too small to do much other than lurch around on unsteady kitten legs and nap a lot. As well as Spartacus, I had two injured pigeons, two feral cats that had received surgery and needed to be rehabilitated, and Lucifer, the world's meanest tortoise. It was lucky for the world that he was incredibly slow, but he definitely had snapping turtle somewhere back in his ancestry.

"Keep your big mouth shut, Truett. Most of these

guys will be rehomed by the time my parents get back, but the animal rescues couldn't take them immediately, and I wasn't about to let them get put down." I stared him down, my hands on my hips, and a flash of amusement crossed his face. I hated that expression, like he found me entertaining. I wondered if I could junk-punch him just once. Then he wouldn't find me so amusing.

"What you keep in your house is between you and your parents, OJ. As long as they have four legs." He glared at Lancelot again.

"You bitch-ass motherfucking shitstain!"

Truett jumped as he turned to the last cage in the room, and I grimaced.

"Give me my fucking money!"

Rufio was an African Gray, who'd been rescued from a crack house. I was only holding him until the parrot rescue in the area could find the right home for him. Unfortunately, it was hard to find experienced bird handlers who didn't have small children, or shitty neighbors who'd definitely complain when Rufio screamed the C-word at them every morning on repeat. For an hour.

Despite his colorful language, he was a sweet boy. Walking over, I put my hand out so he could step onto my arm. "Hello, handsome," I murmured, and he walked up and down my arm. He really was an amazing bird, but way too intelligent.

He eyed both Lancelot and Truett with the same beady-eyed stare, like he was plotting their demise. I scratched the top of his head for a minute, then put him back on his perch. If he was here much longer, I'd have to convert one of the ensuites into a bird room so he could get more enrichment.

Weariness washed through my body. There was always something.

The front door opened and closed, and we all turned in that direction. "Hello? Tillie? Uh, did you know there's a three-legged dog in the foyer?" My stepbrother's voice echoed along the halls, and I rolled my eyes. Man, I was going to have to do this whole speech again.

My heart fluttered in my chest, the way it did every time I saw Sonny. If being in the presence of Truett made my blood run hot in my veins, then being near Sonny made other parts of me burn. I kept that feeling locked *right down,* though, because he was my stepbrother, and this wasn't a porno.

"In the garage!" I yelled back.

In response, Rufio screeched, "You fucking cocksucker, you ate the last of the Cheerios!" It would be even funnier if whoever had taught him these phrases hadn't had a deep voice, because the lines were always delivered in the creepiest demon tones.

Truett snorted a laugh, but left the garage, probably to meet Sonny halfway and tell him about Lancelot. Sighing, I looked over my shoulder at the man in question and gave him an apologetic expression, but followed Truett out.

Lancelot whistled, and his dog, Akio, appeared. I

smiled down at the German Shepherd, as much my hero as Lancelot had been. "Hey boy, were you napping?" I asked, scratching his ears as we walked further into the house.

Sonny was there in the foyer, inexplicably holding Doodles in his arms. The scrawny little dog was wiggling like a worm on a hook, trying to lick the inside of Sonny's mouth. Sometimes I could relate to that impulse.

Smiling at me, Sonny put the dog back on the ground. "Hey, Tillie. It appears that Noah's Ark exploded in here, and you seem to have a mismatched parade of weird animals?" He came over and kissed my cheek, and I tried not to flush. He was just being friendly. Familial, even.

Don't make it fucking weird, Otillie-James Baler.

"They're just boarding here for a bit while I find them homes." A lie. Fifty percent of these animals were unhouseable, so until someone found a better place, they'd live here permanently. But I wasn't about to tell Sonny that. Or Truett.

He put his hands on my shoulders, holding me away a little so he could take me in. "You're okay? Truett said you'd been picked up by the cops." His eyes ran over me, like he was searching for injuries, both physical and emotional.

I glared over at Truett, because of course he'd made it sound worse than it was. "Just a little misunderstanding. It'll be fine once I get a good lawyer."

Sonny snorted, used to my bickering with his best

friend. "Truett's the best, and we both know it." He looked past me to Lancelot. "New friend?"

Sonny was an Alpha, but unlike Truett, he didn't try to beat you over the head with it. No, there was a steady confidence to his aura; you knew that Sonny had your back. Need a snack? Sonny had one. A Band-Aid or a tampon? Sonny had a special pouch in his rucksack filled with supplies, no matter where you were bleeding from. Need a shovel to bury a body? Sonny had one in the back of the truck and would even help you dig.

He might have a more congenial nature, but he was still an Alpha, and I knew he'd side with Truett on principle, especially when it came to threats to the people he considered family.

I sighed. "Yes. This is Lancelot. He's also living here for the moment. Can we have breakfast now? Some of us have been sitting in lockup all night. I'm starving."

I stomped out of the entryway and further into the house, a small trail of animals behind me. Looking over my shoulder at Doodles, Honkers the Lab, and Kevin the pig trotting behind me, I couldn't help but smile. I might be impulsive, maybe even a little irresponsible, but I was changing their lives, and that brought me joy. I didn't really care what Truett said, or Sonny, or my dad and Citrine. I was doing what was right.

I decided on a pastrami sandwich, because it was more brunch time than breakfast, and besides, it felt like a faux pas to eat a BLT with Kevin in the room. Now that Spartacus the rooster was around, maybe I'd have to cut out the chicken for a little while too. As long as I didn't rescue a cow, we were fine.

Surprisingly, the guys didn't follow me into the kitchen, but Akio did, coming to sit by my feet, on alert. Akio was a strange dog, both flighty and well trained. Terrified of the thunderstorm we'd had earlier in the week, yet had stood between me and... the situation I'd been in when I first met him and his owner.

He didn't mind the other animals always bouncing around him, especially Doodles, but it was almost like he didn't know how to play. He tolerated them all, even the kittens, but he was more like an old soul than an animal.

Despite that, he was sweet and loyal, and I sometimes wished there were more people with those traits. Grabbing ingredients from the fridge, I gave everyone a small treat. Doodles didn't know how to sit, and Honkers physically couldn't sit yet, but he was losing weight every day on his special diet, so I hoped he might get back more mobility soon. I'd take him out for physiotherapy in Citrine's heated pool later. I was going to have to get a pool guy in to clean out the filters before the parents came home, because I was pretty sure they were clogged with Labrador fur.

I even gave some pastrami to Kevin, who had no qualms about eating another beast of burden.

Washing my hands, I started constructing sandwiches for me and Lancelot. If I didn't make him food, or insist he ate the stuff in the fridge, he wouldn't eat. It was like he was waiting for me to yell at him for taking more than was explicitly offered—which was why I wasn't worried about the things Truett had mentioned.

Huffing a sigh, I also made a sandwich for the asshole in question, and Sonny too.

Ridiculously loyal assholes.

Four

Edison

Getting a text from Truett that he was collecting Otillie-James from the police station had been surprisingly unsurprising. Tillie was disturbingly unfazed about breaking the law in pursuit of what she thought was right. It was something I'd always admired about her.

Years ago, when she'd finally settled into society, she could have played the game all debutantes played, being demure and charming while trying to catch a rich husband. As an Unshown, though, her options would be limited to other undesignated society members, or maybe a Beta. Even undesignated, she would have had a good match, because she was beautiful, sweet, and smart. She drew your gaze with her looks, but kept it with her personality.

And her body was made for sin, though that wasn't something I should be thinking about at all. Her father would murder me, and my mom would probably help him hide my body. I stuffed the thought down and met my Packmate's eyes, trying to judge the seriousness of the situation.

Truett looked exasperated and a little pissed, which was actually reassuring. He didn't like that this guy was here, but he hadn't immediately set off his instincts. A good sign.

I'd come over after my shift, as promised, but this other guy in the house was a surprise. He looked forty? Or twenty? Maybe sixty? Who fucking knew? He had more facial hair than I could ever dream of growing, and his hair was a pale ash color, which could've been gray or could've been blond. He was a Beta, but he was only an inch or two shorter than me, and had solid shoulders. He held my eyes, but eventually, his gaze slid away.

Strong Beta, then.

Tillie had introduced him as Lancelot, but I doubted that was his real name, unless his parents hated him.

My instincts also weren't screaming at me that this guy was a threat, but I'd reserve judgment for now. I reached out my hand to shake his. "Nice to meet you. I'm Edison Chalmers, Tillie's stepbrother. I'm going to assume your name isn't really Lancelot."

He eyed me with an expression that was disconcerting, but eventually, he gripped my palm. "Lance Alcott. When I met Otillie, she must have misheard, and I haven't corrected her."

I nodded, but Truett narrowed his eyes. "So she

couldn't identify you if she went to the authorities?" I knew Truett would get someone to run the name Lance Alcott the second he got back to his apartment tonight.

The guy shook his head. "No. If she'd asked for my real name, or ID, I would have handed it over." He shrugged. "I liked being someone's white knight, I guess."

I snorted a laugh, because it was a feeling I knew all too well. "Tillie has that effect. You think she needs saving, but eventually, you realize she's fierce, and maybe you're the one who needs saving." He frowned, and I cleared my throat, letting all the mirth leave my face. "I trust her judgment"—I ignored Truett's scoff—"but just know, if you mess with her in any way, I'm going to fuck your life up so bad that living under a bridge will seem like paradise. I can make you disappear forever, and not even your dog will mourn you."

If I'd bet on him being angry or incredulous toward my threats, I would've lost. He merely nodded his head and turned toward the kitchen. Spotting the flash of silver around his neck, I realized that there might be more to Lance Alcott than simply being an out-of-work, down-on-his-luck Beta.

Truett was watching his departing back too, then turned to me with wide, disbelieving eyes. "She moved a man in here, Sonny. Some fucking hobo. You have to talk to Buck and Citrine, get them to come home."

Yeah, no. There was no way I was calling Buck and saying, "Oh, hey, do you remember when you told me to look after your only child? Well, I got busy at work, and she moved in a whole petting zoo and some strange man."

Hard pass.

"I don't get bad vibes from him, True."

Rolling his eyes, Truett lowered his voice again. "You're worse than Juice. We know *nothing* about this guy. He needs to go."

"I think he's former military," I told my friend quietly. I'd seen my share of veterans; some came into the fire department after they were discharged from the military. They held themself in a particular way—their movements were always considered, and their eyes always scanned an area, like they were trying to find threats. Lance Alcott gave me veteran vibes, and the flash of dog tags at his neck only further confirmed it for me.

Shaking his head, Truett muttered, "That might make him more of a loose cannon. She can't stay here alone with him."

Unfortunately, I agreed with him on that. She might be fierce, but she was also vulnerable. My Alpha instincts wouldn't let any threat to her stand. "Guess I'm moving back in then."

He stared at me like I was an idiot, then turned on his heel and strode into the kitchen. I followed along behind him, ready to mediate the Truett and Tillie show. I swear, they bickered like an old married couple.

I saw how he watched her, though, like he wanted to eat her alive. My best friend had had a crush on Otillie-

James Baler for years, and I was a selfish asshole, knowing that he hadn't made a move on her because of me.

We were Alphas. We needed an Omega. And Otillie-James was my stepsibling. She wasn't someone we could have a short affair with, then drop once our Omega came along. I wouldn't do that to her, or to our family.

But if I couldn't have her, he couldn't either. I didn't care how much the idea of her dating and marrying some other fucker made my stomach burn. At least my misery would have company.

I strolled into the kitchen and sat at the breakfast bar, the same one I'd eaten at every day of my childhood. Tillie pushed a plate with a huge sandwich toward me, and I smiled softly at her. She pushed one toward Truett too. Maybe she'd spat in it, but she'd still made it for him. Such a big damn heart.

"So it turns out, Tillie, that my apartment building has termites, and I have to move out for a month. So I thought I might move back in here," I lied easily, taking a big bite of my sandwich so she wouldn't ask follow-up questions. Wishful thinking.

"Oh, really. What fumigation system are they using?"

I blinked at her. "Uh, the one that's like a big tent?" How was I supposed to know fumigation systems? "Super didn't say. Just said we have to be out."

"Where's Mrs. Pentergast going to stay?" she asked lightly.

I didn't fucking know. My next-door neighbor was a hundred if she was a day, lived alone, and I swear, I'd spoken three words to her since moving in there. "Uh, with her son?"

Tillie pointed a finger at me. "You're full of shit, Edison Chalmers. Mrs. Pentergast doesn't have kids, and you can't tent fumigate an apartment building, you big dummy."

I crossed my arms over my chest. "Fine, but I'm still moving in."

She crossed her own arms. "Fine. It's your house."

I winced at the old barb, because it was my house. I would inherit it once our parents died. It would become my Packhouse eventually, and the fortune that we all lived on would one day be mine. Which made me feel guilty as hell.

My father and his family had been rich. High-society rich. When my mom had married Buck, they'd made sure that the entire Chalmers estate would come to me and not to him, partially because they wanted to protect my mother from gold diggers, but also because they wanted to preserve the family lineage.

Granted, that side of the family might have been cursing their decision now, because instead of going to college to earn a degree that'd allow me to take over the Chalmers business holdings, I went and became a firefighter.

I blamed Tillie getting stuck in that tree at our parents' wedding years ago. Climbing that tree, knowing I was the only one who could help her get unstuck, had been satisfying in a way that I hadn't felt before. Truett liked to say that was when I became addicted to being the hero, and maybe he was right.

Whatever it was, I felt like I was finally doing something I could be proud of, and I wouldn't change that for anything, despite the subtle digs my grandparents aimed my way at Thanksgiving dinner.

However, the fact that the house was mine, that the money she was given as an allowance came from the trust funds set up with my money, all that petty shit, it weighed far heavier on Tillie than it did on me. My Alpha had leapt at the chance to provide for the little spitfire. When she was a teen, she'd argued with our parents that it was charity, that she'd rather work than live off my scraps.

And she had. No one could ever call Tillie a freeloader. But I think it still irked her that she had to take some of the benefits, because she'd have to work two jobs to find a place she could afford here, and whatever she found probably wouldn't allow pets. So she was stuck in this house, and I had no doubt that most of her allowance was paying for the food and upkeep of the menagerie of animals.

I didn't care. If that made her happy, she could have a whole fucking zoo. I'd learned really early on that I wanted nothing more than for Tillie to be happy. She deserved the world, and I could give her a small slice of it, with no strings attached.

So I gave her a stern look. "It's your home too; don't be petulant. I won't get in the way of whatever"—I

waved at the zombie-dog, who was licking the floor—
"*this* is." I put my hand over hers, and she looked down at the contact like my fingers were about to burst into flames. "I just want you to be safe and happy, that's it. And I want to be someone you can fall back on while our parents are out of town. Me and Truett."

Chewing her full lower lip, her cheeks pink with embarrassment, she finally nodded. "Okay, sorry. Of course you can stay. I swear, it's not as bad as it seems, and the charges won't stick."

Of course they wouldn't. I trusted Truett to get her off the hook for that. I trusted no one else the way I trusted him; he cared about Tillie as much as I did.

Nodding, I gave her a soft smile. "I guess you better introduce me to the rest of our housemates then." I lifted my chin at the dog so fat, it looked more like a barrel than anything that was supposed to walk on four legs.

"That's Honkers. He's ten, and his owner recently went into a rest home. The rescue said he needed extensive physiotherapy and exercise, but that it would probably be more humane to just put him down." The dog in question looked up at her so lovingly, it was hard to imagine anyone suggesting he be euthanized. She scratched his head equally as adoringly, and I melted.

Late at night, I'd rage that she couldn't be mine. Sometimes I wondered if I could say fuck it to having an Omega, and just keep Tillie. Surely, even if I was depriving my Packmate of an Omega, he could see that Otillie-James would be enough.

But eventually, she wouldn't be. We'd go into rut, and she'd suffer. We might even hurt her. She was Unshown. She wasn't made for my world, my designation. The old ache in my chest burned, and I rubbed at it as she ran through all the animals on the property, along with their laundry list of problems.

But by the end, I found myself smiling more and more. Tillie didn't give up on the hopeless cases. She stood up for the underdog—literally. She believed everything deserved a chance, and that's what made her so damn special.

That's what made me love her.

FIVE

OTILLIE-JAMES

Although I lived in a city, high society was small, and the gossip grapevine was far-reaching and as noxious as a weed. Which meant I wasn't surprised when my dad video-called me later that night. I honestly considered dodging the call and sending him a generic text that pretended everything was fine, but I knew he wouldn't quit calling until he heard my voice. We both knew I couldn't lie to him if I had to see him face-to-face.

Pressing the green answer button, I pasted a cheerful smile on my face. "Hey, Dad, how's Alaska?"

"Good. Saw a Dall Sheep yesterday," he answered gruffly. "How was prison?"

I winced. *Fuck.* "It was only a holding cell, and I was just in the wrong place at the wrong time. Just a big mistake."

"You were *just* mistakenly at a cockfight on the bad side of town during a police raid?"

Damn it. I'd hoped the gossip mill had left out the reason I'd been picked up by the cops. "You know I wasn't participating in a cockfight, Dad."

"Of course not, Peaches, but you were *there*, in a dangerous situation. Willingly, I hope?" he asked lightly. I wished I could lie to him, but he knew me too well. For most of my life, he'd been my only parent, and sometimes the only person I saw for weeks, aside from my online classroom friends. He knew all my tells, knew when I was lying, and he'd call me out on my bullshit in an instant.

Sighing, I pinched my nose. "Yeah, I was there willingly, but I tried to do what you said. I went about everything the right way. I reported that cockfighting ring over a month ago, and they did nothing. How was I supposed to know that the one night they'd decide to actually do something would be the night I decided to rescue the roosters from their painful deaths by the cruelty of man?" Okay, I was laying it on a little thick, but I was in trouble otherwise. "Besides, Sonny and Truett bailed me out, and you know Truett won't let anything serious come of this. He's way too anal-retentive to accept anything but a complete dismissal."

The fact Dad hadn't led with Lancelot being here meant that whoever had tattled to him and Citrine hadn't been my stepbrother or his Packmate.

Dad harrumphed, and I changed the topic to his research up there with Citrine. They were working with some university, and while I didn't understand the complete breadth of their research, it paid them very well to be there in the freezing cold tundras of Alaska.

We talked for a little longer, and I managed to finesse him off the phone without bringing up my charges or court case again. I wasn't fooling myself into thinking that was the last I'd hear about it, but at least I might have more answers when he called again.

Moving back down the stairs to the garage, I did my nightly rounds of feeding and medicine. It was exhausting, but it gave me a purpose. It was something I was good at, and I wouldn't give that up. Eventually, I'd have to, especially once Dad and Citrine returned from Alaska, but that was almost a year away, so hopefully I'd have another plan by then.

Lancelot knocked on the doorjamb of the garage. "Do you need a hand?"

I glanced down at the six kittens, each one mewling and lurching around, like they knew it was dinnertime but couldn't find the food. They had a special incubator they lived in, keeping them warm and helping them grow, but I knew they probably missed their mother. She'd been found dead on the side of a road, with ten kittens in a nest behind a dumpster. The rescue had split the babies, and I'd ended up with six of the worse-off ones. They were hard work, though.

Looking up at Lancelot, I gave him a small smile of thanks. "Please." I handed him one of the tiny bottles, and he grabbed up a kitten in gentle hands. I couldn't help but watch. He had soft eyes; they were the reason I'd brought him home. They held empathy, but also so much pain that it made my chest hurt.

Despite what Truett thought, I hadn't just met Lancelot and invited him home like an idiot. And honestly, he hadn't easily accepted my invitation either. I'd gone back every day for a week, taking him lunch, before he'd decided I was serious in my offer, not just obligated to repay him for his kindness. He and Akio had come home with me, and he'd been nothing but polite and helpful since.

But I knew a creature in pain, and Lancelot was in agony.

I bumped him with my elbow. "I'm sorry about Truett and Sonny today. They're just protective."

He nodded, his concentration seemingly entirely on the kitten in his hands, but something about the tilt of his head, the way his eyes shifted occasionally, that told me he was fully aware of our surroundings. I didn't delve into his past; if he wanted me to know, he'd tell me. But given Akio was so well trained, combined with the dog tags I saw occasionally clanking against his chest, it was easy to guess Lancelot was military.

Despite his silence, or maybe because of it, I continued. "They've always been like that, though. When Sonny's mom and my dad married, we were both teenagers. I thought Sonny would head off to college, and then I'd only see him on holidays, you know? Truett too, though I thought I'd see him even less. But I got stuck up a tree—just one time, I might add—and they've hovered around me ever since, like I'm accident-prone or something.

"They came home every school break, and did big brother things, you know? Scaring off my dates. Calling me Juice." I rolled my eyes. "Sonny took me to get my driver's license. Truett tutored me in History and English. They really adopted me. When they graduated college, I thought they'd leave, maybe get jobs in New York or LA or something. But they just came home. Sonny's with the fire department. Truett joined a law firm in the city. Then they were here all the time, hovering like mother hens." I almost growled at how annoying they'd been, just swanning around the house, being all bossy and Alpha.

"I'd never admit it to them, but it is kind of nice knowing that if things turn to hell, they'll help me, no questions asked. But I wish they'd back off a little. I'm not an idiot." Lancelot was watching me out of the corner of his eye, and I sighed. "What I'm trying to say is that they can be blindly protective, and I'm sorry if they hurt your feelings."

He snorted. "It's fine, Otillie-James." I liked the way he said my full name, like he was rolling it over his tongue, tasting the vowels. I'd always hated my name, but I was finding a new appreciation. "They weren't wrong about my... situation. It takes more than the truth to hurt me." He frowned. "But I'd never harm you. If you ever feel uncomfortable, you can tell me to leave. No hard feelings."

"I know." I kept my voice soft, like he was a wounded animal I was trying to corral into treatment. "I like having you here." Clearing my throat, I dragged my eyes away from his dark hazel ones. "If you ever want to talk about anything, I'm here. I won't judge. I won't even speak. But sometimes if you keep your monsters locked away, they eat you from the inside out."

He didn't say anything, just cleaned up the kitten and picked up the next one. I let it drop; gouging your fingers in someone else's wound wouldn't help them heal.

We worked in silence for a little while, and I was surprised when it was Lancelot who broke it first. "You know my name isn't really Lancelot, right?"

I couldn't help the laugh that burst out of me, which startled Rufio the parrot, making him call me a noisy cocksucker before settling back down to sleep. "I figured. But it suits you, so I decided I'd continue calling you that, until you were ready to correct me." I looked over at him. "Are you ready?"

Lifting his chin, he looked like he might be smiling beneath that bushy beard. "Lance Alcott. It's an honor to meet you."

My smile pulled my cheeks tight. "Otillie-James Baler, and the honor is all mine, Mr. Alcott. Do you mind if I call you Lancelot still? Or do you prefer Lance?"

He chuckled and picked up another kitten. I didn't think I'd ever heard him make that deep, rumbling noise before. He was always so serious. "You can call me whatever makes you happy, Otillie-James."

Grinning, I grabbed the last hungry kitten. "Lancelot it is."

The front door opened, and I heard Sonny announce himself. My heart thumped in my chest, and I told it to behave itself. This stupid crush couldn't go anywhere. What I hadn't told Lancelot was that I'd both hoped for and dreaded the thought of Sonny and Truett leaving to work on the other side of the country.

I knew I needed distance, so I could get over these stupid residual teenage crushes. As in *crushes*, times two. But I would have been devastated all the same, if they'd left.

Falling in love with your stepbrother was cliché, but before they'd registered themselves as a Pack, I'd sometimes thought that maybe I could tell Truett that I liked him. But then I'd decided I couldn't come between them.

I mean, it didn't stop me fantasizing about coming between them. In a more literal sense, though. On those days, my battery-powered arsenal got a good workout.

It would remain a fantasy, because I was Unshown. Worse than a Beta, I couldn't calm an Alpha's emotions. I couldn't provide what they needed during a rut. I'd never be able to bear their children. Couldn't take their knot.

No, it was better if I moved on, and to do that, they

needed to be far away, where I didn't have to see their pretty faces every day. Or worse, where I didn't have to see them get a beautiful Omega girlfriend, who'd turn into a fiancée and then a wife.

I wasn't sure I could deal with that kind of heartache.

Sighing heavily, I cleaned up the last kitten. "Let's have some dinner and watch a movie. What do you think?"

Lancelot hesitated. "Sounds good. But, uh, do you think I could borrow a pair of hair clippers first?"

I kept my smile to myself, putting on my best poker face. "Sure. I'll grab them for you now."

We were making progress, and that felt like something important. I wouldn't dwell on what I couldn't have, and instead find joy in what I already did have. That was all I could do.

SIX

LANCE

Akio whined and leaned hard against my legs as I used the clippers to shave off the bulk of my beard. I was shaving into a hand towel, and I'd put it outside for the squirrels or birds or something to make nests with, because Otillie-James would like that.

More and more, I worried what that girl—who was nearly a decade younger than me and far more innocent—would think of my face. I cared about what she'd like.

And as I unveiled the scars on my cheeks, I worried if they'd scare her. They weren't pretty. In fact, they were red and raised, and tended to terrify small children. It was why I'd let my beard get so bushy; it covered the places that couldn't grow hair anymore because of the scarring.

I was breathing hard by the time I'd trimmed it down, until it was less than half an inch long. I looked at the mangled wreckage of my face. The scars were still pink and raised, but they were starting to fade. Akio barked softly, barely more than a chuff really, and I reached down and buried my hands in his fur, centering us both.

Akio wasn't my dog, but when we'd both been medevaced from our mission, we'd been the only surviving members. We were partners. Kindred spirits. He'd saved me more times than I cared to think about over the last six months.

Wetting my dry lips, I looked down at him. "What do you think, boy? Will it scare her?"

He tilted his head at me, the golden-brown of his eyes feeling far more intelligent than they should be. He'd seen things; we both had. Things I couldn't explain, couldn't relive—not to the VA shrinks or my family, or even other veterans. Things I just wanted to forget.

There was a loud knock on the door, and my heart leapt in my chest as I reached for my knife.

"Lancelot? It's just Tillie. I brought you some of my dad's old clothes. You're about the same size. I thought you might... I don't know. Um, it just occurred to me that you might find it offensive that I brought you clothes. But you don't seem to have many, and my stepmom said to me, 'Three t-shirts and a holey pair of jeans does not a wardrobe make' once upon a time, and I didn't know if you'd like a few options or something, so... yeah." There was soft muttering behind the door, and I could almost hear her chastising herself.

I chuckled softly, a sound that had been almost foreign to me until a week ago, and walked over to the door. Opening it on a pink-cheeked Otillie-James, I watched her eyes widen, then they wandered south, before snapping back to my face.

Fuck. I forgot my shirt.

Shutting the door quickly on her, I grabbed a shirt and threw it on. Panic set in, gripping my chest in a vice that squeezed, and Akio whined louder. He licked at my fingers, mouthing them gently, distracting me from the panic attack that was trying to creep in.

I concentrated on the warm slobber, the feel of his teeth against my curled fists, and pushed the panic back down. It was okay. This was my body now, and although I didn't know everything there was to know about Otillie-James Baler, I knew she wouldn't care about my wounds.

Sucking in large breaths to fill my constricted lungs, I pushed the panic from the edges of my vision, straightening. I felt so stupid, worrying about something as inconsequential as how I looked, when most of my team had come home in pine boxes. Guilt sat like an anvil on my chest, a familiar tormentor.

"Lancelot?" Her light voice was filled with worry, contributing more guilt to the already overfilled well of it that sat in my stomach.

I opened the door again, ignoring the questions that were written all over her expression. I reached out and took the clothes from her, hoping I could divert her from what she saw. "Thank you. Are you sure your father won't miss them?"

Picking up my cues, she made a skeptical sound and waved a hand. "Most of them still had tags. He's been wearing the same threadbare band shirts and flannels since I was four. Citrine likes to shop for him, though, so he has a closet of clothes he's never even seen. Trust me, it'll be fine." Her eyes ran all over my face, as if she was assessing me for injuries, like the banged-up rooster or a three-legged mutt. "Your beard looks nice. Rugged."

"Not like a hobo from underneath Wildcat Creek Bridge?"

She winced guiltily. "He's an asshole."

Yeah, he was, but I didn't blame him at all. If I found someone who looked like me in a house with my sister, I'd assume the worst.

Narrowing her eyes at me, she chewed her plump lower lip. "Would you like me to give your hair a trim? I cut my dad's hair until I was sixteen, and he managed to bag the most eligible widower in the Southern states, so I come with good reviews." She waggled her eyebrows at me.

Fuck, she was cute. And good. Way too good for someone like me. I didn't deserve to even think dirty thoughts about someone this sweet.

Still, I found myself nodding, and she pushed me toward the toilet seat. "Sit, sit. I know I left the scissors in here somewhere." Deciding I was now okay, Akio trotted out of the room. "I'm in charge of all the grooming at the pet daycare where I work, so I have a pair of shears here somewhere." She looked up at me and winced. "I mean, they've been cleaned and sterilized, and dog fur and human hair are basically the same thing." I liked how she looked at me, as if I'd be offended she was using the same scissors on me as she did on some fluffy dog, like she hadn't *literally* found me living under a bridge.

I raised an eyebrow back at her. "There've been worse things in my hair." *Like mud, sludge, my best friend's internal organs...*

Pushing the darkening thoughts away, I concentrated on the way she moved. She seemed to take up too much space in the tiny bathroom, but not because she was physically large. She couldn't be more than five and a half feet. She seemed to have terrible spatial awareness, though. She'd already jammed her fingers in the second drawer and banged her elbow against the towel rail, and given the way she barely flinched, I was fairly certain that was something she did often.

"Ah-ha! Here we go!" Pulling out a little pouch, she unzipped it and eyed her tools seriously. Settling on a set of shears, she moved closer. She wrapped a hand towel around my shoulders, her fingers touching me lightly.

I bit the inside of my cheek so I didn't focus on that sensation. I had no right. If I kept repeating that to myself, it might eventually sink in.

"So, what are we thinking? Your options are basically short back and sides, or a poodle bouffant."

Chuckling, I shook my head. "I'll leave it up to your creative direction."

She cackled evilly. "Brave man. Poodle bouffant it is."

Spraying down my hair with a bottle she got from beneath the sink, she went to work. Silently at first, and I could see her concentration in the vanity mirror. A crease worked its way between her eyes, her tongue peeking out from between her teeth.

I didn't interrupt her, happy that the comfortable silence between us gave me the opportunity to watch her work. She kept the thoughts away, even for a moment, and that was enough for me.

Tufts of hair fell to the floor at our feet, until eventually, she broke the silence. "I wanted to thank you again. For what you did when we met. And for not telling Truett and Sonny about it."

I didn't say anything, because I wasn't sure I shouldn't mention it to her brother. She had put herself in such a dangerous situation, and I was fairly sure she didn't have any regrets about it.

She'd been down off the freeway, by herself, after hearing a report of a dumped mother cat and kittens, or so she'd told me later. What she'd found instead was a group of local teens trying to drown them. Instead of deeming it unsafe, Otillie-James had thrown herself into the group and attacked them. There'd been six of them, who'd probably never seen any kind of discipline, like the rules of society didn't apply to them. They'd decided that Otillie-James would be better sport than the kittens.

I shuddered, though I kept it locked down, as the what-ifs rolled through my mind once more. What if I hadn't been nearby? If they'd been a little older, had been

Alphas instead of still undesignated? If I didn't have the experience I had? If I hadn't had Akio with me?

All the possibilities of those what-ifs made me shudder. The bright, pure light that was Otillie-James would have been snuffed forever, for no reason, other than that humans were cruel and preyed on those they considered weak. As it was, by the time I'd stumbled upon them, her shirt had been ripped, and someone had pulled a knife.

Sucking in a deep breath, I gently chastised her. "You risked your own safety. You have to promise not to do that again. Call for backup or something."

She chewed her lip. "If I'd waited for backup, the kittens would be dead."

"If I hadn't been there, *you* would be dead, or wish you were." There was nothing gentle about that—it was a harsh, ugly reality. Even though I'd been there, it still hadn't been a sure thing. Six on one wasn't easy, despite what the movies would tell you. I was a Beta, albeit a well-trained one. It would've only taken one or two with an Alpha designation to shift the tide of that fight. People also didn't tend to wait until their turn; they'd rush with fists and weapons, trying to swarm you until you were under boots, being crushed one kick at a time.

Luckily, they'd been young and inexperienced, and Akio was a well-trained dog of war. It had evened the odds.

Otillie-James was silent as she threaded my hair between her fingers and snipped at the ends. I reached up and gripped her wrist, stilling her hands. "Better the kittens than you. Wait for someone else. Call me—I'll drop everything and come straight away. Never alone again, okay?"

I could feel the quick beat of her pulse beneath my fingers. She met my eyes in the mirror, and I tried to make my expression as authoritative as my Beta designation would allow. I couldn't bark her into submission like an Alpha. She needed to promise me this of her own volition. The idea of a world without this girl caused an ache in the place my heart should be.

Finally, she nodded. "Okay, I promise."

Something settled in my chest. I might not always be around, but while I was, she would be safe.

SEVEN

TRUETT

"I don't know, Truett. Where did you say you got this name?"

I cleared my throat. "It came up as a person of interest in a case that I'm working on." Which wasn't a lie. It had come up in OJ's case.

"Definitely military, but his file is locked down tight. Was discharged six months ago, though no fixed address, according to his VA records. He was pretty severely injured by an IED, and has more metal in his body than the Terminator. No records between the time he enlisted in the Marines to the time he was discharged. A ghost in the wind, basically."

My buddy Tim over at the VA had done a search on the name Lance Alcott for me, and I wasn't really surprised by those results. There was an underlying feeling of danger around OJ's new housemate, and it had set all my senses tingling, despite his designation.

"Tim, you sure this is our guy? How old is he?"

"Caucasian, aged thirty, six foot three. Sound about right?"

My jaw tensing, I made an affirmative noise. Who the fuck did OJ have living with her? "Yeah, that's him. Anything in his file that suggests he might be mentally unstable?"

Tim laughed. "We're all a little unstable, Truett. But whatever he saw, they gave him a service dog to help, so yeah, I'd say he has a good dose of PTSD." He paused. "Actually, the service dog is a retired MWD. That's a military working dog."

Yeah, that sounded like the antsy German Shepherd who'd eyed me like he wanted to rip my arm off at the front door.

"Thanks, Tim. I appreciate the help, man. We should have drinks sometime this month." We made a little more small talk before I hung up, slumping back into my office chair.

Corporal Lance Alcott from Wisconsin. What was he doing here in South Carolina, and what was he doing in my best friend's childhood home, befriending his stepsister?

I went back to looking at the police report from OJ's arrest. As Frankie Gunnar had told me over the phone—when he'd giddily informed me he'd taken her to lockup —she'd been caught fleeing the crime scene with a half-dead chicken under her sweatshirt. Frankie had said that if it had just been him, he would've let her go. But his partner was a hardass and followed the rulebook like it was his religion, so Frankie had been forced to take her in.

The investigation around the cockfighting was rushed and hasty, and if I was representing one of the ringleaders who'd been caught in the bust, it would be easy enough to pick it to pieces. However, I was fairly sure that OJ would skin me alive if, while getting her charges thrown out, I got everyone else's thrown out with them.

I had to find a way to extract OJ, and somehow use her to solidify the remaining charges. I needed to convince the DA's office that it would be more hassle than it was worth to pursue baseless charges.

Which meant talking to Strat Wilmington. *Pompous asshole.* There was something about his good old boy, affable nature that always pissed me off. It wasn't because he was an Omega, either. I was totally okay with Omegas in the workforce. Respected it. Citrine was like a mother to me, and she would beat my ass with a Manolo if I ever suggested that Omegas shouldn't get higher education and a chance at their dream careers, just because of their designation.

Stretching, I rolled to my feet with a yawn. OJ wasn't the only one who'd been up all night. But despite my tiredness, when I lay down on my bed in my penthouse apartment, the only place I wanted to be was back at the Chalmers estate with Sonny and OJ. I wanted to be wherever her chaos was.

I contemplated messaging her, but instead, I texted Sonny. If I tried to talk to OJ again today, she'd probably find a way to castrate me.

> Me: How's Juice?

> Sonny: Annoyed. Maybe a little guilty. She's playing barbershop with her white knight.

> Me: My contact at the VA says he's a former Marine. PTSD. He needs to get out in case he snaps and hurts her.

I felt like an asshole, but I would fucking piss off every person between here and D.C. to protect the people I considered mine.

And Otillie-James Baler was definitely mine.

> Sonny: He seems all right. I'll watch him, though. Maybe we should make sure one of us is here whenever he's around. I have some leave saved up anyway.

Yeah, OJ was probably going to be the one to snap if we were around all the time, but I didn't care. Her safety came first.

I grinned at the idea of riling her. Fuck, she was something to behold when she was angry. You could almost *feel* electricity crackling off her skin and you didn't know whether she wanted to kiss you or punch you in the face. She was passionate, and in our world, that was something rare. In high society, they bred women the same way they bred frou-frou dogs—even-tempered and with a good pedigree.

Grabbing my laptop, I took it into the living room and tossed it on the couch, before pouring myself a couple of fingers of whiskey. I loved my apartment, but tonight, it felt empty. I mean, it *was* kind of empty; the interior designer had called it minimalist.

Sonny and I had been talking about buying a Pack-house for a while now, but while it was just the two of us, it hardly seemed necessary. We could wait until we found an Omega, and she could choose where we lived when we started our Pack life together. Still, tonight I wished that we'd taken the plunge already.

Slumping down on the couch, I turned the TV onto the news channel and opened my laptop to view the files sent to me by Frankie. I'd put in the formal request, but Frankie had helped me out by getting it to me earlier.

It seemed pretty basic, as far as an investigation went. Kind of run-of-the-mill police work. After three complaints by a member of the public—no awards for guessing which member of the public that was—an investigation had been opened in coordination with the ASPCA. There were notes about conversations with informants, followed by a little lapse in any groundwork before the animal welfare officer contacted the police with information about a possible event being held last night.

The reports from last night's raids were all pretty succinct. At least twelve people had been picked up, but they'd clammed up almost immediately. Some had previous charges, ranging from assault to animal cruelty, which wasn't a surprise. There was also a note about a suspect being arrested in possession of a bird, and I rolled my eyes.

Damn Otillie-James Baler.

There were just lists of names. Eventually, more accounts would come through once I got the official reports, but in the meantime, I stared down at the list of names and mugshots. None of them meant anything to me, but it wouldn't hurt to do a little research. I sent off a request to the district attorney's office to get a meeting with Strat Wilmington, then shut my computer.

Strat and I had been in the same year at Berkeley, competitors in every way, despite being in the same frat, the same classes, the same everything, except I was an Alpha and he was an Omega. Not that his designation hindered him in any way. We competed for grades, girls, and extra-curriculars.

No one had been more surprised than I was when he became an assistant DA, but I had no doubts he had something bigger planned. This was just a rung on whatever ladder he wanted to run up, probably to become a judge. Or maybe President. Strat always had some lofty goals, along with the cunning to achieve them.

Fucking dick.

Exhaustion raced through my body, and I laid my head back on the overstuffed cushions of the couch. It had been my only demand of the interior designer. I didn't want to sit on some skinny, hard couch at the end of a long day. I wanted something soft that molded to my body.

I snorted. What I *really* needed was to get laid. Opening a designation-only dating app on my phone, I spent thirty minutes flicking through profiles. They all looked the same—a reflection of what society thought men wanted. They were mostly Betas, but there were a few Omegas on there, even a couple of ballsy Unshowns.

But no one was right.

Who was I kidding? They weren't right, because they weren't my best friend's stepsister. I was so fucking screwed.

So for the millionth time since she'd landed in my arms as a teen, I found myself opening my pants and pulling out my cock. Spitting on my hand, I stroked myself to the thought of Otillie-James Baler.

Her plush mouth. Her curvy little body. Her lush tits.

I imagined her on her knees in front of the couch, licking her lips as she eyed my cock in my hand. I'd tell her to suck me, and her eyes would flash with defiance, warring between wanting to taste me and telling me to fuck off. And then, when she was good and ready, she'd take my cock in her mouth and swirl that pretty tongue around my head. She'd suck me down until I hit the back of her throat.

Gripping my dick harder, I pulled it almost violently. Spreading around the precum, I imagined pulling her onto my lap, pushing myself inside her, my face right between her tits.

Fuck. Fuck...

I stroked harder and faster, my imagination getting more and more depraved as I imagined all the ways I wanted to fuck her. Imagined placing my teeth on the curve of her shoulder and biting down, claiming her as mine.

My release shot up my spine, and too soon, I was blowing my load all over my abs. I let my head flop back onto the couch again, sighing as the pleasure gave way to the guilt chaser that inevitably followed.

We weren't that far apart in age, but something about jerking off to OJ always felt forbidden. Like I was sullying something good and perfect.

Sighing, I used my shirt to clean myself up and hauled myself to the shower.

EIGHT
OTILLIE-JAMES

You didn't rescue animals for a hobby without befriending a vet or two, and Anakie Remorne had quickly crossed the line from professional acquaintance to friend. As I stood Spartacus on the metal table in front of her, she was trying hard not to laugh as I explained that I'd been picked up for cockfighting, then been busted by Truett and Sonny for having a veritable farm at the house.

Anakie was a few years older than me, a Beta in her late twenties, and she ran the vet clinic with her husband Rex, a six-foot-six former Australian rugby player, who was one hundred percent Alpha. They had an Omega and another Alpha at home, who would all tease me just as mercilessly next time I came to dinner.

"You should've called me. I could've picked up the rooster and treated him, rather than putting that on your new... friend." Unlike Truett and Sonny, Anakie didn't think I was an idiot. However, when I'd brought the kittens in for their vaccinations, I'd mentioned Lancelot. Rex and Brock—Anakie's other Alpha—had appeared at my house that night and "talked" to him. I didn't know what had been said, but I assumed it was to tell him that they could murder him and no one would ever suspect a thing.

I raised an eyebrow at her. "Well, I didn't have a lot of time to give instructions, considering I was in the back of a cop car. By the time Truett bailed me out, Lancelot had already patched him up, or I would have brought him in myself."

Anakie hummed, but listened to Spartacus's chest and checked his lacerations, giving him the full work-up. I couldn't do half the rescues I did without her help. I wasn't an endless fountain of money, despite Citrine giving me a credit card and telling me that I could use it for whatever, whenever. I really didn't want to take her money. I had a work ethic, even if this wasn't a typical nine-to-five job.

I worked at a doggy daycare three days a week to pay for most of the food costs for the animals, but medical expenses were another thing altogether. Sonny would probably give me the money in a heartbeat, but I didn't want to rely on him for that. I'd hate for him to think I was a gold-digger. I'd heard it enough when I was in high school—how my dad was only with Citrine for her money, that we were trash, trying to slither our way into polite society. All that crap.

It was complete bullshit. My dad *adored* Citrine. He would love her if she had nothing. He'd lie down on a fire ant nest for her. Fight a grizzly. Even wear a tuxedo.

Finally, Anakie wrapped her stethoscope back around her neck. "He's in generally good health, considering his lifestyle before you rescued him. I'll give you antibiotics for his wounds, but you should still keep an eye on them. If they start to weep or smell bad, bring him back. You know the drill." She peeked around the doorway toward the waiting room, before leaning closer. "Mrs. Pilzner and her schnauzer are out there, so be quick. How's your stepbrother reacting to your new roommate? I bet that came as a surprise."

I shrugged, because honestly, Sonny had been pretty chilled out about it. "Not bad. I gave Lancelot a haircut, and he shaved yesterday, which makes him look a lot less..."

"Wild?" she supplied, and I nodded. I swallowed hard, hoping Anakie wouldn't read too much into it.

More than just looking more civilized, Lancelot now looked handsome. So fucking handsome. Battered and scarred, but instead of making him less attractive, it somehow made him beautiful. Like he was a brass statue that had once been shiny and new, but now he'd patinated into something breathtaking.

I didn't know his story; I hadn't pried. But the amount of damage he had on his body, especially his face and chest, told me he'd been through something. That he needed more help than I could give him. It was more than just needing a hand up, a warm place to stay, and food in his belly. It felt like he also needed a professional to heal the wounds festering below the surface.

I knew he was wounded there too. It was in the way he'd watched me last night, his gaze as injured as the skin of his cheeks. And his very fine chest. And abs.

Man, his abs.

"What's that face?" Anakie asked, eyeing me suspiciously.

I wiped my expression clear. "What face? I better go. I might introduce Spartacus to Gert today, so he has a bit of company." Gert the goose was grumpy, but she could be a real mother hen when she wanted to be. She'd once adopted two baby birds. And a baby bunny that had appeared from god knows where. I'd even had to steal one of the foster kittens back, after she'd managed to herd it into her nest. She wouldn't take Spartacus's shit, but she'd take him in.

Anakie's snort was sympathetic as she stroked Spartacus's head. "Good luck, buddy. You'll need it with that old battle-ax." We talked a little longer about everyone else's needs, and I got more kitten formula.

Then, as I was leaving, Rex appeared. "Come for dinner this week. We'll put something on the grill and have a few beers. You can even bring your mate Lancelot." He grinned, showing dimples that I knew had suckered Anakie in the first time they met. "We'll even bake you a cake with a nail file in it... You know, for next time."

I flipped him the bird, very subtly since there were other people here, and I'd already embarrassed my family enough for one day. "Better come to mine instead, so Anakie and Sophie can get white-girl wasted with me." Sophie was their Omega. "Besides, Sonny's staying at my place too, and he'll be sad if he's left home alone. Also, my dad got one of those Blackstone things before he left, and I'm pretty sure he said I was supposed to use it."

Rex looked horrified, muttering about seasoning and regular use, like outdoor cooking was a religion. Shaking my head and promising to call, I paid my bill, got the meds, and headed back to the estate.

After dropping Spartacus back home, I immediately left again to run errands. Lance and Akio weren't at home, and I tried not to worry. He was a grown-ass, capable man. He didn't need me to coddle him. It was good that he was leaving the house.

But still, I felt anxious.

I distracted myself by going to the tractor supply store on the outskirts of town to pick up my weekly feed order. I also grabbed a cheesecake from Jill's Cheese-Cheeks, which was a bizarre name, but they made a Basque cheesecake that could make you weep tears of joy.

When my phone rang on my trip home, I almost didn't answer it. Truett's name flashed across the screen, and I was already rolling my eyes. "Hello, you've reached Finding Screamo, South Carolina's only sex store and bait shop. Unfortunately, we can't come to the phone right now—"

"*Otillie-James,*" he said in an exasperated tone.

I snorted. "Oh, Truett, it's you. What can I do for you?" I'd never admit it, but I'd always lived for the snarky relationship I had with Sonny's best friend. He challenged me. He didn't look at me like I was a vulnerable piece of glass, the way my Dad—and even Sonny—did. He looked at me like I was a honey badger about to gnaw off his hand. I loved that, even if he did drive me insane.

"I need you to come down to my office today. I've got a meeting with the assistant DA, and I was hoping you'd come with me—maybe give him that look, like butter wouldn't melt in your mouth, and convince Strat to change his mind about prosecuting you."

I raised my eyebrows. "Strat Wilmington?" There couldn't be that many men named Strat, even in the South. "I was friends with his little sister Elizabeth before she moved to California." Elizabeth Wilmington was beautiful. An all-American kind of beautiful, like a doll with a perfect heart-shaped face, a button nose, and dazzling blue eyes.

But she listened to metalcore music and hated the world, high school, her parents, and anything to do with high society. We'd bonded immediately, outcasts of the upper class. No one had been more surprised than me when she'd designated early as an Omega, then immediately ran away to California to be a model.

While I'd never out her, I was fairly sure she was gay. It was part of why she'd rebelled so hard. If being poor and from the sticks was a reason to be ridiculed, being a lesbian and an Omega would have been abhorrent to the society matrons. She'd been expected to marry young, produce blue-blooded Alphas, and live miserably ever after, just like they had.

I was glad she'd gotten out.

Truett grumbled. "Yes, that Strat. He prosecutes for the district attorney's office now, and he's got the animal cruelty case."

Well, that was a relief. I'd met Strat a couple of times during my friendship with Elizabeth. He was around the same age as Sonny and Truett, but they'd gone to different private schools. Elizabeth had been kicked out of that school for smoking in the bathrooms, which was a well-kept secret. Publically, her parents had just suggested that the new school was better suited to her ambitions. Her ambition had once been to overthrow a government, so I wasn't quite sure how another snooty private school would have helped that.

Either way, I'd found Strat to be nice. Elizabeth had adored him, and she'd tended to hate everyone else, and even barely tolerated me, so if that wasn't an excellent reference, nothing was. He'd been polite and welcoming, basically the exact opposite of his parents.

I knew he'd gone on to become a lawyer, but half our graduating class had gone on to be a lawyer, or business consultant, or a banker. Some big-money bullshit that was generational, rather than earned.

What I hadn't realized was that he knew Truett, or

that they operated in the same circles. I hadn't spoken to Elizabeth in far too long. I made a mental note to catch up with her, maybe send her a message.

"Well, that's good news. He must know I'm not out here killing chickens for fun. So why do you sound like someone just pissed in your Wheaties, True?"

He growled down the phone line, and the noise made something tighten low in my abdomen. I squashed down the feeling. I was only allowed one inappropriate crush, and right now, I was pushing my luck with Lancelot. And Sonny.

Who was I fucking kidding? Truett had been a frequent star in my dirty dreams for a long time, not that I'd ever admit it to him or anyone else. Ever.

"I just don't like the guy, that's all."

Hmm. I had a suspicion that it was more than that, but Truett was a surly bastard, so maybe it was that Strat rubbed him the wrong way.

"Can you make it?"

I looked at the cheesecake box, knowing it would be a giant waste of time to go all the way home to put it in the fridge, only to trek back down the freeway again. "Fine."

Twenty-five minutes later, we stood outside the DA's office downtown. Truett was dressed in a beautifully tailored three-piece suit that made him look delectable, if it wasn't for the scowl on his face.

"If you aren't careful, the wind will change, and your face will look like a cat's butthole forever," I teased him lightly. "You don't have the personality to pull off a butt-hole mouth and still get laid."

Giving me an annoyed look, he gently nudged me into the foyer and past the security desk. The guard eyed the box of cheesecake suspiciously, but seemed to decide it wasn't anything nefarious.

Jabbing the button for the elevator, Truett looked at the box with annoyance. "I can't believe you brought a fucking cheesecake to a meeting with the person who literally wants to put you in jail."

I shrugged. "Citrine said it was polite to bring a gift anywhere you go." I didn't add that the whole thing had originally been for me. Better he thought I was just embracing Southern hospitality. His expression said he knew I was full of shit, but fortunately, I was saved by the elevator doors opening.

There was a reception desk, the assistant behind it a stunning redhead. She gave us a bright smile, her eyes lingering on Truett. "Mr. Heathstone, welcome. Mr. Wilmington will be with you shortly. Can I get either of you coffee, water?"

I shook my head, though she wasn't even looking at me. Truett gave her his most charming smile, the one that didn't quite reach his eyes. "No, thank you. We'll wait over here for Wilmington." With light fingers on my spine, he directed me toward the leather couches that were too low and hard to be even remotely comfortable. Taking the cheesecake from my hands, he rested it on his own lap. "I understand that you know Strat, but please, let me do the talking. Don't mention anything incriminating. If he asks you a direct question, try and keep your answers as vague as possible."

I rolled my eyes. I'd do my best, though. I wanted this to all be over just as much as he did, if not more. It was my criminal record on the line, which could affect my plans for the future. My dreams of my own farm, where I could take as many animals as I could. Where I could finally put my connections to good use for once.

Finally, Strat appeared, the look on his face warm but professional. He was handsome, his blue eyes almost mirthful. Didn't seem very lawyer-ish, but Truett was my baseline, and he was a surly bastard at the best of times.

"Truett, come on in. Bring your client."

Maybe Strat didn't remember me after all. He led us through the spacious hallways, filled with bland art and beige carpet that must've been a nightmare for the janitorial staff. Finally, we reached an office with Strat's name on the door, and he indicated we should enter.

"Please, grab a seat." Shutting the door, his smile got wider. "When I saw the name in the case files, I thought there was no way this could be the same girl who was friends with my little sister, but how many Otillie-James Balers could there be in the world?"

Truett raised a brow. "If we're lucky, only one." He pulled out the file from his briefcase. "Let's get down to business—"

But Strat ignored him. "Is that a cheesecake from Jill's CheeseCheeks? That place is my dirty little secret.

It's around the corner from my gym, and I've definitely undone my hard work on the way home more than once. Their Nutter Butter cheesecake..." He drifted off, longing on his face, and I laughed.

Opening the lid of the box, I showed him the half cheesecake. "Unfortunately, it isn't Nutter Butter, but you're welcome to a piece of my Basque cheesecake."

He clapped his hands together with a grin. *Man, did he get more handsome in the last few years?* He'd always been very pretty, in the same way his sister was. Great cheekbones, golden skin. He was a little like Truett in that way.

"I'd like that, Otillie-James. Every day is a cheat day if there's cheesecake involved—wouldn't you say so, Truett?" Walking over to a coffee machine that sat on an antique side table, Strat pulled out three small plates and teaspoons. Of course he'd have a coffee machine and plates in his office. Why not?

"I'm a bit of a coffee snob, so this was the first thing I bought for my office when I got the assistant district attorney job. Can't burn the midnight oil if you aren't properly caffeinated."

He placed everything on his desk, and I used the knife he'd produced from somewhere to slice up the cheesecake and move it messily to each plate. I wasn't going to win Hostess of the Year anytime soon—yeah, that was a real thing down here. A way for Omegas to woo the Alphas. Thankfully, I'd only been dragged to a couple, though the canapés were usually good, and everyone generally ignored me, so it wasn't too painful.

After passing a slice to Strat, then another to Truett —who begrudgingly took it—I sat back down. "Sorry. I was on my way home with it in the car when Truett called, and I didn't want to waste it."

Strat groaned around his fork. I totally got the food porn thing now. Watching his tongue flick out and get a piece of cheesecake from his lip was absurdly attractive.

Clearing his throat, Truett eyed me, his expression telling me to behave. What did he think I was going to do? Climb across the desk and offer myself up for Strat to use as a plate? Unlikely.

Though that one might go in the Flick Folder for later, once I was home alone.

Strat gave me a warm look that told me he knew exactly where my thoughts were, and I suddenly realized why he was so different from Truett. Physically, they were quite similar: stacked and strong, wearing the hell out of their tailored suits. No, it was their auras that were different.

Strat Wilmington was an Omega. An Omega district attorney? *Hell yeah.* A sexy-as-fuck district attorney.

"So, if you're amiable to doing a little work on your break," Truett snarked, shaking me from my lustful reverie, "could we talk about the charges against my client here?"

Strat met my eyes, and I thought perhaps he was

laughing at Truett. "Of course, Truett. I haven't forgotten that you're all work and no play. The evidence isn't circumstantial, but I also know that if this goes to court, you'll be able to drag enough character witnesses from the woodwork to have her declared a saint, my own family included." He lifted his chin in my direction. "Otillie-James, patron saint of strays and lone wolves." I flushed, but he continued. "So how about you tell me what you were doing there?"

"You already have her statement," Truett argued.

Shrugging, Strat forked another bite of cheesecake into his mouth. Chewing slowly, he just smirked. "Be that as it may, I'd like to hear it directly from her—if that's okay with you, Counsel."

Truett looked like he was going to argue again, and I placed my hand on his thigh to stop him. It was a hard thigh. Obviously, he didn't skip leg day.

Wait, what am I doing again? I really had to get my libido under control, before I ended up cellmates with someone named Barb the Bitchmaker.

"It all started with some kittens..."

NINE
STRAT

Although her name had been familiar, I hadn't remembered much about Otillie-James Baler. She'd been Elizabeth's friend from her school days, but I'd already graduated high school by the time she started coming around.

Whenever I saw her, it was usually just in passing if I'd had to come home for something, a situation I tried to avoid wherever possible. While I used to miss Elizabeth, I'd found it better to pick her up from school and take her out for ice cream or some shit, rather than to come back to the house and risk a possible run-in with the parents.

The person I did know—and know well—was Truett Heathstone. He had some kind of big idea that we were archnemeses or some such shit, but really, I just loved to get him riled up. Even in college, he'd been a hot-blooded Alpha. Anytime I beat him in anything, he'd get all red in the face, his sharp jaw flexing angrily. It had been kind of hot.

It made my Omega nature purr that he never gave me an inch of leeway, despite my designation. He wasn't disrespectful, but he never stepped aside just so I could come first. No, that first fiery look had been all it took to make it my mission in life to piss him off as much as possible.

I was bisexual, and I definitely got the same vibes from Truett, but I'd never heard even a rumor he played around with guys as well as girls. Maybe he kept it under wraps; god knows I did. Especially after Elizabeth had told our parents she was a lesbian after she turned eighteen, and that they should go fuck themselves. I didn't quite know what they'd do if we both came out. Probably write us both out of their wills, pretend we were dead, and adopt another child to replace us. They were vindictive like that.

At least I'd managed to talk them around, ensuring that they didn't cancel Elizabeth's trust fund from our grandparents in a fit of homophobic rage. I'd play the good straight son for a few more years until Elizabeth got her money, then I'd see how things unraveled.

The true joy of being bisexual was that in front of me was a smorgasbord for all senses. Separately, they were attractive. Truett, with his flexing jaw, hard edges, and overwhelming Alpha energy. Otillie-James, with her soft curves, big eyes, and full, soft lips. She was Unshown, but I didn't care about those kinds of labels.

When she put her hand on his thigh, I briefly wondered if they were together. My dick hardened at just the thought. To play with these two would be something else.

"It all started with some kittens. Well, no. It started with a three-legged bait dog that another animal fosterer told me about. She told me that there was a cockfighting ring somewhere on the east side of town that happened every weekend, and that they couldn't find it. She told me to make a police report, because hers had gone nowhere, and the more we reported it, the more they'd *have* to look into it.

"That was just over a month ago, maybe? I followed it up, but I got the runaround. Anyway, I kind of forgot about it, until I got a report of a stray cat colony down beneath Wildcat Creek Bridge, including a litter of kittens. But by the time I got there, the kittens and some of the other cats had been picked up by a group of teenagers, who were"—she cleared her throat, her wide eyes getting damp—"making a game out of disposing of them. I overheard them talking about maybe giving them to someone who did dogfighting, but I missed his name.

"Then one of the others talked about how his uncle went to cockfights at the autobody shop on Lafayette Street. That the fights happened every weekend, and that they should all go." She cleared her throat again. "That's when I approached them and told them to give me the kittens."

Truett's head whipped toward her. "You did fucking

what?" Ah, so he didn't know this part of his client's story. The way his eyes burned with disapproval, though, I got the feeling that Otillie-James was more than just another client.

She, to her credit, ignored his anger completely. "Obviously, they didn't take kindly to being told what to do, and things got a little... hairy. Anyway, that's beside the point."

Truett gripped her arm and tugged her in his direction, and I narrowed my eyes. "Easy there," I warned. I didn't think he'd hurt her, but she seemed so delicate. I didn't want him to bruise her without thought.

"Fuck off, Willmington. I would cut off my arms with a rusty saw before I'd hurt OJ." He looked back down at her. "Why didn't you tell me this?" he rumbled, his voice even lower, because he was clearly pissed. "You *can't do that,* OJ. You could have been..." He trailed off, and he didn't need to say what could have happened. We saw it all too much in our line of work.

Shaking loose his hand, she reached over and wrapped him in a quick side hug. "I know. I was fine, though—that's when I met Lance. He rescued me, him and Akio." She turned back to look at me. "I'm sorry, we're getting off topic. Anyway, after I got home, the kids' words played in my head. I reported it to the cops, because they had an open investigation on it, right? Then I went and staked the place out. I sat in my car with the doors locked; I didn't do anything stupid." She screwed up her nose. "That time, at least."

The reason she was here sat heavily in the air between us. Shaking my head, I gave her an encouraging smile. "Obviously. Please, continue."

"But the cops never showed. So I went back the next weekend, and again—no cops. Same the following weekend. I watched them throw the bodies of all those dead birds right in the dumpsters, like they didn't even care about getting caught." Her cheeks were now flushed with outrage. "So the weekend after that, I took matters into my own hands."

Truett cleared his throat, and she looked away to the left. Classic sign she was about to lie.

"Uh, then the following weekend, on that particular day, I was walking down that street and found an escaped chicken, which I caught to return to its rightful owner. I definitely didn't know that the junkyard belonged to that auto body shop."

It was such an outrageously awful lie that I laughed. "Is that so?"

Before Truett could counsel her not to, she shook her head. "Obviously not. I broke in there with the idea that I could save a few of those birds, but then the cops decided to *finally* pull their thumbs out of their asses and actually turn up. I made a run for it with one of the roosters, and got busted." She licked her lips. "Does it say in your files what they did with the other animals they rescued?"

I flicked through my notes, and my heart sank. "They were euthanized."

She hissed out a sigh between clenched teeth, her shoulders curling in. "So it was all for nothing. They all died anyway." The hurt in her voice tugged at my chest.

Truett reached over and pulled her close. "They went to sleep, rather than brutally fighting to the death, OJ. That's something. And Spartacus gets to live out his days on a giant estate, being coddled like a baby."

Spartacus?

The way she molded into his body, allowed him to bring her comfort, told me these two were definitely more than casual acquaintances. Was he her Alpha? I couldn't see any claiming marks on her, but that didn't mean they weren't hidden beneath her clothes.

I'd watched her pretty, heart-shaped ass as she walked through my office door. If I was her Alpha, that's where I'd bite her. It seemed unlikely, though. Alphas didn't claim Unshown, especially not ones with the pedigree of Truett Heathstone.

I tried to remember what else I knew about Otillie-James Baler. She'd definitely gone to that preppy school with my sister, but nothing else rang a bell. I'd have to call Elizabeth tonight and discover a little more. I wasn't even going to lie to myself and pretend the interest was professional.

"I'm sorry, Otillie-James. If it appeases you even a small amount, I'm going to make sure that the people who profited from this blood sport get punished to the full extent of the law." Leaning back, I look over at Truett. His eyes were full of fire, and he still didn't release the girl. "It's obvious to me that you really were in the wrong place at the wrong time, and it would be a waste of this office's resources to pursue a case against you. You're free to leave and to go about your life, Miss Baler."

I gave her a soft smile. "But for everyone's peace of mind, I'd appreciate it if you took someone with you on your rescue missions from this point on. It's always good to have a collaborative witness, if for no other reason." Like ensuring she didn't end up at the bottom of the river, or in a dumpster beside dead fucking chickens.

Nodding solemnly, she stood. "Thank you, Strat. I appreciate you taking the time to meet with us. Give my love to Elizabeth the next time you speak with her?"

I reached out to shake her hand. She placed her much smaller one in mine, and I marveled at how soft and delicate her skin felt. I didn't have farmer's hands by any means, but hers felt like silk beneath mine. I wondered if she was this soft everywhere.

Truett cleared his throat, and I realized I'd been holding on a little too long. Releasing her hand, I looked up at my surly counterpart. "It was good to see you again, Truett."

He held my gaze, his own burning. "Likewise," he muttered. "I owe you one."

Well, that was unexpected, but I wasn't about to look a gift horse in the mouth. "I'll hold you to that," I murmured back, as he ushered Otillie-James to the door.

He looked over his shoulder. "There was never any doubt about that."

I watched them until they turned the corner and were out of sight. My office still smelled of Otillie-James's soft, sweet perfume, and Truett's Alpha scent. One should cancel out the other, but instead, they blended perfectly.

I was going to have some seriously inappropriate fantasies of fucking Otillie, while being topped by Truett. It was inevitable.

But first, I had a promise to keep.

TEN

EDISON

My captain at the station hadn't been happy when I'd told him I needed to take a few weeks' leave, but considering I hadn't had even taken a single sick day over the last three years, he'd eventually relented.

I didn't think I needed to be here at the house, but that didn't mean I didn't *want* to be here. I'd picked up a giant bag of carrots from the grocery store and was currently bribing the goats away from my mom's azaleas. They were greedy little bastards, and two of the three were currently running at me like a stampede.

As I snapped a carrot in half, it made a louder than usual cracking sound. One of the goats let out a fearful bleat, went stiff, and fell over. I waited for it to stand back up, but nothing happened. A minute went by, and it stayed prone on the ground.

Fuck.

"Oh shit... Oh fuck!" I rushed over, but it was like the animal had rigor mortis. "Please tell me you're a fainting goat, and don't have some kind of neurological disorder," I muttered, trying to put the goat back on its feet, but it just toppled to the side again. Its little friend seemed completely uninterested in the fact its compatriot was having a medical episode, just fishing a whole carrot out of the bag that I'd dropped.

"Come on, little guy. Get up," I hissed, but it was literally immobile and unblinking. Did it have epilepsy? Was it a Russian sleeper spy, and I'd just activated it with a carrot snap?

Fuck, five minutes, and I've already killed one of Tillie's pets. Maybe I needed to go back to work, where I could stay out of the way.

"Do I need to take you to the vet?" I asked the goat, like it would answer me.

What was the acronym for resuscitating a goat? Was it the same as for a human? They'd drilled the ABCs into us at the academy—it couldn't be that different, right? It was still a mammal.

A was for airways, but I couldn't pry the goat's mouth open without sticking my thumbs at the back of its snout. It was gross, but I had to try. What if it was choking on a piece of carrot, or maybe it had been poisoned by azaleas? Should I Google if they were poisonous to goats?

I couldn't see anything lodged, and I could feel its hot breath, so I thought it was probably breathing and didn't need mouth-to-mouth. Probably ruled out compressions too.

There was a choking noise behind me, and I spun to see an amused-looking Tillie. Guilt washed over me. "I think I injured your goat. Can they eat azaleas? How do you check a goat for poisoning?"

She looked beautiful today, in tight, faded jeans with a hole in the knee, and a white camisole that showed the golden tan of her skin. She wasn't dressed up, or dressed down. She just looked like everyday Tillie, and that's what made wanting her so damn hard.

I gave her a stern look. "Don't stand there and laugh! What if something's really wrong with it?"

Shaking her head, she patted me on the back. "The only thing wrong with Scaramouche is that you're traumatizing the hell out of her by sticking your fingers in her mouth. If you just step over here for a minute..." She led me a few feet away, then after a few seconds, the damn goat perked right up.

"For fuck's sake. Why didn't you do that in the first place?" I muttered at the goat, who happily joined its friend. "Wait, did you say its name is Scaramouche? What kind of name is that?"

She shrugged. "Her friend over there is Beelzebub, and over near the fountain is Fandango. She just doesn't like people very much."

"Their names are Scaramouche, Fandango, and Beelzebub? Whatever happened to Daisy and Milly?"

Rolling her eyes at me, Tillie went over and scratched

Beelzebub behind its floppy ears, as it chewed on the pilfered carrots. "Boring. Life's too short for that."

I kept a wide berth from the goats. Obviously, they weren't my biggest fans, and I'd traumatized Scaramouche enough for one day. Or maybe she'd traumatized me. "I've taken a few weeks off work. I was due some holiday leave, and it looks like you could use a hand."

She gave me a stubborn look that I knew all too well. "I can handle my responsibilities just fine."

I raised an eyebrow at her. "So can I."

"I'm not your responsibility," she snapped, and I lifted my hands.

"Whoa, I never said you were."

She let out a frustrated noise. "But you insinuated it. Don't gaslight me, butthead."

I sighed, because she was right. I was fucking this up. "Otillie-James, you are the most capable person I know. I'm kind of glad you're a good person, because I have no doubt that if you had a villain origin story, you could've raised an army to bring down nations by now." She frowned at me, but I saw the corners of her lips twitch up. "Honestly, I need a break. Plus, I did a head count, and Tillie, you have *thirty-seven animals* here. You need help, and that's okay."

She shrugged. "I've got Lance."

I didn't want to say that he was the other reason I was staying, because it'd offend them both, but it still hung in the air between us. "Well, now you'll have me too."

I also didn't say that she looked tired. I'd thought it had just been from staying up all night at the police station, but really, she didn't look much more rejuvenated today. She was clearly burning the candle at both ends, and we could both use the rest.

She shrugged. "It's your house."

I reached out and gripped her forearm. "Stop that. It's your house too. When Buck married my mom, this became his home and yours. I hate that you still feel like a guest here." Her skin was so soft under my fingers, and it felt almost electrified. I spent so much time trying not to touch her that these small actions, these inconsequential brushes, felt like so much more. Her head tilted softly to the side, and I wanted to put my mark right there for the world to see.

In a different world, she would be mine.

When she looked down at where my hand was holding her arm, I released it quickly, hoping she couldn't see me flush. Her own cheeks were pink, and I tried to tell myself it was from anger, not from anything else. Because if it were anything else...

God. How could I resist her?

How could I look her father in the eye again?

How could I look anyone in the eye again?

She was my stepsister. We sat down to Christmas mornings together. We celebrated birthdays. The society gossips wouldn't care that I hadn't met her until we were almost adults. They wouldn't care that we weren't physically related in any way, shape or form. Along with the fact that she was Unshown, it would be a scandal, and I wasn't sure anyone would forgive me for it.

I almost didn't care.

She chewed on her lip. "Come on. If you're going to hang around all the time, I'll teach you how to feed the kittens. They need feeding at least every three hours, and I think both Lance and I would appreciate the help."

That was a big admission, and I couldn't help the smile that spread over my face. "It would be my pleasure, Tillie."

We walked slowly back toward the house, and just being with her made my heart happy. I followed along as she told me about her day. About what the vet had said about the chicken she'd saved. About her run-in with Truett and how he'd gotten the charges dropped. About Strat Wilmington, who was an Omega and an assistant district attorney.

I noted how her eyes sparkled as she said Strat's name, and I tried to curb my jealousy. I wasn't an idiot; she wasn't going to be single forever, though both Truett and I had done a pretty admirable job of chasing off potential boyfriends during her high school years. Since then, she'd had a few, but no one seemed to last more than a few months.

I thanked the universe for small mercies, because seeing her in love with someone else would be like putting my balls in a vice and squeezing every single time. It made my Alpha irrationally angry. I'd have to move to

Antarctica or Australia, just so I didn't have to see someone else making her happy.

She stopped at the tree, the infamous one that she'd fallen out of all those years ago, changing my life. "You know, there's still a nest of squirrels up there. I think they're the same ones, or at least their offspring."

I laughed, looking up at the very top branches where I'd found her. She'd been so stubborn, and I'd been so fucking scared. When she'd fallen, my heart had stopped. It had been the longest ten seconds of my life, watching her hit every damn branch on the way down.

I raised an eyebrow. "Rumor has it they still pad out their nests with periwinkle-blue Vera Wang."

"Bougie." She stopped, chewing her lip and looking up at me, and my whole world stopped once more. She was staring at me like I was her hero, with her big blue eyes staring right into my very soul, capturing it as her own. "You know, I don't think I ever properly said thank you for climbing up there and rescuing me all those years ago. If you hadn't helped me, I might still be there."

Stepping closer—because I had no choice; I was being pulled as if magnetized—I gave her a soft smile. "No, you would have made it down. You're too resourceful not to handle yourself. I have total faith in your abilities, Tillie. I just also know that even if you need it, you won't ever ask for help."

We were close now. Too close. Her lips were parted, and my eyes kept being dragged back down to their pillowy softness. What would happen if I just leaned down and took them with my own?

Her tongue darted out, wetting her lower lip, and I bit back a groan. I dragged my eyes back to hers. I wanted to interpret the look in them as desire too, but I couldn't be sure. And I couldn't ruin everything, just because I'd judged wrong.

She cleared her throat a little. "Thank you." Her voice was soft and a little rough, and I shook myself out of my daze.

If I wasn't reading her signals wrong—if she wanted me too—would I really risk everything just to be with her?

The answer was easy and immediate.

Absolutely.

I needed to speak to Truett.

Eleven

Otillie-James

I needed to get laid. Not just laid—I needed to get tag-teamed by Casanova and Don Juan, so that any thought of my stepbrother fucking me would disappear entirely from my brain.

There'd been a moment. I was almost sure of it.

But as soon as we reached the house, he was all business, asking about how much to feed each kitten, their schedule—anything but the way we'd been standing under the tree outside, and the way his eyes had snagged on my lips as we spoke.

Just going to lock that shit back down where it belonged, as late-night fodder for my vibrator collection. After we finished up with the kitten care explanation, I quickly retired to my room and to my waterproof rabbit.

Lance and Akio still hadn't returned, though, and I was a little worried. Maybe they were gone for good, but would Lance really leave without saying goodbye? I wished he had a phone, or some way to contact him, so I didn't have to worry. I just had to remind myself that he was a capable man, not some injured fawn I'd collected on the side of the road. He had his own things to work through, and he couldn't do that if I was hovering around him.

But when I woke up the following morning, and Lance was in the kitchen, I couldn't help the flood of relief that washed through my body.

"Good morning, Lancelot."

He gave me a small quirk of his lips, but his eyes were warm. I wondered if the scars on his face pulled painfully if he smiled.

"Good morning, Otillie-James. I've given the kittens their morning feed."

I took my mug over to the machine and set it to make me a latte. "Thank you. I have work today, for a few hours, but I wanted to warn you that Sonny is staying for a little bit. He's taken time off work, because he needs a 'break.'" I did air quotes with a sigh. "But I think he just wants to keep an eye on me, to make sure I don't break into some science lab and liberate the monkeys or something."

He raised an eyebrow. It was dark and straight, and kind of attractive. "Was that something you were looking at doing?"

At least once a year, every year since I was about thirteen, but I didn't tell him that. I just shook my head. "Not lately." I reached down and scratched Akio's ears. "I just didn't want you guys to be surprised, if you stumbled across him this morning. Sonny's a nice guy. He won't get in your face."

Lance gave me a strange look, his head slightly tilted. "This is your home. It's his home too. I'm the guest here."

I rolled my eyes at him, bringing my coffee to my lips and sighing happily before leaning back against the island countertop. "I know that. But it's always good to know who's haunting the place."

A little bit of stubble had grown back across his face, enough to just see the slashes of scarring across his cheeks. There was one that dissected his upper lip almost to his nostril. His eyes were dark this morning, and not to brag, but I'd done a fantastic job on his hair. He seemed to be wearing new clothes, just basic ones—a soft flannel and light-wash jeans that fit him perfectly, clinging to his thighs just right. He looked so fucking handsome, it was almost painful.

Burying my face back into my coffee, I pushed that attraction back down too. Maybe I was ovulating or something, because I'd wanted to climb every attractive man in the vicinity for the last forty-eight hours.

But what would it be like to run my tongue up the strong column of his neck?

Oh god. Time to leave.

Lance's face was unreadable as he sipped his tea, seemingly oblivious to my horny turmoil. Clearing my throat and hoping my face wasn't on fire, I downed the rest of my coffee. "Okay, off to work I go. Call me if you need me." Then I remembered he didn't have a phone. "Or, like, send a carrier pigeon or something. Pepe would probably do it."

Pepe was an injured pigeon out in my coop, with his girlfriend Sweetpea. None of the other rescue places would take them, because they were just pigeons, right? Rats with wings. But pigeons had once been domesticated, to the point they no longer knew how to operate as wild birds, and then someone invented the telephone, and what? We abandoned them back on the street? They'd even forgotten how to properly nest. Nope. Not on my watch. They'd get the same treatment from me as the dogs and cats.

I shrugged. "You'll figure it out." Lance chuckled, and I hustled out of the room before I said anything embarrassing.

I worked across town for Fur Babes Doggy Daycare, which was usually eight hours of pure chaos, but I loved it. I'd tried college, and while I'd made good grades, it wasn't for me. I didn't want to go into research, or become a corporate powerhouse, or whatever the hell kind of careers other people wanted.

Maybe it was because I'd lived the first part of my life homeschooled, free and without structure. It hadn't made traditional education any easier for me. It had then been compounded by the assholes at that stuffy private school Dad had made me attend, who'd made the remainder of my teenage years hell.

Yeah, college hadn't been for me, but the problem was, I didn't know what *was* for me yet.

I turned into the staff parking just as the bus pulled up. It was basically a school bus for the doggos, and honestly, it was my favorite thing. Terry, the bus driver, opened the door, and the cacophony of barking immediately made me smile.

"Morning, Terry! Just in time, as always."

"Morning, Miss Otillie. Only eleven today. Aruba Smith is having dental surgery." Aruba Smith was a mixed-breed stray, adopted by Paul and Lionel Smith on their honeymoon in—you guessed it—Aruba. He was surly around strangers, but spent most of his days sitting beside my feet, looking at all the purebreds with something akin to disdain. He'd definitely punish his parents for the indignity of oral surgery.

Sasha, the daycare's owner and hardest worker, bustled through the front doors of the building and onto the bus with me. "Morning, Terry. Morning, Tillie." She smiled at the dogs, still attached to their seats by clips on their collars. "Morning, fur babies! How are we today?" she cooed, and the bus went wild.

Laughing, I went to work unclipping dogs and attaching them to leads on my belt harness. We never attached more than two at a time, just for safety. I started at the back, while Sasha started at the front.

Unclipping Bacon and Eggs, a Beagle brother and sister, I attached them to the leads. "Good morning, lovelies. Are we going to have a good day today?" Walking down the aisle of the bus, I scooped up Smilow. He was an elderly gentleman, who was maybe part Chihuahua with a grumpy attitude, but I'd won him over on my second day by giving him some of my fries.

Making my way through the air-conditioned office to the kennels, I attached everyone's kennel tags to their collars. Each dog's collar tag would only let them in their own kennel, so they could get a little peace and quiet if they ever wanted out of the communal areas. Bacon and Eggs got to share one, though, because they preferred to curl up together and would cry if separated.

Shifting through the tall gates, I let the Beagles off their leads, and they raced straight into the common area. Then, moving further down the rows, I put Smilow in our geriatric section. This was for our elderly puppers, who wanted to nap, eat, and lie in the sun without being jumped over by more rambunctious dogs.

As I put Smilow in, he gave me a look that said I probably could've been quicker, and I was lucky he wouldn't talk to my manager, then went to lie under the blanket on his fluffy bed.

Grinning, I went back out to the bus to let in the next lot. And the next. Before I knew it, I was smiling widely and chatting away to my favorite friends. I loved all of the dogs, from the wild, enthusiastic Shepherds like

Apollo and Aksel, who seemed to run and play from the moment they arrived to the minute they left.

Or Tank, who was always holding at least two tennis balls in his mouth, even when I hadn't put out any balls yet. I'd swear he kept them in his cheeks and would just spit them out when he wanted to play.

Or Mika the Goldendoodle, who had an emotional support blankie that she spent all day carrying around.

I kept an eye on them all as they played, the ever-serious X the Doberman at my side surveying the shenanigans. "They're in a good mood today, wouldn't you say?" I said to him conversationally. "You wouldn't believe this, because I'm sure you're a law-abiding citizen, but I got picked up by the police on the weekend. You're being supervised by an almost-convicted felon." X gave me the side-eye, like he was reevaluating our friendship.

Drax and Loki were getting a little rowdy, so I stood and went over to do my job. The second I unzipped the pouch on my belt, every dog in the yard stopped, their attention immediately on me.

I looked down at them with my most authoritative expression. No one else in life listened to me, but when I told these guys to form an orderly line, they did. Grinning, I fed the first one a treat, then the next, and so on.

What a job.

I was exhausted when I made it home that night, my feet and knees aching from standing in the yard most of the day. I'd been tired for weeks now, and when I walked through the door to the smell of dinner already cooked, I could have wept with relief.

Kicking off my boots and hanging my bag in the coat closet, I walked into the large kitchen. A shirtless Sonny was cooking something on the stove, and I swear, drool welled in my cheeks. Sonny was *beautiful*. Soft, golden skin stretched across flexing muscles, unadorned by anything. No tattoos. No scars. Just smooth perfection that you wanted to mark up with your teeth and nails.

I wasn't surprised to see Truett sitting at the island across from him, typing on his phone. He'd lost his suit jacket, just in his vest and white dress shirt, but underneath the soft white cotton, I could see the tattoos that flowed up his arms. I knew they ran over his torso too, some even spreading down his thighs. I'd really enjoyed the family pool parties over the years, just so I could watch him in his swim shorts, moving around like a work of art. Or a wet dream.

Those slutty thigh tattoos had been a focal point in many of my teenage fantasies. Also, my adult fantasies.

What was weird about the scene, though, was Rufio perched on Truett's shoulder. The bird looked absolutely ecstatic to be there, clinging to genuine Armani.

Shaking my head, I strode into the room, like I hadn't just been loitering in the hall, perving like a creep. "That smells amazing," I told Sonny, and when he looked up and smiled at me, my heart flip-flopped in my chest.

Fuck. So beautiful.

"It's just cheese and garlic pasta, but I'll run to the store tomorrow and get supplies for something more substantial for the rest of the week." Was there slight disapproval in his voice that the only thing I had was deli meat and frozen pizza?

I was busy. I didn't have time to cook elaborate meals. So I nodded noncommittally, walking over to Rufio. Bending closer, I put my hand out for him to step on. "What are you doing up here, Mister?" I asked, but the question was really for Truett.

The Alpha in question shrugged. "I walked past the cage, and he said, 'Let me out of here, fuckface.' Who am I to argue with a request like that?" He looked at the bird with amusement. "I kind of like his audacity."

I just bet. "You're never going to find a permanent place with language like that, Rufio."

"RUF-I-OOOOH!" the bird chanted back at me.

Laughing, I walked to the bird stand in what had once been the dining room, but now housed both Pepe and Sweetpea the pigeons, and Elvira, the umbrella cockatoo with a plucking problem. An experienced parrot handler was coming to get Elvira at the weekend, and I was glad. Whatever had happened to her before she was rescued had made her withdrawn, and I didn't have the time nor the skills to bring her out of her shell. She needed specialist care.

I sat Rufio on top of Elvira's cage, which had all the parrot toys and enrichment laid out. That should keep him busy for a little while anyway.

When I walked back into the kitchen, Sonny and Truett were laughing together, looking like the teenage boys I'd fallen in love with all those years ago, making my heart ache. One day, they would belong to someone else.

I pasted a smile on my face and went to join them. They might belong to someone else eventually, but today, I'd pretend they belonged with me.

TWELVE
LANCE

Self-flagellation was kind of becoming my thing, and nothing was more painful than watching Otillie-James smile and laugh with the other two guys in the house, knowing I would never be a part of a dynamic like that.

Couldn't be, really. I was a danger to anyone I loved. Akio was the only being I could care about, and that was only because he could read my moods before even I could.

I'd stayed here too long, and now leaving would be like a festering wound. Still, I couldn't make myself go. Yesterday, I'd packed up all my stuff, and Akio, and moved on. Ten hours later, I'd found myself right back in her kitchen, waiting for her to wake up before work.

I rested my head against the cool, stacked stone of the patio pillar, and tried to talk some sense into myself. She wasn't for me.

The French doors opened, making me stiffen. I willed myself to relax, to not turn around, to not assess the threat. Some of those instincts were so ingrained into me now, through training and trauma, that it was like fire ants crawling on my skin to keep my back to a possible threat.

But Akio wasn't worried, and my senses told me that it was Otillie-James's stepbrother. These logical assessments meant nothing, though. I still wanted to reach for the knife in my boot.

He edged around me, coming into my peripheral vision more than an arm's length away. *Smart Alpha.*

He was holding a bowl and a can of Coke. "Dinner. Tillie said you wouldn't come and take it yourself, that it had to be explicitly offered. And I didn't know if you imbibe or not, but there's beer in the fridge, if you'd prefer."

He thrust the bowl at me, and I met his eyes. I couldn't get a read on this Alpha. He seemed to genuinely care, but I'd met a lot of Alphas in my time. Most of them were arrogant and high-handed, especially around Betas and Unshown. But not this guy. He might only care because Otillie-James cared, but it was more than he *had* to do.

So I took the bowl and the Coke. "Thank you."

Sitting down on the short retaining wall that ran around the edge of the paving, he looked over at me. "I'm sure Tillie has already said this, but you're welcome to help yourself to any of the food or amenities here. We wouldn't be good Southern hosts if it wasn't implied that my house is your house."

I sat down on the wall too, facing back over the expansive lawn. "She has strongly suggested that I should help myself many times. I just don't want her to feel like I'm taking advantage."

He didn't deny I was taking advantage. She'd literally fished me out from underneath a bridge; nothing I offered her in exchange would trump putting a roof over my head. "I'll add my offer to hers, then. Make yourself at home for as long as you're here, and I'm here too."

There was a subtle warning there, or maybe not so subtle. Maybe it was more like a sledgehammer to the temple.

"I would never hurt her," I defended quietly, and he gave me an empathetic expression.

Shrugging, he turned back toward the lawn too. "I believe you. But I've been around long enough to know that sometimes the man is not in control of the monster. If anyone knows that, it's an Alpha." His jaw flexed. "You don't have to tell me about all the skeletons in your closet. Truett looked into you enough that I know that those skeletons probably carry heavy ghosts."

He didn't seem apologetic that they'd done a background check on me, and I didn't blame him. I would've done the same thing.

He continued. "I'm sure Otillie-James has told you that if you ever need to talk, she'll listen. But some things, you can't talk about to a person like Tillie. She's sweet and good, and lives in a world where confronting a bunch of hoodlums for kittens doesn't end up with your throat slit. So, I'm adding my offer there too. If you want to talk, I'm here. If you want to talk to a professional, I'll pay. Someone better than the overworked VA shrinks, anyway."

I shook my head. "I don't want your money, either."

Edison huffed a laugh. "She once told me that she pitied me, that my money was a burden she wouldn't want to shoulder. I didn't understand at the time; I thought she was just being a stubborn teenager. But now, I get it. At best, people might be using me for access to my inheritance. At worst, any offers might look like I'm trying to buy a person. I promise, none of this comes with strings attached."

He didn't understand, and I found myself wanting someone to comprehend just how fucked up I was. "I was in the Special Forces. I saw... things. I was the only member of my company who made it back, except Akio."

That was all I'd say about the horror of my service, but it was enough, I think. He didn't say anything else, didn't probe for more, just continued to watch the setting sun beside me. There was no pity on his face, and that was a relief. Me and this rich boy were about as far apart as we could be, but in this moment of quiet solidarity, it was nice to share the burden.

"I owe her. I owe her more than she can ever know," I told him quietly. "She saved me in a moment when I was so hopeless..." I couldn't go on. Not then, and not now.

"She says you saved her too. I know you did. Which means we all owe you in return. A world without Otillie-James is a world that's darker than before. So let's call it even." He stood, brushing the dust from the back of his jeans. "I'll leave you to eat, but tomorrow, come and have dinner with the rest of us, okay? She'd enjoy it, and so would we."

I wasn't sure what took over my tongue—maybe the demon of hope—but I stopped him. "Otillie-James... is she yours?" She'd only said he was her stepbrother, but the way they watched her, their possessiveness—it was a little more than familial, at least in my opinion.

He narrowed his eyes, and I wondered if he was about to revoke his dinner invitation. "I'd defend her with my very last breath," he replied, and it was my turn to give him a hard stare.

"That's not what I asked. Is she a part of your Pack, or is she just your little sister?" She was Unshown, but it was obvious that didn't mean he cared any less.

"She's mine," he growled, the Alpha really coming out to play now.

My spine straightened, ready for a fight, and Akio weaved closer to me. "Does she know that? Or are you going to just string her along and chase away all her other chances at happiness?" I had no right to say these things. No right to bite the hand that was literally feeding me. But I owed Otillie-James the hard questions.

He met my eyes and stared me down, until I was forced to look away. He was dominant, that was for sure.

I could hold my own against weaker Alphas, but Edison, and his Packmate Truett, weren't weak in any way.

Letting the dominance loosen, he slumped back down beside me. "She's my stepsister. And an Unshown. She'd be ridiculed in my world. Sneered at by people we've known for years. I can't do that to her." Shaking his head, he sighed heavily. "Truett would lose clients, and maybe his chance at a partnership. The Chalmers business holdings would take a hit at the scandal, and people would lose their jobs. Can I put them both through that, just because I have an inappropriate crush?"

Otillie-James was right; his money was a burden. "You'd protect her from that." It wasn't a question. I barely knew this Alpha, but I knew how he felt about her. "Isn't she worth it?"

"What if we find a scent match? What if Truett falls in love with an Omega who hates her?" I noted he didn't say what if *he* fell in love. Because he was already one hundred percent in love with Otillie-James.

I held back my snort. People-watching was something they'd taught us to do in specialist training, analyzing the smallest flickers of body language, and deciphering what they meant. However, there was nothing small about the way Edison felt about Otillie-James. He watched her like he wanted to gobble her down. He wanted her so badly, it was almost painful to witness.

The way she wanted him back.

Maybe this was the way I could repay her for her

kindness; I could help her get her Alphas. I couldn't have the girl, but they could. Everyone just needed to get out of their own way. Then, when she was happy, I'd be able to leave.

Self-flagellation was the only mistress I'd need.

Thirteen

The investigating detectives had been less than impressed when I told them we didn't have enough to charge the only person picked up in the cockfighting raid who'd actually been in possession of a rooster, but once I'd explained her statement, and the corroborating evidence, they'd eventually come around.

However, they'd had a single proviso, one that I'd agreed to, merely because I wanted to see Otillie-James Baler and Truett Heathstone one more time.

The phone line rang, and I tapped my fingers against my desk as I waited for them to answer.

"Heathstone." The gruff, one-word greeting was exactly what I expected from Truett.

"Truett, it's Strat Wilmington." Silence. *Surly fucker.* "I just wanted to let you know that Miss Baler's charges have been dropped completely. However, the Rock Hill PD has requested that she come down and look at a lineup of possible suspects to see if she can place any of them at the scene of the cockfight."

"We politely decline," he answered almost immediately.

I sighed. I should have known he'd say that, just to bust my balls. "You don't want to talk to your client about it, perhaps? Maybe I'll just give her a call myself."

The idea of talking to the gorgeous Otillie-James Baler made my dick throb. I wish I knew what it was about her that made my Omega purr, but it was something. And unlike an Alpha, who was all angsty about choosing their one mate, Omegas could choose as many as we damn well pleased, and if you wanted to be part of that, you'd just have to get on board, whether Alpha, Beta, Omega, or Unshown.

It was one of the few freedoms that came with the designation.

"Isn't it unethical to lust after possible defendants?" He sounded so snarky and high-handed, it made me smile. I loved cutting him back down to size.

"Obviously, you weren't listening. All her charges have been dropped. What goes on now is between yourselves and the police department." I almost purred as I delivered the next line. "But it is still my job to put the rest of those scumbags away, and I think I'd like to work very closely with Otillie-James to achieve that. Maybe I'll take her to dinner to discuss it."

The noise he made down the line was borderline

rude. "Over my fucking dead body, Wilmington. Leave OJ alone."

Oh, that sounded possessive. Maybe I'd read it wrong, and they *were* together. "Is she yours? I didn't hear anything about you or Edison Chalmers claiming another Pack member, but I'm not exactly hooked to the grapevine, you know."

Maybe they had an Omega already. The thought made something that felt a lot like jealousy churn in my chest.

Silence again. "We're still in the early stages of courting."

I'd been an ADA long enough to know that he was full of shit, but I let it slide. "I see. Well, as her Alpha and her lawyer, I'd be happy to discuss it with you also. Say, tonight? At Le Luxe?" I rattled off a fancy French place downtown, even though I was more than happy with hot wings at my local dive bar. His pride would demand that he come, and his need to impress both Otillie-James and me would mean he'd probably pay and burn about it the whole time.

"I'll make a reservation. We'll see you there at seven." He hung up on me, and I laughed. Alphas were so predictable.

Although it was suit and tie attire, I dressed down a little in tailored dress pants and a white dress shirt, with two buttons left undone. Washing out the hair gel, I just ran my fingers and a little mousse through the tousled lengths. It made my hair shine gold in my bathroom lights.

I looked less like the ADA and more like a man. No, more like an Omega.

I'd hated my designation when I first presented. My parents had wanted an Alpha, of course, and they'd made their disappointment very clear. When Elizabeth had designated as an Omega too, their parental disappointment had been all-encompassing.

Not that I gave a fuck what my parents wanted. But I'd had a dream since I was a kid, and it was to be a Supreme Court Justice. Being an Omega would hinder that if I let it. If I showed an ounce too much compassion or empathy—if I was anything but a cutthroat asshole—they'd shunt me to some backwater office and let me live out my little career, until an Alpha could come along and take care of me.

I didn't want that. I wanted to earn my place. I wanted to be competitive. I wanted to take on my peers and win, fair and square. Truett had been the first of my classmates who hadn't given a shit. Even now, he didn't care that I was an Omega—only that I was a worthy adversary in the courtroom.

Handing my keys to the valet, I walked into the restaurant. Smiling politely at the *maître d'*, I gave her Truett's name, and she directed me toward a table by the windows. I spotted Truett immediately, his dark hair shining almost mahogany under the chandelier. He stood as I arrived, and I took in his outfit quickly. In dark blue dress pants and cream cashmere sweater, he looked like he just stepped off the pages of GQ.

I'd spent many a heat with nameless heat helpers, imagining they were Truett Heathstone. And Henry Cavill. And Kate Beckinsale, particularly in that vampire film from the 2000s. But you know, an Omega could dream.

He thrust out his hand, and I took it immediately, shaking with as much firmness as you'd expect from an Alpha. It wasn't a dominance thing. No, it was a confidence thing. The power of a handshake couldn't be underestimated.

He grinned at me, all teeth. "Glad you could make it." We both knew I'd backed him into a corner.

"Wouldn't miss it for the world," I snarked back, then turned toward Otillie-James.

And stopped dead, my lips parting gently. She looked...

Wow.

"Otillie-James, you look beautiful," I said softly, and I meant it with every fiber of my being. She was in a soft, champagne-colored silk wrap dress. Its pretty embroidered bodice was tight across her breasts, and the skirt skimmed her hips, somehow making her curvier and more delectable. I wanted to unwrap her and eat her for dessert.

She stood and smiled, taking my hand. I shook it only a tad less firmly, because I wasn't about to treat her like she was anything less than a capable woman, especially when I'd been struggling to fight past my own designation bias all these years.

"You look very handsome too, Strat." Her voice was husky, and I moved behind her as she retook her seat, tucking her chair back in before she realized just how attracted I was to that voice. Its very physical effects were rapidly becoming an obvious bulge in my pants.

Truett gave me the stink-eye, obviously knowing exactly where my mind went. *Whoops.* I grinned unapologetically at him and took my own seat. "Thank you for coming, both of you." If this wasn't a business dinner, I would have them both coming in a different way. "I'm delighted that your charges are officially dropped, Otillie-James, and that deserves a glass of champagne." I signaled the waiter. "I don't know if your Alpha told you, but the detectives have asked you to attend a lineup and see if you can place any other suspects at the garage that night. We'd appreciate your assistance in getting anyone who attended punished."

The burning sensation told me Truett was glaring at me. Otillie-James raised her eyebrows. "*Truett* told me, yes. I'd like to help. Anything to get the ringleaders put away, and the people who profited off the misery of those birds punished." She didn't deny he was her Alpha, but she still seemed surprised.

The waiter appeared, and I ordered champagne. A bottle of their best vintage, of course.

Beaming at her, I nodded. "I knew you would, Otillie-James. You have that look about you."

She smiled. "What look is that?" she flirted back.

"Audaciousness?" Truett suggested sarcastically, and she gave him an annoyed look.

Shaking my head, I held her eyes. "Empathetic. A defender of the weak. That's why I became an ADA—I wanted to protect the people of the city. It doesn't pay the best, but I don't need the money."

Her lips curled softly at the corners, her eyes dancing. I wanted to steal those small smiles from her for the rest of the night. Maybe the rest of the weekend. I gave her my own lopsided grin in return.

As the champagne was poured, I told her that I'd contacted Elizabeth, who'd wanted me to tell Otillie-James that she said hello, and that she was doing wonderfully. I'd happily talk about Elizabeth all night; that's how proud of her I was. After she'd quit modeling, she'd become a fashion designer with her partner, Alexandra, and they were taking the West Coast fashion scene by storm—part grunge, part sustainable high fashion. I couldn't be more proud of my sister and her flourishing business venture.

Shaking my head wistfully, I was trapped in Otillie-James's eyes. "She did it without the support of our parents, or their money, or even mine. She went over there and worked hard, and everything she has, she built herself." I loved my sister. She was the best person I knew.

Beaming, Otillie-James grabbed my hand. "I knew she'd be amazing, no matter what she put her mind to. Though, I'm not going to lie, I'm glad she went into fashion and not destabilizing governments, like she wanted to when we were seventeen."

I threw back my head and laughed so loudly that several diners turned toward our table. "I'd forgotten about that. I'm happy she didn't become a guerilla too."

When she removed her hand, I tried not to pout. Instead, I looked up at Truett's hard stare and grinned. "So, how long has Truett been courting you?" I asked lightly. When Otillie-James's eyes immediately went wide, I knew he'd been full of shit.

"Objection!" he muttered, but she'd already whipped her gaze his way.

"Truett isn't courting me. He's in a Pack with my stepbrother." She frowned. "I'm Unshown."

I shrugged. "I'm an Omega. Means nothing to me; we can bond with whoever we like without fear of disapproval. If my Omega wanted you, I'd court the hell out of you." I let my tone be teasing, but I could see that Truett saw the truth in my words.

She giggled self-consciously. "That's unconventional too, right? Don't people normally court the Omega, not the other way around?"

I shrugged. "Conventional has never been a personality trait I aspire to embody." A server came with the first course, a tiny little nibble of food that had crumbs and foam, and I regretted not having this meeting at

Bucket'O'Wings night at my local bar. "So, if Truett is being a dumbass and *not* courting you, is there another Alpha in the wings treating you how you should be treated? Or maybe another Unshown? A Beta?" I knew there wasn't another Omega; I'd have smelled it on her.

She smelled so sweet, like orange blossoms and gardenias, something light and floral and delicious. I wanted to roll in that scent. At first, I'd thought it was perfume, but perhaps it was just her natural scent, given the way my Omega reacted to it. Though it was very strong for an Unshown.

Could Truett not scent it? If he could, how did he resist her?

She shook her head. "Uh, no. Not really. I've been busy with my job, with my rescues."

I asked her more questions, watched her face light up when she spoke of things she enjoyed, her anger at the cockfighting ring, her joy at the rescue animals and their antics. She was enchanting.

We were now on the third course of the set tasting menu, something she seemed to be enjoying, if the sweet little noises were anything to go by. She spoke to me animatedly, but I didn't miss Truett swapping out his full plate for her empty one. She didn't seem to notice, but it prolonged her happy food noises even longer. I might pay for dinner, just because they'd made her emit those sounds.

While I might be learning everything there was to know about Otillie-James Baler, she'd also managed to pull more than a few facts from me, as if she were a CIA spy. Like the fact I also had no Alphas, and wasn't being courted. My career had kept me busy, and I couldn't risk an Alpha making me quit my job.

Truett scoffed at the idea. "Why would any Alpha make you quit? You're a fucking great lawyer, and they'd want you to what? Sit at home in your nest, fussing with the house all day?" He snorted. "Ridiculous."

My heart pounded in my chest. Every Alpha I'd gone on dates with since I'd designated had basically insinuated that if we Packed up, I could quit my job and do whatever I liked with my days. Like they'd be doing me a favor.

Truett was the only one who seemed to understand being a lawyer *was* what I wanted to do with my days.

I looked over at this Alpha I'd spent far too many years challenging. I enjoyed riling him, but I'd also had more than one late-night fantasy about him too. Was he interested in me like that? Were he and Edison Chalmers looking for an Omega, or were they happy with Otillie-James?

Did it have to be an either/or situation?

As the night progressed, a plan formulated in my mind—one where I got the girl *and* the Alphas, and we all lived happily ever after.

FOURTEEN
OTILLIE-JAMES

Strat Wilmington was charming, sexy, and as our night went on, my body got warmer and warmer under his unwavering attention. I didn't think any designated person had paid me this kind of attention, ever.

It was like he wanted to know everything about me. Maybe it was professional curiosity, but as the night went on, the casual touches got more and more frequent, until my skin felt like it was electrified.

Maybe I was just being sensitive. Possibly I needed to get out more. Because there was no way this gorgeous Omega was flirting with me. I must be misreading his body language.

"Tell me more about your Lancelot," he asked lightly. "You said he'd been unhoused when you met him."

I stiffened, ready to defend Lance again. Actually, Truett had thrown in that little tidbit earlier in the night, and had completely ignored me when I kicked him. "He was. Now he lives with me. He saved my life, and I owe him for that."

But Strat didn't seem to judge. "We all owe him for that. What's he like?"

My cheeks flushed pink. "Kind. Quiet. Maybe stoic would be the right word. Polite. Disciplined, definitely. He was a former Marine, I believe." Polite, to an aggravating degree at times. "Handsome," I added, and Strat's eyes danced.

He grinned. "I'd like to meet him one day."

"You should come around this week for dinner," I offered. "We're having a cookout with friends on Saturday, if you want to join us?"

He gripped my fingers and squeezed lightly. "I'd love that."

I bit my lip as I looked down at where his long fingers covered mine. They were pretty hands. The kind of hands you fantasized about running over your body or fisting silk sheets.

Fuck, what was *wrong* with me? If I was getting my period, it needed to skip to the chocolate-bingeing, hot-water-bottle stage already, because my libido had gone off the rails.

We were interrupted by the server coming over to artfully compile the dessert course on the table in front of us. Right there, on a shiny piece of plastic, they put elaborate chocolate swirls, biscuit crumbs, fresh fruit, and that was just the garnish.

Truett bitched under his breath about fancy restaurants, but I knew he had a sweet tooth and would be diving into this table dessert as soon as the server left.

Strat's eyes danced with delight. "I am absolutely going to devour this. I love sweet things." He held my gaze as he said the words, and I realized he actually *was* flirting with me. This wasn't me misreading signals at all.

Strat Wilmington wanted me.

Holy shit.

I'd never had an Omega flirt with me before. I was Unshown. Omegas weren't interested in Unshown.

It wasn't that the Unshown were badly treated. After all, we made up sixty percent of the world's population, though only six percent of the upper class of society. No, we weren't badly treated—we were just Unshown.

We were just average at most things.

We just smelled normal.

We just had normal anatomy.

We were just... never quite enough.

So this was definitely an anomaly.

Truett cleared his throat, and I realized I'd been sitting here, gaping at the man before me. Giving an awkward chuckle, I hoped my face wasn't as red as it felt.

"I like sweet things too, but no one would ever accuse me of being sweet. Maybe a little salty. Like that one time I put salt in my cookies instead of sugar. That was shocking." I picked up one of the tiny little cubes of dessert. I didn't even know what it was, but I stuck it in my mouth to stop the words. The flavor burst on my tongue, and my eyes went wide. "Holy crap, this is *amazing*." I turned to Truett, picking one up and stuffing it between his lips before he knew it was coming. "Taste this!"

He reared back, but eventually started to chew, his face lighting up in pleasure. *Man, he's handsome.*

I looked over at Strat, who was watching us both intently. *Shit.* Maybe I'd misread this situation entirely. Maybe Strat wasn't flirting with me. Maybe he was flirting with Truett.

That'd make sense, because they had some serious tension between them. I'd thought it might be professional tension, but maybe it was sexual tension.

I tilted my head at Truett, realizing I didn't actually know if he was into guys. He and Sonny didn't seem like a couple. They didn't touch any more than most guys who were best friends, which mostly was inappropriate jokes about touching each other's dicks and wrestling in a display of Alpha-ness. But as they'd gotten older and grown out of it, there hadn't been any indications they were lovers.

We would've all happily accepted it if they were. I knew they'd both had girlfriends in college, which had kind of burned at the time, and I didn't like to think about it too much..

Truett gave me a disgruntled look. "It's good."

I gasped. "It's better than good. It's sweet and salty and a little tart. The balance is mindblowing. Strat, try one and back me up!" I implored the Omega, who was looking between us with a grin now.

"Will you feed me one too, Otillie-James?" He fluttered his eyelashes, and I had the distinct feeling he was laughing at me. I straightened my shoulders, raising an eyebrow in challenge before picking up the little cube of truffle between my fingers and holding it out to him. Smirking, he leaned forward and took the bite from my fingers, his full bottom lip brushing against my skin.

Fuck. Is it hot in here?

Pulling back, he closed his eyes and chewed slowly, his tongue coming out to clean up the small crumbs of chocolate that were perched there. I was transfixed. The restaurant could burn down right now, and I'd be too focused on watching Strat enjoy his dessert to evacuate. My whole body felt flushed, so I knew my face had zero chance of not looking like a hot mess.

I needed to go home ASAP. I needed to grab every vibrator hidden around my room and engage in a battery-operated orgy. I cast a quick look at Truett, who was also focussed on the Omega in front of us.

Yeah, Truett Heathstone thought Strat Wilmington was hot. He wanted to sit in a tree and do a little K-I-S-S-I-N-G. They'd make a cute couple. Or throuple, I guess, if you added in Sonny. Did Sonny like boys too?

The sudden idea of the three of them having sex had my whole body clenching.

Fuck. Okay, time to go.

Looking at my non-existent watch, I pushed back my chair. "Oh crap, is that the time? I need to work tomorrow so I better head home. You two stay, enjoy dessert. Strat, it was lovely—"

"Sit down, OJ," Truett commanded, just short of a bark. "I'll get dessert boxed up."

It was a testament to how flustered I was that I didn't tell him to go get fucked. Instead, I just planted my ass back in the chair.

Truett got the server's attention, and the guy came over with a small container, placing the pieces of dessert —and some of the other components that I hadn't even realized *were* dessert—inside. We all sat in heated silence as he finished, and I gulped down the remainder of my champagne.

Tugging at the neckline of my silk dress, I wondered if it was actually just hot in here. Maybe my body wasn't on fire just yet. Truett and Strat seemed to be having a battle of wills over whose black Amex was going in the little folder to pay, but eventually, Truett won. As we waited for his card to be run, the silence at the table was loaded. I didn't look at either of the men beside me, instead checking my phone for messages.

There was one from Sonny, showing him curled up on the couch with kittens sleeping across his chest. Beside him, a little out of focus, was Lance, kittens resting on his abs. I smiled softly, my heart feeling full.

> Sonny: Fed the babies. Putting them down for their nap. Unrelated question—how many cats do I have to own before I'm labeled a crazy cat man? It's seven, right?

I laughed. We only had six kittens, but I purposefully didn't remind him about Sparks, the half-feral cat with one eye and a bent tail, who hid from everyone but me. He lived outside with Gert and now Spartacus.

"Who has you smiling like that?" Strat asked softly, and I turned the phone around to show him the photo.

His lips curled into a lopsided grin. It was boyish and sweet, and kind of sexy. "Edison Chalmers was always too attractive for his own good. He doesn't need to add baby animals to the mix. It's just unfair."

Truett cleared his throat again. "If you're both done?" He stood, holding my chair for me as I rose. My head felt a little whirly, but I hadn't had that much champagne. In fact, I'd probably had so much food that I looked like I was having a food baby, which would have soaked up every ounce of alcohol in my stomach.

I snorted a laugh, leaning over to Truett and patting my stomach. "Thank goodness I'm wearing a wrap dress after that meal. Otherwise, people would think I'm pregnant." His eyes dropped to my stomach, but he didn't laugh, just indicated that we should leave.

Strat held out an arm. "Allow me to escort you to the valet."

I wrapped my hand in his elbow, trying to ignore the envious looks of the people around me. They could tell I was Unshown, and the whispers told me that they didn't understand why I was with the two men currently bracketing me.

Still, I was Otillie-James Baler. I didn't cower. So I lifted my chin, met their eyes, and dared them to say something.

Truett might be an asshole, but he was a protective asshole, and whether he wanted to or not, he would come to my defense every single time. Not that I needed him to defend me. I could kick ass all on my own.

But no one said a word. They'd silently judge, but would never go up against two people so well connected.

Strat dropped my hand as he gave over his valet ticket, and I tried not to pout. He was just being polite. Those Southern manners were indoctrinated into us early. He turned to me as the valet walked away.

"Thank you for being such an amazing dinner companion, Otillie-James. You definitely make up for Mr. Tall, Dark, and Broody over there." He lifted his chin at Truett. "I'll give you a call later in the week when the Rock Hill PD have organized their lineup. I'll accompany you personally. Perhaps we can get lunch afterwards?"

I tried not to grin. "I'd like that."

He turned to Truett. "It's always a delight, Heathstone." He was clearly teasing him, and I wasn't sure if the flush on Truett's cheekbones was anger or a blush.

"Indeed, Wilmington. Until next time."

Why did that sound like a promise? The tension was definitely sexual. Oh man, I couldn't wait until I got Truett alone. I was going to grill him about his past with Strat.

Strat's Audi pulled up, and he kissed my cheek. He smelled like summer, like sea salt and champagne and long nights. I wanted to roll in his scent. "I'll be seeing you, Otillie-James."

Then he was gone. *Holy shit.*

FIFTEEN
TRUETT

That had been fucking torture. My balls felt like they were going to explode.

I'd sat across from Strat and Otillie-James fucking Baler, watching them flirt and eye-fuck all night long. When she'd fed him that piece of chocolate, I'd contemplated picking her up, laying her across those damn desserts and fucking her right there, in front of Strat damn Wilmington and the whole world.

Then, when the only person she could think of was me, I'd spread Strat over her and fuck him too.

I clenched my jaw so hard, it was a wonder it didn't break. OJ kept looking at me with those inquisitive eyes that saw far too much, and I knew that as soon as the door closed on my Maserati, she was going to bombard me with questions.

As I pulled out into traffic, I was proved wrong—she waited until we were on the freeway. "So, when did you realize you wanted to bone Strat Wilmington? Is it a new thing or...?"

I growled at her. "I don't know what you're talking about."

She snorted a disbelieving sound. "Bullshit. You looked at him like he was a lollipop you wanted to suck all day long."

I shot her a disapproving look, but she glared back at me defiantly. Something about that look made me want to put her on her knees and watch her suck my cock. I had no doubt she'd even blow me defiantly, looking up at me with those wild eyes that made me hard as fuck.

She reached across and put her hand on mine over the gearshift. "I don't care if you like men, True. Or women. Or whatever. I don't think Sonny would care either. I mean, if he doesn't already know."

For fuck's sake. "I'm bisexual, Juice. Is that what you want to know? Sonny already knows. That's definitely something you should talk to him about, though." I wasn't here to out my best friend.

She tilted her head. "Is that why you guys don't have an Omega yet? Do you and Sonny...?"

"Fuck?" I supplied. She nodded, and I sucked my back teeth. "That's none of your business."

She huffed, and it was cute as hell. I couldn't tell her that the main reason we didn't have an Omega was because of her, though. That Sonny and I both had unresolved feelings for the woman beside me, who I'd lusted after and resented in equal measures over the years.

Crossing her arms over her chest, she gave me a grin. "Fine, but you *can* tell me if you find Strat Wilmington attractive. Actually, you don't need to. I know you do; I'm not blind."

That was debatable, considering that both Sonny and her new friend Lance looked at her the same way, and she was wildly oblivious.

"Fine, I find Strat Wilmington attractive. Are you happy?"

Smug little wench just smirked at me. "Yes, I am. You should pursue him. He wants you too. He kept throwing you longing looks."

"Jesus, Otillie-James. I don't need a matchmaker. I get laid just fine."

Her eyes shuttered, and I wanted to bite off my tongue. She was silent for a moment, and then continued, her tone no longer teasing. "I just think you'd be good for each other. You respect his skills as a lawyer. He's handsome, intelligent, and would push your buttons. Sonny would enjoy spoiling him, even if he doesn't like to be spoiled. He'd be good for you both. That's all."

I was fucking this up.

Screw it.

I pulled over into the parking lot of a big box store. Shoving the car into park, I looked over at her. This was a bad idea, but enough was enough.

"Sonny and I aren't looking for an Omega, Juice." Sucking in a deep breath, I hoped Sonny would forgive me for what I was about to say. "We aren't looking to add anyone else to our Pack. Because we've both been in love with *you*, ever since you fell out of that damn tree and right into my arms. We don't have an Omega, or a Beta or anyone else, because no one ever measures up to you."

I was breathing heavily, my heart pounding in my ears as she stared at me, her lips slightly parted. She was frowning, like she couldn't understand my words.

Leaning forward, I captured her lips with mine. Maybe she would understand this better. I poured every ounce of yearning into what might be my only chance to kiss her. I was going to make it memorable. I'd have to hang onto the memory for the rest of my life if this went badly, so I was going to make it worth it.

She was still beneath my lips for a moment. So long, that I began to panic that I'd fucked everything up. Just because I wanted her, didn't mean she wanted me too. Maybe I'd misread everything.

But then she kissed me back, and it was with such fervor, there was no doubt in my mind. I unclipped her belt and grabbed her up, pulling her into my arms and onto my lap without removing my lips from hers. She had these sweet, soft curves, with skin so smooth, I had dreams about touching every inch of it.

"Truett," she breathed, and I groaned. I'd dreamed of her saying my name like that. I reconnected our lips, plundering her mouth with my own. My Alpha was rolling around happily inside me, demanding we fill her up, knot her, bite her, make her ours, but I pushed all that down. She couldn't take my knot, and I would *never* hurt her. Never.

She was making breathy little moans, and I swallowed them down like the sweetest candy. *God.* I had to stop before I fucked her in a damn parking lot.

Drawing back, I tried to suck in air. She looked at me, wide-eyed and almost shocked, and I was at a loss of what to say. My dick was hard as a bar beneath her asscheeks, and I was hoping she was confusing it for the steering wheel or something.

I cupped her face lightly. "I'm sorry for the... ineloquent way I said all that. But I meant it, OJ. You've always been the one for us."

She shook her head, and my heart fractured a little. "No, you've had girlfriends. You're a Pack. I'm Unshown. You've never said anything. I don't... I don't understand."

Blowing out a breath, I knew I should put her back in the passenger seat for this conversation. But I couldn't, because this might be the last time I got to hold her like this. "You have to know that you being Unshown means less than nothing to us. We don't want you for your designation, OJ. We've always loved you for your heart." I'd just dropped the L word again. Sonny was going to kill me.

"At first, you were too young. And you were his step-sister. Then you seemed happy when we left, so we thought maybe it was one-sided. We couldn't stay away, though; we had to move home. While we were gone, you turned into this strong, independent woman who didn't need or want us. We decided not to say anything—we didn't want to blow up your family, just on the off chance you might want us too." It all seemed like such bullshit now.

Oof. I hadn't expected her to punch me in the chest, though when it came to Otillie-James, maybe I should have.

"Are you telling me, Truett Heathstone, that the *six years* I've been pining after you assholes, you've been pining after me too? Do you know how *ridiculous* that is?"

Now it was my turn to blink uncomprehendingly. "You've been pining?" The idea of OJ pining over any man, Alpha or not, seemed ridiculous. She'd barely liked Sonny when they first met, and honestly, everyone tended to like Sonny. I was more of an acquired taste, and I hadn't thought it was a taste OJ ever intended to try.

"Uh, it appears so." Instead of saying anything else, she gripped the back of my head and kissed me again. Her tongue battled with mine, and her sexy little body turned, so she could put a knee on either side of my thighs. Her breasts pressed against my chest, and I held her hips tightly against me.

This had to be a dirty dream. Everything about this night had been straight out of a fantasy. There was no way that Otillie-James was on my lap, grinding down on my cock.

Fuck.

I wasn't sure how long we kissed for, but eventually, she pulled back, her lips pink and swollen, her hair messed up. Her wrap dress had slipped to the side, and her lace-covered breast was right there, in front of my eyes. Better yet, in front of my mouth. I leaned over and took her rose-pink nipple between my teeth, and sucked hard.

"Oh my *god*," she moaned, and I knew this was getting out of hand. With willpower I didn't realize I still possessed, I pulled back and lifted her carefully back onto the passenger seat. Breathing heavily, I tried to get my Alpha under control. I desperately wanted to drag her into the back seat and fuck her senseless.

But I also wanted to do this right. Which meant I was going to have a stern word with my Alpha *and* my dick about the benefits of delayed gratification.

"Otillie-James Baler, if you'll let me, I'd like to court you." The solemnity of the statement was lessened a little by the bulging tent in my pants and the breathlessness of my voice.

Her smile faded a little. "What about Sonny?"

"I'll talk to him." And by talk, I meant he'd kick my ass across the Chalmers estate and back again.

She shook her head slightly, like she was mentally going through all the ways that this wouldn't work. "What if you find an Omega, and she hates me?"

"What if we find an Omega, and he wants you just as much as we do?" We both knew I was talking about Strat Wilmington.

She swallowed hard. "What if I like someone else too?"

I had a feeling she wasn't talking about Strat. I had a feeling I knew exactly who she was referring to, and I wasn't quite sure how I felt about that.

Shaking my head, I gripped both her hands. "We can play the what-if game all day, OJ. The fact is that I would do just about anything, accept just about anything, to have you."

Because when it came down to it, I'd tried the alternative. I'd tried a life without her, and now that I had the taste of her on my tongue, I knew I'd never be able to live without her again.

Sixteen

Edison

Truett: We need to talk. My place. 🐱

There was a mind-blown emoji, which meant this was serious. Truett's text had been ominous, and the fact that he'd dropped Tillie off and then left almost immediately didn't bode well. She'd gone straight to her room; I'd heard the shower running, making me worry that she might be crying on the bathroom floor.

If Truett had hurt her feelings, I was going to punch the asshole. We'd never really talked about our feelings for Tillie, but he knew that she was special to me.

She was a taboo subject for us. It would be too easy for our Alphas to be riled if they realized we both wanted her. They'd say fuck it. It wouldn't matter what our families, society, hell even Tillie would think. The Alphas wanted her, and that's all that mattered to them.

No, we talked about Tillie, but we never really *talked* about her. About the fact that I'd had recurring fantasies about her since I was eighteen. About the fact she was perfect for us, for our Pack, for everything.

Sighing, I climbed into my car and headed over to Truett's apartment downtown. It was a nice place, if a little soulless. Close to his work, but not to mine. We'd been waiting on creating a Packhouse together until everything was more settled.

Parking in the guest spot, I caught the elevator up to the penthouse. The place might be soulless, but the view at night was amazing, the lights of the city twinkling beneath us.

"Truett?" I called, heading into the kitchen to grab a beer from the fridge. I wasn't sure what had told me that this was going to be a beer conversation; maybe call it natural instinct.

Truett appeared, no longer dressed for dinner, instead in sweats and an old college shirt. I'd known him so long that sometimes I felt I knew him better than I knew myself. And guilt was written all over his face.

"What the *fuck* did you do?"

Tillie and Truett had a contentious relationship, but I trusted him with my life. More than that, I trusted him with her life. I didn't think I was wrong about him, but I was beginning to panic.

"I kissed her."

Relief whooshed out of me. *Okay. That's okay. Almost inevitable.*

"And then I told her that we were both in love with her, and that we wanted her to be Pack." It came out in one garbled, run-on sentence, so unlike Truett's normally eloquent speech. At first, I thought I'd misheard him. But his words slowly filtered through my shock.

"Are you fucking insane?!" I shouted, launching myself toward him. "Why would you do that without asking me first? Why would... Just *why?*" My skin felt hot and cold at the same time. Maybe I was having a heart attack.

Fuck. Was that why she'd run straight to her room? Was she disgusted with us now? What kind of man would think about fucking and biting his stepsister? *A pervert, that's who.*

Truett was shaking his head, even as I gripped his arms, like I wanted to shake the shit out of him. "You don't understand, man. She was sitting there, eye-fucking Strat Wilmington all night, and they were flirting and touching, and my Alpha was all riled. Then she was in the car, talking about how we should pursue him, asking about me and you and if we had sex, and how we should find a nice Omega... My Alpha was roaring in my head, and I just snapped and told her everything."

He dropped his eyes, his Alpha apologizing too. "There's no excuse, but it just all bubbled up and spewed out. She looked so beautiful. And I kissed her..." He trailed off again, and I sighed, looking at the ceiling and counting my breaths.

One.

Two.

Three.

Gripping his shoulders, I pulled him closer to me and hugged him tightly. I could feel his guilt down our bond now. He must have been blocking me before. "It's okay, True. It was bound to happen eventually. We'll deal with the fallout together. I'll talk to Buck, and apologize to Otillie-James personally. Maybe we could move to Charlotte or something, keep out of her way."

Truett was shaking his head, pulling away from me. "No, you don't understand. She said she's wanted us forever too. Actually, she tit-punched me and said, 'You mean I've been pining after you assholes for six years, and you've wanted me too?'" he said in a mock-Tillie falsetto.

I stumbled backwards and sat on the couch, shock robbing my knees of strength. "What?"

Striding toward me, he dropped to his knees in front of me. "She wants us too. She doesn't care about your family or mine, what society thinks, none of that. She wants to be part of our Pack." His eyes were wide and imploring, but I didn't know if I could believe him. I needed to hear it from her.

But I was scared. What if he was wrong?

He grabbed my knees, pulling himself closer to me. "I told her I wanted to court her. And I do, Sonny. I want it more than anything." He cleared his throat. "And maybe Strat Wilmington too."

I slapped a hand over his mouth, because I couldn't take much more of this. "In five minutes, you tell me you want to court my stepsister, and an Omega, who you considered your archnemesis all throughout college. Is that correct?" He nodded, then licked my palm, making me drag my hand away. *Gross.* "Do you want to give me a goddamn heart attack?"

He shrugged, and in his grin, I saw something that I hadn't seen in a long time on the face of my best friend. Excitement. Hope. "Better to get it out there in one go, like getting your asshole waxed." He sat on my lap, and I wrapped my arm around his waist. "You don't have to decide about Strat now. He's coming for dinner this week —Tillie invited him before all this happened. See if you get along; see if you feel the same draw as I do. Baby steps."

I huffed a laugh. We could do this. We could have it all. However, I'd start with my dream girl first. I buried my face in Truett's chest.

We'd fucked over the years, but we were both Alpha. We enjoyed it, but we were both too dominant to truly relax into a relationship. We found comfort in touching each other, and snuggled a lot. Spooned on days when we were tired or stressed. It was a tactile relationship that sometimes slipped into something more, but there was something missing. That something was Tillie between us.

Leaning down, he kissed me, and even his kiss was fervent and a little feral. I gripped his head, imagining I could taste her on his lips.

We were doing this.

I left Truett's house the following morning, at the same time he went to work. I wanted to miss Tillie before she went to work, because quite frankly, I was a chicken shit and needed a day to come up with the words to tell her that she meant the world to me. Flowers too. I needed flowers. Maybe I could get the goats in on it—those little bastards owed me one.

When I got back to the house, it was empty again. I didn't know what Lance and Akio did during the day, but most of the time, they weren't home whenever Tillie was at work. I could have used the distraction.

Six hours later, I'd fed, watered, and changed the bedding for most of the animals who needed it, but I still didn't know how I was going to tell Tillie that I loved her.

No, you didn't start with the L word. I'd tell her I wanted to court her. That was the right idea.

I'd made dinner, a pot roast that was slow cooking in the oven. I'd also messaged Truett to stay home, so I knew we wouldn't be dominating the moment, being all Alpha. I felt like I needed this moment to be just me and Tillie. She had to be one hundred percent in, and Truett had a way of wearing you down to his way of thinking.

The door opened, and my heart leapt in my throat, but it was only Lance. I could hear the clip-clopping of Akio's nails. When he walked into the kitchen and saw the candles and flowers, he raised an eyebrow. "Uh, I don't think this is for me?"

I shook my head. "No. Well, I made you a plate. It's in the microwave." I reached down and patted Akio, who was sniffing at my jeans. Man, I hoped I didn't stink. "Truett told Tillie that we wanted to court her."

I didn't miss the flash of something sad in Lance's eyes before it was replaced by a small, happy expression. "Congrats. I haven't known you that long, but I'm pretty sure I should say 'about time.'"

I was still thinking about that flash of disappointment. Did Lance want her too? I mean, how could he not?

I liked the man in front of me; his actions now were much more important to me than his past, and my Alpha liked the Beta. So did Tillie. I'd thought she'd make a move on him, honestly, and maybe if she wasn't so damn noble, she might have. Shaking my head, I pushed the thought away.

A problem for another day.

I reached for a bag beside the kitchen door. "I got you something, but I'm not sure it's something you want, so feel free to say no." I handed him the paper bag with a smartphone inside. "I put my number on a sticky note in there, in case you need it. Whenever you need it." I looked around the kitchen nonchalantly. "There's some good apps on there for mental health. If you can't take any big steps, maybe just small ones will help for now."

Something about the big Beta tugged at my heart. I knew instinctively that he didn't want pity or sympathy, and some other part of me knew that he had no one else to lean on. He was a mystery, a wounded soul that I wanted to help. Maybe Tillie and I were more alike in that way.

He eyed the bag, but eventually, breathed a long sigh. "Thank you."

I shrugged. "Like I said, keep it if you want, or not. You can just leave it somewhere if you don't want it, no hard feelings. Keep my number, though. You might need that one day."

There was the crunch of gravel, and both the man and the dog turned to the sound. Lance stepped toward the microwave, grabbing out the plate of food and moving toward the stairs. "We'll leave you to it. Good luck, and... thanks for this." I wasn't sure if he meant the food or the phone. He whistled for the German Shepherd, and they quickly left the room.

Shit, here goes nothing.

SEVENTEEN

OTILLIE-JAMES

There were candles and flowers and a nervous-looking Sonny to greet me when I arrived home. I edged into the dining room, my eyes flicking everywhere, trying to take it all in at once.

"Sonny?" I asked softly, because I didn't want to assume this was for me and be wrong.

He licked his lips, a motion I watched with rapt fascination. "Uh, hi. I thought I'd make dinner."

God, this is so awkward. "Is Truett coming too?" Obviously, they'd spoken. He wouldn't be doing this if they hadn't had some kind of Alpha-to-Alpha conversation.

He shook his head. "No. I thought dinner with just us would be nice. Unless you want him here too? Or, uh, Lance? He's home, up in his room, I think."

I'd never seen my self-assured stepbrother so jittery. "No, this is fine," I reassured him softly, placing my bag by the door. "I'm going to assume that Truett spoke to you about what happened."

"Yeah, I went to his place last night, after he dropped you home. Come and sit down. I'll pour some wine, and we can talk." He grabbed a bottle of my favorite wine from the ice bucket. How did he know it was my favorite?

I could smell something baking in the oven, definitely some kind of bread. Cooking was one of Sonny's many talents, and I'd taken advantage of his kitchen skills over the years. We'd sat down for dinner so many times I'd lost count, but this was the first time it had ever felt awkward.

He stepped toward me, then stilled. "Oh, fuck it." Grabbing me up in his arms, he kissed me. Hard. A possessive kiss, filled with so much longing that it made my chest ache. I stood there, shocked, but my body knew what it wanted, and she was happy to take over while my brain caught up.

I threw myself into the kiss. The kiss with Sonny... I'd thought about what these lips would feel like so many times over the years, but it didn't do justice to the way they moved across mine. Dominating but soft, it was like we were dancing. He was leading the kiss, but tempting me to follow.

He tore his mouth away, his pupils blown wide. "I'm sorry. I should have checked with you if that was okay. I've wanted to do that for so long, and I—"

Instead of letting him go on, I grabbed the soft curls

of his hair and pulled his lips back to mine. I was kissing Edison Chalmers. One of the two men I'd loved forever. One of the two men I never thought I'd have. And if this was a fever dream, I was going to enjoy every second and pray I never woke up.

He lifted me easily and sat me on the table, slipping between my thighs like he was made to be there, his mouth covering mine like he wanted to memorize the feel, the taste, the sounds of us kissing. I was right there with him. I wrapped one leg around his, holding him tightly to me, letting my hands wander. Being able to touch him how I wanted...

"This is a dream," he breathed against my lips, leaning me further back as he echoed my earlier thoughts. "Tillie, you don't know how long I've wanted to do this."

Definitely as long as I have.

I grabbed his lapels, pulling him against me as I leaned back, kissing him with almost desperation. What if this was my only chance?

But I didn't need to worry, because Sonny followed me. He kissed me and kissed me, and I got lost in his heat. His scent was deep, like the forest and bourbon and the sweet lick of flames.

Actually, that burning scent was new.

"Tillie!" Sonny shouted, wrenching back and smacking at my head. "You're on fire!"

I screamed, and he threw a glass of white wine on my head, splashing it down my face. He was still patting the back of my head as Lance and Akio raced into the room, Doodles the dog skidding in hot on their heels, losing traction without a second back leg and sliding into the wall. Even Kevin the pig bounded in, grunting loudly. Lance must have been looking after the animals.

I didn't miss the knife in Lance's hand, but as he appraised the room, with me covered in wine, and Sonny carefully holding the back of my hair away from my body, he slipped it back into his boot. I hadn't even known he carried a weapon with him.

"What happened?" he asked calmly. Doodles came over to lick up the wine from the floor, and I nudged him away with my foot. The acrid smell of burned hair had now permeated the room, stinging my nose.

Sonny looked pale. "Her hair brushed against the candle flame and just went up like a fucking roman candle!"

Yeah, well, I had erratic frizz hair, and sometimes, it took a lot of product to keep it looking presentable.

Sonny was looking at my skin. "You have a slight burn on your neck. I think we should take you to get checked out." Lance reappeared with a cloth soaked in cold water, holding it to my nape.

"I'm okay, I promise." Actually, it stung like a bitch, but I didn't want to sit in the emergency room for hours. I paused. "How's my hair?"

They both winced, which was not a good sign. Sonny cleared his throat. "It's not too bad. It mostly burnt up the ends." He blew out the remaining candles. "I think we might get battery-operated ones from now on. Come on, I'll drive you to Urgent Care."

Ugh. "Sonny, I'll just go run it under cold water in the shower. It's really not—"

He turned, and I could see the guilt and the residual fear on his face. "Please, Tillie."

Huffing out an annoyed breath, I stood. "Fine. But when we're sitting there for hours, remember we could have played naughty nurse and recalcitrant patient in my bedroom, instead of trying to get comfortable on hard plastic chairs."

I woke to the sound of my phone ringing.

It had been a long night. Truett had appeared at Urgent Care just after we'd arrived, and had chewed Sonny out for so long, it was a wonder he hadn't needed burn care too.

As I'd suspected, I had a couple of first-degree burns, but honestly, it wasn't nearly as bad as it could have been. I had some burn cream, along with instructions on how to care for it if it blistered. The guys had dropped me back home at two a.m., tucking me into bed. I hadn't even protested, because I was literally dead on my feet.

Rolling over, I slapped my hand around, searching for my phone. Finding it under my pillow, I lifted it to my cheek. If it was work asking me to come in to cover someone's shift, I was going to hang up on them.

"Hello?" I mumbled.

"Otillie-James? It's Strat."

I blinked awake. "Hey, Strat. How are you?"

"I'm good, thank you." He hesitated. "I didn't wake you, did I?"

I looked at my phone, suddenly realizing it was eleven in the morning. "No, of course not," I lied. "Sorry, I was just, uh, watching the finance channel." *Oh my god, I'm such an idiot.* "What can I do for you?"

His low chuckle told me he knew I was full of shit. "The police have arranged a lineup for this afternoon and would like for you to attend, if you're free."

I stood, like being vertical meant that I was a constructive member of society. "Sure. What time?"

"Around three?"

I looked over at the mirror. Half my hair was gone, just charred ends standing up like frizzy little pubes. "Sure, three sounds good. Unrelated, but you don't happen to know anywhere I could get an emergency hair appointment?"

Luckily for me, Strat Wilmington was well connected. He'd managed to get me an appointment with one of the best salons in the city, and had promised to collect me from there personally to drive me to the station for the lineup.

My hairdresser was a sweet little Beta with a heart-shaped face and a button nose, who giggled when I recounted what happened. "I don't think I've ever had a kiss that hot," she chuckled as she chopped inches and inches off my hair. "No one's ever set me on fire like that."

I mock-glared at her. "Ashley, I swear I will not tip you if you keep making fire jokes."

She just smirked. "It might actually be worth it."

Apparently, the damage to my hair was worse in some parts than others, and it had caught in the center of my hair and not on the ends, so by the time Sonny had put it out, a lot had burned off.

Fuck my life.

Ashley had told me to trust her, then put me in front of a station with no mirror. That was probably for the best. Otherwise, I might have cried.

"At least you have the bone structure for a shaggy bob. It could be worse. You could have dead straight hair, and I'd have to give you a buzz cut," she cajoled, and as long lengths of my hair fell around me, I tried to see it as a silver lining. I'd been meaning to make a change for a while.

But what if the guys don't like me with shorter hair?

I wanted to punch myself in the ovaries. Who cared what they liked? If they only wanted me for my hair, then this accident was definitely a blessing in disguise.

"Okay, I'm almost done. Let me just blow dry this." I closed my eyes as she dried and styled, and I mentally prepared myself for something hideous.

The door to the salon opened, and Ashley sighed wistfully. When Strat Wilmington appeared beside my chair, I looked up at him and burst into tears. How fucking embarrassing. Over hair, of all things.

This PMS was getting wild, because I'd never been one of those people attached to their hair, or so I'd thought. This was harder than I could have ever guessed. I was out of control of my emotions.

Strat leaned down and nuzzled my face. "Oh sweetheart, you look beautiful. Don't be sad." He kissed my cheek, and I wasn't quite sure when we'd reached that stage of our friendship, but I let him. It made me feel better.

"Do you promise?"

He stood back up and nodded. "You'd look beautiful with no hair, but"—he looked at Ashley's name badge—"Ashley here has done a spectacular job. You look gorgeous."

As if to punctuate his words, Ashley whipped away the covering on the mirror, and I let out a relieved puff of air. It was a wavy little bob that sat around my chin, and it looked cute. Not nearly as bad as I'd thought. It wasn't my normal long blonde locks, but it wasn't bad.

I gave Strat a watery smile. "It looks good." I met Ashley's eyes in the mirror. "I'm sorry I doubted you. I swear I'm not normally like this. The last few days have just been a lot."

She waved a hand at me. "I know what you looked like when you came in. I get it. I'll get all this stuff off you, then I'll meet you up front." Removing my cape, she disappeared out the back.

Embarrassment flooded my cheeks. "Sorry for crying all over you," I murmured to Strat as he helped me out of the chair. He hugged me close, and I leaned into him.

Why did that feel so nice? I barely knew Strat. I knew I liked him. I thought he was hot, obviously. But normally, this level of casual affection would make me feel uneasy.

Maybe it was his Omega vibes.

"It's okay, sweetheart. Let's go. I'll grab you a deli sandwich from my favorite little place on the way to the station."

EIGHTEEN

STRAT

Something about Otillie-James was riding my Omega. He just wanted to put her on his lap and snuggle her for the rest of the afternoon. The last thing I wanted to do was take her to a police station to look at a bunch of criminals.

I hadn't been appeasing her; the new hairstyle made her look like she'd just been thoroughly fucked for a few hours, and I was dying to see if I could recreate the style back at my house, maybe in my nest.

So as I escorted her into the police precinct, it took me every ounce of willpower to wear a professional mask. I talked to the desk cop, and he buzzed us back. We were met by Detective Perkeski, an aging Beta cop who was just about done with the force and people in general. His hair had gone prematurely gray, his face was covered in more potholes than the Jersey turnpike, and he was generally just over people's shit.

"Mr. Wilmington, if you'll come this way?" He ignored Otillie-James altogether, and while normally that would irritate me, today it made my Omega rage. Maybe I was coming up to my heat? I'd have to look at my calendar when I got back to the office, so I could book the leave accordingly.

It was one of the reasons I'd gone with public prosecution and not into a private firm. I knew I'd never make partner, having to take a week off for my heat every three months. Bigoted old fucks probably did it themselves with their own Omegas, but they saw it as optional for Alphas, whereas there was no way I could just "push through" my heat.

Swallowing down a growl, I met Otillie-James's worried look with a smile. I was fine. I'd definitely figure this out later. I didn't want to go through my heat just yet; I had plans. Or at least, my Omega had desires, and it was up to me, the man, to make them happen. I couldn't just pout and whine and hope that the Alpha I wanted, and the pretty little Unshown, would fall into my nest with me.

I wanted to reconnect with Edison Chalmers, the other Alpha, first. I remembered him in passing from our teenage years, but that was it. I also wanted to meet Otillie-James's Beta, at least to see if he was right for her.

They led us to a viewing room, and the other detective, Hopkins, was there. He was a middle-aged Alpha, but he'd always treated my position with respect. He shook my hand, nodding respectfully, then did the same for Otillie-James. "Good to see you again, Miss Baler."

Flushing, she shook his hand. "I mean, same, I guess? I really am sorry about wasting your time, though."

He gave her a narrowed-eyed look, like he was trying to decide if she was really a criminal mastermind or just an idiot with a chicken. I could have told him she was neither of those; she was a beautiful soul, who just wanted to save the creatures that had no one else to save them.

He just grunted something and picked up the comms phone in the corner, telling them to send in the lineup.

Perkeski looked bored. "Just let us know if you recognize anyone as being at Hooley's Garage that night."

Of the fifteen men they showed her in the lineup, she was able to say for certain three had been there. One guy she remembered spitting on the cement near where she'd been hiding at the back of the garage. Another guy, she'd seen laughing and grinning at his winnings, though he seemed a lot less jovial now. And a third guy was Spartacus's owner, who'd tossed him back in his cage, brutalized and broken. I was glad he was here to get his comeuppance.

She indicated that there were two more who looked familiar, but not enough to say without a doubt they'd been there. She studied one in particular for a long time, a red-haired guy, who looked a little like he'd had his head shoved in a toilet bowl too many times. In the end, she said she'd seen him before, but couldn't place him at the cockfight specifically.

By the end, she looked flushed, and maybe a little anxious. This was a lot for most people; the weight of people's lives resting on your memory, but her word wouldn't be the smoking gun to put anyone away. There was still a fair amount of police work to be done, building a case on my behalf, before people got punished.

As I spoke softly to Hopkins about the next steps, there was a tug at my sleeve. I looked over my shoulder at Otillie-James, a frown immediately folding my face. She was looking more than flushed now. She was sweating lightly, her skin oddly waxy and her eyes feverish.

It was warm in this tiny room, but not unbearably so.

"I don't feel so great. I'm just going to go. I'll get a cab home." I shook my head immediately, but she stopped me. "No, I know you're still working. Don't rush off on my account," she croaked out. Her hands were shaking.

Did she have food poisoning? Was she having a panic attack? She looked wrong.

"I'll take you," I said firmly, then looked at Hopkins. "Call the office later."

He nodded, his eyes watching Otillie-James in a way that made me want to growl like an Alpha. I hustled her out of the station and to my car at lightning speed. My Omega was thrashing around inside me, and I didn't know why.

But as I closed my door, and her sweet floral scent hit

me square between the eyes, I knew. My Omega knew too, and he was *panting.*

Fuck.

"Otillie-James, are you okay?" I asked her softly, and she gave me a panicked expression.

She shook her head almost violently. "No. My body aches," she whined, curling over. "Maybe I ate something bad?"

She was twenty-three, which was old for this. It was extremely rare, but not unheard of.

"Sweetheart, I think you might be going through your designation and your first heat all at once. I think you might be an Omega."

Her pretty eyes flashed to mine. She looked at me like I was stupid. "I'm Unshown, Strat. I'm okay with that."

I shook my head, holding back a chuckle, because it wouldn't be helpful at this moment. "Does your belly feel like it's burning, yet you feel so slick that you're worried I'll be able to see it leaking down those pretty thighs? Does your skin feel so sensitive that even the smallest breeze feels painful, yet you know that if I touched you, you'd feel better?" Okay, that was a little presumptuous on my behalf. But I definitely hoped that it was true. "Do you feel hot and cold and so needy that you just want to peel off your skin?"

"Yes," she breathed through gritted teeth.

"Then babe, I think you're an Omega, and you're going into heat. There are a couple of options now," I tell her, pulling out into traffic. I had to get her somewhere fast, because I finally realized why my Omega had felt so off all day. She was pushing me into a sympathetic heat. Probably because it was her first one, and probably because it was delayed, it was going to be a doozy, and my Omega pheromones were all too happy to join in on the fuckery.

"I can take you to a heat house, and hand you over to some lovely nurses, who'll have some Alphas who've all had health checks and criminal checks, and signed agreements to keep you safe. They have all sorts of safeguards to protect Omegas during their heat. I've been to a few myself. I can drive you there personally." I cleared my throat, keeping my voice light, which was harder than expected. "I think you're throwing my Omega into heat, so we could ride it out together. It won't be perfect, and we'd be pretty mindless, so if there's someone you trust to check on us and make sure we aren't dehydrated husks, it would be best to call them." Her pheromones were starting to make my mind fuzzy now. "Alternatively, I can drop you home to your Alphas, if you trust them to get you through your first heat."

"Home," she breathed. A whine slipped from my lips, disappointed that it wouldn't be me and her, but I understood. When you were in the haze of heat, your instincts naturally wanted an Alpha. We were literally made for each other.

"Okay, sweetheart. Hold on." Using the car's bluetooth system, I pulled up Truett Heathstone's phone number. Then I reached over and wrapped my fingers in hers, holding her steady, pushing calming pheromones her way.

I remembered my first heat. It had been terrifying. I'd designated almost a year earlier, though, so I'd had time to plan and prepare, both emotionally and physically. To get a double whammy all at once must be so scary.

The phone line clicked. "Heathstone."

I almost panted at the sound of his voice. I was going to have to deliver Otillie-James and head straight to a heat house myself. My Omega whimpered.

"Hello?"

"Truett, it's Strat. Uh..." *How do I say this without sounding insane?* "I need you to meet me at the Chalmers Estate right now, and call your Packmate too."

"Excuse me?"

"Otillie-James has just been through designation, and her first heat is hot on its heels. She's an Omega."

The silence down the end of the line was so loud, I could almost feel it hum around the car, only broken by the sound of Otillie-James's whimpers of pain.

"Truett?"

"I'm sorry, I swear you just said OJ was an Omega."

I growled. "I *did*. Now get your ass home and attend to your damn Omega, Heathstone, or I will." I jammed the end call button and squeezed her hand. "Almost there, sweetheart. I promise, your Alphas will make it all better."

Or I'd kick their asses myself.

NINETEEN
OTILLIE-JAMES

I was an Omega. Holy shit, I was an Omega. This would change everything, and a little part of me mourned the life I'd had. Even though Strat was a lawyer, and Citrine was a geophysicist, they were the exceptions rather than the rule as to what was expected of Omegas.

It was generally assumed that Omegas would be homebodies, caring for their Packhouse, their nest, their offspring. None of those things sounded bad to me right now—especially the idea of a nest, and a lot of breeding so I could have offspring—but the logical part of me knew I'd soon be sad that I couldn't just walk down the street by myself anymore. I'd need an Alpha or a Pack member with me, in case an unscrupulous Alpha decided to bark me into submission. The world was a lot more dangerous for Omegas, despite being coddled and loved.

A stabbing pain in what I assumed was my uterus—

like a period cramp from a taser—had me folding in half. However, that was nothing in comparison to the clenching need inside, like if I didn't get a cock inside me ASAP, I might actually scream.

This was insane. I clung to Strat's hand as if he was my only anchor to reality. His scent washed over me, and I lifted his wrist to my face, breathing him in. It appeased that feeling inside me, so I didn't resist. I'd probably be embarrassed as hell about this later, but right now, I needed him so damn much. His scent was like a Vicodin straight in the veins.

His jaw was tight, and he didn't speak after he got off the phone with Truett. At the thought of the Alpha, my body clenched around nothing, and I whined. This was *awful.*

Strat laughed, and I realized I'd spoken out loud. "Don't worry, sweetheart, it definitely has its perks later. You'll quite like being an Omega when you have your big Alphas filling you up over and over. It's a couple of days of only telling yourself yes. Taking what's offered, without thought of propriety or other people's needs. It's all about you." He sounded wistful, like it really was something nice. I couldn't imagine how anything about this misery could be construed as nice.

He hit another button on his screen, and I realized he was starting a voice memo. "Okay, Otillie-James, while you are still coherent enough to think this is miserable bullshit, I need you to tell me who you want in your nest with you."

"Truett and Sonny," I said immediately, and my body clenched at the very thought of those two big Alphas wrapped around me, making me feel good. I looked over at Strat. "Uh, you. If you want. No pressure, though."

He lifted our still-entwined fingers to his lips. "I would be honored. We should talk to your Alphas first, though, because you are definitely throwing me into heat as well." His cheeks did look flushed, his eyes wide and wild. "Anyone else?"

I chewed my lip, worried about this next name. What if he felt pressured? My Omega didn't care at all. She wanted her Beta, even if he really wasn't hers, and logical me didn't understand the impulse to *own* people.

"You can ask for whatever you want, Otillie-James. Doesn't mean they have to give it to you. It's a consensual transaction, always."

"Lance. I want Lance." Damn, I'd been hiding from my attraction to Lance, ever since he'd let me get a glimpse under the wild-man hair he'd been using as camouflage. It was wrong to want him there, to make him feel obligated to cross that line for me. "If he wants to be there. No pressure."

I folded over again, moaning through the pain. This was miserable.

Strat stroked my thigh reassuringly. "I know, baby. I know. Don't worry, the memo is just for the guys to know that this is what you want. I won't even play it for them, unless they're worried about your consent, as they should. But you're already doing so great."

I didn't feel like I was doing great. I felt like I was on fire.

He pulled in through the gates of the estate, and I whined loudly, before slapping a hand over my mouth. Strat laughed, but didn't get to say much because when the car slowed at the front of the house, Sonny was already there, opening the passenger door and dragging me out.

Well, there wasn't much dragging happening, because I was propelling myself into his arms like a torpedo. I buried my nose into his neck and breathed deeply, filling my lungs with him.

"Truett called. What happened?"

I couldn't answer; all I could do was whine. I looked past him at Lance, who was standing in the doorway, looking worried. I made a little grabby-hand motion before I could stifle it. If I really was an Omega, I didn't have any self-control. My brain was screaming that this was terrible timing, unfair to everyone. We weren't at this stage in our relationships, and when it came to Lance, he didn't even know I wanted him like that.

When he didn't walk closer, I buried my face in Sonny's neck, and he stroked my back. But when a hand gripped mine behind Sonny's back, I opened an eye. Lance was there, his calloused fingers holding mine, feeling cool and perfect.

"Are you okay, Otillie-James?" he asked softly, and I shook my head.

"No."

"I'll handle everything here. Don't stress about it," he soothed.

My Omega whined. She was happy that our Beta was taking care of our house, but she wanted him in the nest with her too. I didn't even *have* a damn nest. I didn't want to use Citrine's; the idea of using another Omega's nest made my stomach heave.

I chewed my lip, my sane brain trying to push back my brain-addling hormones. "Will you stay with me? In my nest?" I asked him, and he looked so shocked, you'd think I'd slapped him.

His face went through a whole range of emotions, some I couldn't even name before they were gone, eventually settling back on his normal, neutral expression. His voice was soft. "I'm not sure I can."

Swallowing hard, I blinked back tears. That wasn't fair of me. It wasn't even fair to ask. "That's okay. Thank you for taking care of everything." My little Omega heart was breaking, but I tried to keep that from my face.

I realized Sonny and Strat were speaking to each other in low voices. "You really had no indication?"

Sonny was shaking his head. "No, though I guess our Alphas had picked it up, because they've been a little less restrained toward her lately. It was impossible to keep the distance."

Strat gave a strained laugh. "Hooray for bad Alpha control." He was beginning to sweat too, and I wiggled in Sonny's arms.

My Alpha—yes, *mine*—stared at Strat. "Omega, are you okay?"

Strat shook his head. "No. I'm going into heat too." He cleared his throat, but I could sense the strain in his tone. "Otillie-James has indicated she'd like me there during her heat, but I think that unless all the Alphas are on board, having two Omegas in heat would make it harder on Otillie-James."

I whined again, but suddenly, Truett appeared, and it became too much. Everything was too much now. I sucked on Sonny's neck, and he groaned, gripping my ass as I wrapped my legs around him. I ground my core against his abs, and normal me would've been horrified, but right now, I didn't give a flying fuck.

He buried his hand in my hair and pulled it back slightly. "Calm, Omega. I'm going to make everything better, I promise."

Everything was hazy. I reached for Truett, and finally, he was there, taking my lips with his and kissing away the pain. *Yes. This is what I need.* I climbed from Sonny's arms to his and gave him long, sucking kisses that were sloppy and desperate.

Truett pulled back, heaving in oxygen. "Baby girl, this is a surprise."

I wanted to say *no shit,* but I had better things I wanted to do with my mouth than verbally spar with him.

A scent hit me between the eyes, and I moaned. It wasn't Truett, though he smelled like heaven. It wasn't even Sonny, with his warm, earthy scent. No, I knew who it was, and I was *hungry*.

Pulling away, I looked over at Strat. "Omega," I growled. He was in heat too, and I was going to fuck my Omega. He was mine. "*Mine.*"

Wiggling out of Truett's arms, I went straight to Strat and climbed him like a tree. Bless his horny Omega heart, he didn't even hesitate, taking my lips with his and giving me a scorching kiss that just made me even more desperate. We fed off each other until I was clawing at his shirt. I needed his skin. I needed to touch it, to taste it.

"Jesus fucking Christ," someone groaned. "Omega, we would be honored if you let us see you through your heat also." I realized it was Sonny, and he wasn't talking to me, but to Strat.

"I accept. Thank you, Alphas," he mumbled against my lips. I pulled away so I could look at him. Did I look like that too? Flushed and wild?. "And thank you, my little Omega."

Holy shit. Why did that make me gush? He was also an Omega—it shouldn't have the same effect, should it?

"Now if you can point me in the direction of her bedroom, I'm this close to losing it and fucking her on your front porch."

Someone breathed the word *fuck* again, but it didn't matter to me anymore. The haze was fully down, and the Omega was in charge.

TWENTY
TRUETT

I was reeling. Not a lot of things in my life threw me for a loop, but Strat Wilmington calling to tell me that not only was OJ an Omega, but that she was in heat, well... I doubted I'd ever top it.

I'd expected neither of those things when I woke up this morning. I especially didn't think I'd be helping two Omegas through their heats.

Fuck. We were going to die. But what a way to go.

Male Omegas were reasonably rare, and people who bonded male Omegas coddled them, like they were some kind of rare and expensive creature. To have a male *and* female Omega during a heat was almost unheard of. I was kind of hoping, for the sake of all our health, that their heats would almost feed off each other.

We hovered behind as Strat carried OJ up the stairs, not even removing his mouth from hers to watch his step, either trusting himself or us to ensure he didn't fall to his death, taking her with him.

I moved closer behind him. He was a big guy, but I was bigger. The combination of their scents was enchanting. Beguiling. I was like a rat following the pied piper to certain death with a smile on my face. Strat was fucking gorgeous, his well-muscled body flexing as he strode up the stairs with self-assurance. His ass was so fucking biteable, I could barely resist the urge to lean forward and take it between my teeth.

I still couldn't believe Strat was here. My brain kept feeding me scenarios and positions, and each one got filthier and filthier, until I was fairly sure my cock was about to burst through the seams of my pants.

This was fate. Or luck.

Sonny and Strat had apparently come to some kind of agreement, and my Packmate was also staring at the two with stars in his eyes. Once we made it to the landing, I grabbed his arm. "No biting, Edison."

It wasn't the right time. She'd had enough upheaval; she needed to come to terms with that before we brought her into the Pack. But she *would* be Pack. She'd be our Omega.

Sonny nodded. "No biting. Not this time, anyway."

In agreement, we stepped through the door to OJ's bedroom, and obviously, we'd taken too long having our thirty-second conversation, because they were already naked. It was almost a superpower.

They were gorgeous together. Hard lines and soft

curves, pale skin and golden tan. They were perfect, two sides of the same coin. And they'd be mine for the next week. My Alpha roared to the surface, and I moved toward them. I wanted to watch, but I wanted to taste even more.

I ran my fingers up OJ's spine, feeling that creamy skin beneath their tips. "Hello, Omegas," I growled, and the combined noise they made was like a symphony. I was going to record that sound and use it as my morning alarm. My ringtone. My car horn. Everything.

I leaned closer, running my nose across her shoulder and burying it in her neck, groaning as she tilted her head. Jesus, she was already offering her throat up for my claiming bite, and we'd barely started. I was going to be a mess by the end.

"Do you want to suck down your sexy Omega while I eat that pretty little pussy, baby?" She mewled her agreement, and I grinned. "Good girl. Present for your Alpha. I'm going to lick up your juices until you come all over my face."

She pushed Strat back on the bed, and any semblance of the put-together lawyer was gone. He was all Omega now. Although she shoved him back into the mattress, his hands never left her skin, never stopped kneading and stroking. He'd hardly even looked at us Alphas yet, but it was coming. I knew it was. He was in the early stages of heat, or at least, I thought he was. I'd never helped an Omega through their heat before.

What if we fucked it up? What if I couldn't keep my teeth to myself and claimed OJ? Or fuck, claimed Strat?

Now wasn't the time for those worries, because my beautiful OJ, the girl of my dreams, was bent over in front of me, her ass in the air, her naked pussy dripping and delicious right there.

I snapped. I dove headfirst between her cheeks and plunged my tongue inside her. Gone was any finesse I'd ever had. I was operating one hundred percent on enthusiasm alone.

Sonny had come over, devoid of his own clothes, and he was leaning on the bed, whispering filthy stuff to the Omegas. OJ was doubling down on Strat's cock, and I kind of wished I could watch from Sonny's position. I could see his hand pumping his monster cock, so whatever it looked like, it was obviously hot as fuck.

Not as hot as my face covered in OJ's wetness, but close. I'd have plenty of time to watch her swallow cock, preferably mine. Too soon, she was fluttering around my tongue, the clamp of her fib pulsating around me.

Where Alphas had a knot, locking our cum inside our Omegas, female Omegas had a fib, which clamped around the base of our cocks and practically milked us of our release, stimulating a gland that would help us produce more, with a quicker refractory time.

Male Omegas had almost the lite version of both, and we called them locks, making male Omegas a little like a double adaptor. They had a small knot at the base of their cock—much smaller than an Alphas—to lock onto their female Alphas or mates, and a fib in their ass, helping them take a male Alpha's knot. It was why they were so sought after. They provided the best of both worlds.

Being in bed with both Omegas made me wish I'd paid better attention in health class.

All thoughts of classes escaped me, though, as OJ whimpered, climbing up Strat's body to straddle him. I could see his cock pulsing and hard, and I knew he hadn't come yet.

"Wait!" Sonny yelled, startling us all. "What about birth control?" I grabbed her hips to stop her sliding onto Strat's dick.

Fuck. This was an accident waiting to happen.

OJ whined, trying to move, but I had hold of her. Sonny gripped her chin. "Omega, *still*," he barked, and they both stopped. "Otillie-James, are you on birth control?" His voice was full of so much authority, it almost made me want to get on my hands and knees, and present too.

I snorted. *Not fucking likely.*

"IUD," she breathed, and he stroked his thumb across her cheekbone.

"Good girl. Now take your Omega's cock. He's waiting, and he aches."

I let go, and she didn't need any more encouragement than that. She sank down on his cock so quickly, it was like watching a magic trick. They both moaned something incomprehensible. Then she began riding Strat, and he looked like he'd found the promised land.

"I've never had another Omega before... Oh *fuck*," he groaned. It was slurred and dazed, and man, I got it. I was going to blow just from watching them. I watched the base of his cock swell, smaller than my knot, but still enough that when he pushed it inside her, they both slammed their eyes shut and came on a symphony of moans.

The noise, the view, their combined scents—it was like the best porn I'd ever seen, times a thousand. Unlike an Alpha knot that'd keep her almost prone in one place, there was a little leeway with Strat's lock knot, and he was using it to massage just inside her entrance, making her squirm and whine. Despite the knot, his pounding was making his cum leak out of her hole to drip between them.

Finally, she must have locked him tight with her fib, because he stopped moving and wrapped his arms tight around her waist, and they lay shuddering together. It was so goddamn beautiful and erotic and sexy that I was sure I'd see it every time I closed my eyes.

It only lasted moments until she was moaning and squirming again. Strat pulled her off his cock, his eyes meeting mine. "Take her. I might be Omega, but even I have a refractory time of a few moments," he slurred, falling deeper and deeper into his own heat.

I leaned down and gave him a slightly sloppy kiss. I didn't want the first time I kissed him to be later, when he was completely out of his mind in the heat haze. "We owe you," I breathed, and he just grinned back.

"I'll take it out on your flesh in approximately three hours," he promised.

OJ was trying to strip me bare, and her outrage that my clothes were in the way would have been adorable, if not for the fact her skin felt like it was on fire.

I sat back on the bed, letting her straddle my hips as I caught her lips with mine. I kissed her as she grabbed my cock, moving it to where she wanted it. She must've been able to taste herself on my lips, because she whined softly.

Sonny was there then, catching her lips with his own, and I watched them kiss. It was like a match dropped on a pyre; the heat between them was wild. I lifted her, turning her around, so her back was to my chest, and Sonny quickly dropped to his knees to claim her with his lips.

Finally slipping inside her, I groaned, my vision going white as my eyes rolled back in my head. Nothing had *ever* felt this perfect, not in my whole life. She rode me frantically, chasing the pleasure and relief, and I moved her hips, slamming her up and down on my cock.

"I'm going to knot you so tight, lock my release in that tight little pussy until I'm painting your womb," I groaned, and she screamed with pleasure. Sonny was still drinking down those moans, alternating between her lips and her tits.

Too soon, my knot was swelling, tightening like a fist inside her, and it felt like I was going to black out from the sheer pleasure of it. I held her hips still, grinding up but not allowing her to bounce around. I didn't want to dislodge my knot and hurt her.

"That's it. Look at you taking my knot, like a good little Omega. God, I've loved you so long," I whispered. That last bit just slipped out, though I was fairly sure she couldn't even hear my words right now. She was a ball of need, of desire, of heat and pain and pleasure. I would tell her again once she was back to OJ—sweet, sassy, and full of fire.

I'd tell her every day for the rest of our lives, if she'd let me.

Twenty-One

Lance

This was painful. I wasn't just talking about the throbbing of my dick, which had been hard for the last two days. I mean, that was painful too, but it had nothing on the look on Otillie-James's face when she'd reached for me, asking me into her nest. The disappointment on her face when I'd said no.

It wasn't that I didn't want to. I did. God, more than *anything* in my short, miserable fucking life did I want that. However, I knew that if I was with her through her heat, if she invited me into her nest and into her body, I wouldn't ever leave.

So instead of helping Otillie-James through her heat, I was taking care of the other half of her heart. Taking care of the animals here was a full-time job; no wonder she'd been struggling so hard when I first met her. I started at five in the morning and went until ten at night, though it was a little better now that the kittens were starting on solid food. Their feedings were less frequent throughout the day.

But they were only one small portion of her daily routine. Giving medication, feeding and watering, changing out bedding, giving the birds free-fly time and then getting the little fuckers back in their cages—it all took hours. And I was thankful for every single one of those tasks, especially the ones that took me outside and away from the sounds of her cries of ecstasy. Away from the scent of Omegas in heat.

I swore beneath my breath, and even Akio whined. He was picking up on my tension, and I worked hard to soothe my fractured feelings, at least for him, if not for myself.

I was currently lugging hay for the goats and herding them away from the azaleas once more. Yesterday, when the height of the heat had been washing the house in pheromones, I'd built a fence outside. It was only temporary, but it should keep them off the flower beds.

Scaramouche gave me the side-eye as she ate her hay, and if you'd ever had the side-eye from a goat, you'd know it was a little demonic. Something about those slitted pupils made you believe that they were one bad mood away from headbutting you in the balls.

I'd also prepped baskets of food and hydration, leaving them outside the bedroom. I hadn't seen either of the Alphas yet, though maybe I should hook them up to an IV. Technically, I'd been trained to do that in the Marines.

I fed Gert the goose, and the now-besotted Spartacus, who followed Gert around like a lovesick rooster. You'd never even know he'd once been a fighter. The love of a good goose could do that to a cock, I guess. The other day, I'd even seen him trying to swim to the middle of the pond with her. I'd been preparing to dive into the murky little pond to rescue the dumb bastard, but luckily, he'd managed to swim his way out. Now he just waited for his lady love on the banks. Apparently, everyone had to learn a lesson or two the hard way.

There was a collection of cellphones on the dining room table, which had been ringing off the hook, but I didn't feel right answering them. So I'd just been ignoring them, and when either Sonny or Truett emerged, I'd get them to deal with it.

I headed back inside and made some fruit salad. Maybe the Alphas could coax the Omegas to eat something in bite-size pieces.

As if I'd summoned Truett, he emerged from the upper floor. He looked like shit. He was almost haggard, his hair disheveled, and he was covered in bite marks and scratches. He was in a pair of boxer shorts and nothing else.

He staggered a little, and I moved around the counter. I didn't want the big bastard to faceplant, because I wasn't sure I could deadlift him onto the couch. Steadying him, I helped him to a bar stool. "You look like shit."

Truett huffed a laugh. "They're both finally sleeping,

even if it's only for a moment. If I die today, I'll die happy. But dehydration isn't the way I thought I'd go," he said roughly. I walked to the fridge and got him one of the sports drinks I'd borrowed their car to go and buy. Smiling at me, he took it thankfully and downed the whole thing in one mouthful.

I grabbed the basket full of phones also. "These have been going nuts. I thought one of you should look into it."

He picked up his phone and immediately winced. "Fuck." He scrolled through all the missed calls. "*Fuck.* It's Buck and Citrine. Their parents."

I winced too. I wouldn't want to have that conversation. "You should call them before they send the cops around." If they were my kids not answering for days, I'd already have my ass on a plane back to South Carolina.

Truett shuddered, but I could see his resolve. "I know. I will." He looked at me appraisingly. "Why didn't you want to join her in the nest?"

I froze. "I'm not right for her." I didn't deserve her, but I didn't say that to him.

"You don't want her?" There was no judgment in his tone. "You can be honest."

"I want her more than I should. She just isn't for someone like me."

He stared at me with those eyes that were too intelligent. Like he could read me, my intentions, my very heart. "The fact you think that is the very reason you'd be perfect for her. I know you've been leaving the baskets outside the door. I know you've been caring for the creatures she loves. I know you look at her like she's an angel sent down from heaven to save your very soul."

He gave me a knowing smirk. "Despite what you've done in the past, whoever you were in a different life, the man in front of me now is very much worthy of the Omega who keeps asking for him. The Omega who saw something in him, before the rest of us. She might have absolutely no common sense, but she's a good judge of character. So if you can't trust yourself, you should try trusting her." He slapped my shoulder. "No pressure, though. Don't go in there unless you're really sure, because I promise you, once you've bathed in her light, there's no going back to the dark."

Grabbing his phone, he grimaced. "Wish me luck. I have to go tell a man who could crush my head in his hands that his daughter's an Omega, that I want to claim her into my Pack because I've loved her forever, and that me and his stepson are currently fucking her through her heat."

Fuck no. Even the idea of that conversation gave me cold shivers.

Picking up the fruit salad, I walked up toward her bedroom. The door was slightly ajar, and I couldn't help but look. The male Omega was spread across the bed, his head nestled in the crook of a sleeping Sonny's armpit. Dicks were out everywhere. And curled up in a small ball of creamy skin, her head on Sonny's hip, was Otillie-James.

She was beautiful, even though her hair was standing up at weird angles, and her cheeks were flushed bright red. If I had to guess, I would say she was going through another heat spike. I could smell it in the air, beneath the scent of sex and pheromones.

Her eyes blinked open, finding mine immediately. "Lance," she breathed softly, slipping from Sonny's arms and crawling toward me across the bed. God, she was what dreams were made of. I stood so still, I was like a deer in the headlights. "Lance, I hurt," she moaned.

I mightn't be Alpha, but I was helpless to ignore that plea. I straightened my spine and stepped into the room. "Do you want me to wake your Alpha, Angel?"

She shook her head, crawling into my arms. I shuddered, the rightness of her in my arms washing over me like a balm. I ran my hands up and down her naked back. This felt like taking advantage of her, and I couldn't get that out of my head. I tried to keep my hands in respectful positions, but my brain was very much aware that her naked cunt was pressed against my abs, and her chest was pressed against mine. She was one hundred percent Omega right now, and I told my cock to calm down.

"Want you," she murmured, and her lips began to roam over my cheeks and down my neck.

"I want you too, Angel, but not this time. I want you to be with me one hundred percent the first time we make love." Hopefully, I wasn't blowing my only chance to have her. She mightn't even want me, after the hormones of the heat stopped riding her like a bad addiction.

She frowned, then curled in on herself as pain washed through her. *Fuck.* I couldn't leave her in pain. "How about I take the edge off, and by then, Truett should be back. Would that be okay?"

She smiled at me, the expression so wide and joyful that I was stunned. "Yes," she moaned, before kissing me.

Wow.

I'd heard men talk about kissing someone and feeling like all their nerves had come alive, but I'd always thought it was just soldier talk. Everything back home was better when you were stuck in a tent in the middle of the desert —gas station hot dogs, candy corn, and kissing girls all became so much better than reality.

But this... Maybe they hadn't been talking out their ass at all. My whole world had shrunk down to this woman, this moment, this kiss. She held me close and kissed me, like that was all she needed from me, even though I could scent her desire and feel her slick dampening the bottom of my t-shirt.

When I pulled back for air, her face was dazed and wild, but she still winced as the heat made her cramp. I gently laid her down on the rug at the bottom of her bed, glad it was fluffy and soft. "I'm going to eat you out, and I think that should chase away some of the pain," I promised.

Her hands threaded through my hair, tugging gently. "Yes," she breathed.

Spreading her thighs, I stared dumbly at her dripping cunt. *God.* My dick throbbed, and there was no way I wasn't going to come in my pants like a teenager. Thank god she'd never know.

I ran my tongue up her inner thighs, licking up the juices smeared across them. Her fingers tugged at my hair, hurrying me, and I chuckled low. Now was not the time to tease her, but one day, if I got the chance, I was going to edge her for hours until she was whimpering my name.

Stiffening my tongue, I ran it along her seam, from entrance to clit, and she moaned so loudly that there was no way she wasn't going to wake the other two. She gripped my hair hard, grinding herself up against my face, riding it.

I went wild, sucking and licking and fucking her with my tongue, breathing when I could, but if I suffocated—or, given how much she came, possibly drowned—I had to hope one of the others knew CPR. If not, what a way to die.

She kept chanting my name over and over, and it was the best sound I'd ever heard. I murmured encouragement with my mouth on her clit, making her wriggle and writhe, and I wondered if I could just eat her for hours.

After the third orgasm, though, she was panting for my cock, and I froze. I couldn't. Not like this. I wanted her to want me, not just who she thought I was in the heat craze. I pulled back and realized that we had indeed woken up the other two people in the room, as Sonny was now fucking the male Omega right into the mattress.

A hand landed on my shoulder, and I was so blissed out on the taste of Otillie-James, I didn't even startle. Truett was there, giving me a knowing look as he knelt down beside me. "How about you kiss your Beta while I fuck you on my knot, sweet Omega?"

Otillie-James frowned, like she wanted to protest, but once she got a look at Truett's cock, she was all grabby hands. Omegas in heat were needy but simple creatures, and I breathed a sigh of relief for that. Because if she'd insisted, I wasn't sure I'd have the willpower to deny her again.

Truett pulled her to her feet, lifting her easily into my arms. "We are about to get real up close and personal right now, Lancelot," he said, using Otillie-James's nickname. "Better brace yourself."

She wrapped her arms around my neck, kissing herself from my lips. I held myself steady as Truett lifted her thighs and dragged her down onto his dick. She moaned down my throat, like she was feeding me her pleasure. He fucked her hard, trusting me to hold them steady.

As she murmured incomprehensible things against my lips, I wrapped one arm around her ribs and dropped my other hand between her pussy and my abs, so she could grind her clit against my palm.

She went wild. It didn't even matter that I felt the slide of Truett's knot against my palm. In fact, I swear it made him go even harder, so apparently, he didn't mind either. He had his lips pressed against her shoulder blade and a wild look in his eyes, and how they'd resisted bonding her yet was a real miracle.

The friction rubbing on my cock made me blow inside my jeans, and I'd have been embarrassed if this wasn't the fucking hottest thing ever. Finally, she came two more times, and Truett knotted deep inside her, making her sigh with relief. I pressed her back into his chest, and he held her to his body tightly, walking them backwards. I made sure they didn't fall, but her eyelids were already starting to flutter closed. Grabbing some of the electrolyte drink from the basket beside the door, I tempted some between her lips before she passed out completely.

Then I hightailed it out of that room, like the chicken shit I was.

TWENTY-TWO
EDISON

I'd never felt so exhausted and exhilarated at the same time. Tillie and Strat's combined heat had lasted five days, and without Lance bringing us sustenance, I wasn't sure we all would have survived. It had been a blur of sex and knots and so many bodily fluids, it was basically the inside of a teenage boy's tube sock.

The whole place would have to be deep cleaned, and I suspected the mattress would probably have to go. They had special nest mattresses that were fluid-proof, but we'd had no warning to get one of those.

Next time Tillie's heat hit, she'd have a perfect nest, and this would be an amazing experience, not one that came with a heavy dose of *what the fuck?*

I had her on her side, promising her all these things as we made love gently. Truett was covering Strat beside us, fucking him with a dominance he seemed to crave. They were so goddamn hot, and Tillie panted as she watched them. I could feel the frenzy of the heat lessening with every hour, and as much as I wanted to stay in this room forever, there was going to be a world of problems that would arise from this.

Truett had said Buck and my mom were coming home next week, and I was tempted to claim Tillie now so they couldn't take her from me. I would never steal her choice from her, but my Alpha was frantic that perhaps she'd change her mind and we'd lose her forever.

Her fib tightened around me as she came, engaging my knot, and we locked together. I wasn't sure how I knew it was for the final time in this heat; I just did. I held her extra close, nuzzled my nose into her nape, and just breathed her in.

She laced her fingers with mine, her body relaxing for the first time in days. This moment was perfect, and as Truett came along with Strat, sealing it with a dirty kiss, I wondered where we would all go from here.

I hadn't even realized I'd fallen asleep until a gently nuzzling against my chest woke me. The skin beneath my palms felt cool, and I knew Tillie's heat had officially broken. I looked down at the woman in my arms, at the face I'd loved for so many years.

"Hey there," I said softly, not sure how this was supposed to go. Would she want us without the heat driving her? Did we go back to that tentative progress from before?

As if she could see the uncertainty in my mind, she leaned up and kissed me. "Thank you."

I scoffed. *Thank me?* "Don't thank me, Tillie. That was... unbelievable. Something I won't ever forget. Thank *you*." I brushed my lips across hers. I knew the shape of those lips better than my own now. I knew what they looked like as they screamed my name, the shape they made as she came, their stretch when she was in pain. How they looked wrapped around my cock.

She rolled her eyes at me, and as much as I loved Omega Tillie, I loved this one more. The one who called me on my shit, who sparred with Truett, who had such a big heart. "I mean thank you for stepping up and not hesitating, I guess. If I had to go to a heat house, I'm not sure..."

I growled deep in my chest. There was no way a strange Alpha would have taken care of my Omega through her heat. I would have gone in there, taken her back by force if I had to. I didn't care if that made me sound like a barbarian.

She grinned up at me. "At least you aren't settling on an Unshown now."

Shock made me blink. I gripped her shoulders and tugged her up, until we were nose-to-nose. "Otillie-James Baler, I loved you before you were an Omega. I've loved you every day since you stood in front of me, all defiant and fresh from the damn mountains, and the most beautiful girl I'd ever seen. Before this, before you were an Omega, there was only one Pack for you, and it was ours.

The fact you're an Omega now just means that we get to have a hot-as-fuck orgy a couple of times a year, but it changes nothing else. Not the way I want you, or the way I love you."

Her eyes were glassy as she rested her head on my chest, right over my heart. "I love you too," she whispered and I held her tight, this woman who held my whole heart. "Dad is going to kill us."

Yeah, that he is.

Dressed and showered, we all reconvened in the living room. There was a high chance that this was going to be awkward. Strat and I had basically been strangers before this week, and now I knew what his cock tasted like.

Lance had been dragged into the heat. Not against his will—because if he'd said no, I would have enforced it, no matter how much I loved Tillie—but maybe against his better judgment. I mean, his judgment was way off on this, but it still had the potential to get weird.

As if all this wasn't bullshit enough, our parents would be back next week, and we had a house full of pets, a guest room that was now a permanent aviary, and my mother's garden had seen better days.

That wasn't long to set everything to rights and find places for all the animals. Buck and Mom had been pretty tolerant of Tillie's rescues over the years; we'd had everything from baby birds to mangy foxes. But they had a strict rule of only one at a time, and only as long as it needed a home. She was supposed to be actively trying to reintroduce them to their natural habitat or finding them a home. Buck believed that wild animals should be returned to their own ecosystem, and that if you didn't try and rehome the domestic animals, that was one less animal you could save.

I was fairly sure the only thing they'd been actively saving was their sanity.

I looked at the dogs sitting in a huddle with Akio. Let's just say, she'd passed the "only one" rule quite a few animals ago.

Drinking Gatorade, Tillie flopped down on the couch beside Strat, snuggling into his side. Okay, so they were definitely still feeling each other without the heat hormones. That was good. Because I was also feeling Strat without the heat hormones.

I frowned a little. Could we even *have* two Omegas? Was there a rule against that?

Fuck it. Rules are meant to be broken.

Truett sat watching them hungrily, and I cleared my throat. Shaking his head, he put on what I liked to call his business face. It was the one he'd used around Tillie for years, so she never knew that he was secretly in love with her. "So, no point dancing around it. Your dad and Citrine will be back next week. They called while you were deep in your heat, and I had to tell them. Otherwise, Buck was going to send around the cops and make sure we didn't have you tied up in the basement or something."

He was exaggerating. Buck trusted us. But he *loved* his daughter, and he wasn't about to take our word that everything was okay, when we couldn't give any details.

Truett looked guilty. "I know you probably wanted to tell them, but honestly, your dad scares the absolute shit out of me. Then Citrine got on the phone..."

Yeah, the two of them could make quite the convincing pair. The iron fist and the velvet glove.

Tillie reached over and squeezed Truett's hand. "I understand. Honestly, I don't know what I would've said anyway, if I'd had to tell them. I'm kind of glad it was you." She smirked, and I wanted to kiss her. "Sorry you had to be the sacrificial lamb."

Lifting her fingers to his lips, he kissed her knuckles. "There isn't anything I wouldn't do for you, firecracker."

Romantic bastard. It worked, though, because Tillie climbed off the couch and straight into his lap. Seeing them together like this, the girl I'd loved forever and my Packmate, who I'd loved even longer, made my heart swell in my chest. They kissed, and I tried not to stare like a creeper.

It helped that I wasn't the only one watching enviously, as both Strat and Lance couldn't seem to drag their eyes away. While they kissed, and kissed, and kissed, I looked over at Strat. He looked almost...wistful. Envious. It was hard to navigate this part, but I was going to try. I was the head Alpha of my little Pack of two, which meant that it was my job to ensure everyone was happy.

"Omega," I said softly, drawing his eyes. "What do

you need?" It was a rumbling question, almost more Alpha than my own voice.

He shook his head. "So many things, Alpha. Things I'm not sure I'm allowed to have." I wasn't wrong. There was sadness in his tone, and it burned my nose. I held out my arms, and he didn't rush into them, but he edged closer and closer until he was at my side.

I wrapped his large body in my arms, holding him close. "Tell me what you want, Strat, and I'll do my very best to make it happen." I stroked my hand down his arm, until I could entwine our fingers. He had pretty hands. Long, strong fingers and wide palms. I bet his parents had been surprised he didn't designate Alpha, an anomaly for sure, but I thought he was beautiful. "You're so perfect."

I wanted to court him. To ask if he'd let us make him ours, but there was more than just me in this Pack now. I had to speak to them first, even though I was almost sure neither of them would protest.

Instead, I kissed the side of his head and made the only promise I could make. "This isn't an ending, Strat. This is a beginning. You have my word."

He looked at me with wide, appraising eyes, and I left my truths right there, written all over my face. I was having two Omegas, and no one would stop us.

Apparently, Truett and Tillie had stopped making out, because she let out a long, put-upon sigh. "Do you think the parents will let me blame all the animals on my Omega nesting?"

I mean, it was possible, but unlikely. She'd been this way long before she designated.

Truett shrugged. "I can keep a couple at my apartment."

I shook my head. My apartment had a no pets policy, so I was out.

Lance cleared his throat from where he stood near the doorway. "I may have a solution."

TWENTY-THREE

OTILLIE-JAMES

This had been the weirdest week of my life. That included the time I'd picked wild mushrooms for my soup when I was thirteen and gotten one of the wrong kind. I'd spent three days thinking I was a cupcake with special powers, while I recovered in a hospital in Montana.

I'd gone from zero to a thousand with the guys and Strat, and I couldn't even find it in myself to feel bad about it. The whole thing had felt right on a soul-deep level. It was like my heart was *home*.

Except when I looked at Lance. Then all I felt was shame. I'd basically coerced the poor guy into eating me out. *Fuck, I'm an awful person.*

I'd fully expected him to be gone when my heat broke, but I should have known better. Lance was loyal to a fault, and he'd kept this whole animal operation running while

I'd been vagina up for five days. I'd have to apologize. I'd have to find him somewhere else to live. Maybe I could convince Truett to put him and Akio up in his apartment, just until I found something more suitable.

We were all piled into the Range Rover, Akio with his head out the window, Lance in the front seat as he directed us outside of town. We drove about thirty minutes outside of the city limits, and the suburbs slowly turned into more rural areas.

I held my phone in my lap, my screen open on a new text to Strat. I was trying to work out the etiquette around texting after a heat. Did I tell him I missed him already and hated that our group had to be separated? My Omega literally whined at the thought that Strat wasn't right here in touching distance.

And that was a fucking weird thing in itself. Having these opposing feelings, like there were two beings now trapped inside my body. The Omega, whose needs and desires were mostly like mine, with a definite hedonistic tint to them. She really didn't care about logistics—just about what she wanted.

She wanted Strat. She didn't care that she was *supposed* to feel territorial about other Omegas near her Alphas. Actually, the idea of any other Omegas near Truett, Sonny, or even Lance made me growl low in my throat, making Truett throw me an appraising glance. I swallowed it down.

Strat was definitely the exception to the rule. Because

the idea of anyone else touching Strat that way also made her mad.

Fuck it.

> Me: Miss you already.

I sent the message, then tossed my phone face down across the seat. *Jesus. How desperate can I be?* What if he'd just wanted some heat partners and that was it? What if *he* didn't want to share Alphas with another Omega?

I was all about my own wants and needs, and I hadn't even thought about anyone else.

My phone vibrated, and I snatched it up. I really had no chill.

> Strat: Not as much as I miss you. Let me know what you find on Lance's mystery tour?

> Me: I will. You should come around this week. Would that be okay?

I wanted to slap my forehead. I sounded like such an awkward weirdo. The bubbles bounced at the bottom of the screen for a long time, like he was deleting and rewriting the message a dozen times. Probably trying to work out how he could tell me he wasn't interested in me like that, without hurting my feelings.

Maybe I'd misjudged. Maybe the heat hormones had colored the whole experience, and he hadn't been as into it as I was, without his own heat hormones feeding off mine.

I was convinced he was writing a message to let me down easily, and I wanted to throw my phone out the window, but I couldn't take my eyes from the screen.

Strat: If I had my way, I'd never leave.

Happiness flooded every single one of my limbs, and I bounced a little in my seat, trying to control my excitement.

Truett reached out and gripped my hand. "You okay there, OJ?" I showed him my phone, and he grinned back. "You like your handsome Omega, huh?" He said it lightly, but I could feel the weight behind his words.

Tilting my head, I raised a brow. "Don't you?"

He dragged me closer to his side and kissed my head. "Absolutely. And I think we should court him as a group, if you're happy with it, and your Omega doesn't mind." He lowered his voice. "When it comes down to it, you're our first priority, OJ. Later, as our Pack grows, the Pack as a cohesive whole will be a priority, but you're the girl we've wanted forever. Loved forever. Your comfort means the most to us right now. When you're ready to court Strat, let us know. If you're never comfortable enough to have another Omega in the Pack, so be it."

He placed his lips beside my ear. "If you want to bring in a certain Beta, we'd be okay with that too," he whispered lightly, so the guys up the front couldn't hear.

"This Pack is yours now, baby. You shape it however you feel is right."

I blinked up at him, trying not to cry, trying to find the words I needed to tell him how I really felt.

"We're here," Lance said softly, something slightly off about his tone. I dragged my eyes from Truett to look out the window.

My breath caught in my throat. "Holy shit. Who owns this place?"

A huge house sat perched in the middle of rolling pastures. Trees bracketed the back of the house, making it feel secluded and private. I looked down at my outfit. Maybe I should have dressed nicer.

Lance opened the passenger door. "I do," he replied quietly, climbing from the car and walking toward the pasture.

I blinked. I didn't understand. Not at all.

I looked over at Truett. "Did you know about this? Did it come up in that background check I know you did?" I knew this Alpha—the first thing he would've done when he'd met Lance was a police check, then a more thorough background check. Always looking out for my safety, even if I did want to throat punch him at times.

He shook his head. "No. Not a single word." He kissed my fingers. "There's only one way to find out. Let's go ask the man in question, shall we?"

Wherever we were, Akio was familiar with it, because he was trotting around like he owned the place, looking more like a dog than I'd ever seen him. Lance was standing beside the fence, looking out over the pasture, like looking at the house caused him physical pain.

I indicated the guys should stay back, and walked toward him. "Lance?"

His jaw was flexing, tension radiating from his body. "I know what you're thinking. If I have a place like this, why am I mooching off you? Maybe it was an elaborate scheme to take advantage of you."

I screwed up my nose at him. "Actually, that hadn't even crossed my mind." I placed a hand on his lower back, feeling him practically vibrating with tension. "Can I hug you? You look like you need it, and it's sending my Omega a little crazy." He looked down at me, his eyes wandering over my face incredulously, but eventually, he lifted an arm, and I snuggled in beside him, sighing happily at the contact. "Talk to me, Lance. I'm not going anywhere." I kept my tone light, but I was imploring him to trust me. There had to be a reason he'd been living under a bridge, instead of in the million-dollar farmhouse in front of us.

He sighed and pulled me a little closer, as if I gave him comfort. I didn't think I'd ever been prouder in my life. I rested my cheek against his shoulder silently; he'd speak in his own time.

"I inherited this place when I got out of the Marines. It shouldn't even be mine." He was silent again for a long time, and I was beginning to wonder if that was all he was going to give me. "I was a foster kid. In care since I was four, shoved around from place to place until I ended up with a bad attitude, and eventually, a juvenile record. When I was at a careers day thing at school—I got free food, so I never skipped—there was a military recruiter there.

"He took one look at me and said, 'Son, you're at a crossroads. For someone like you, there's prison, or there's the military. One road leads you to being nothing more than a lifelong drain on society. The other lets you be a hero. You choose.'" Lance huffed. "Obviously, I chose the military. Went through bootcamp. Went on to become a Marine. Got accepted into one of their spec-op units. Still waiting to be the hero."

Honestly, it was more words than I'd ever heard him speak in a row. I just squeezed his hand. I didn't want to interrupt, but I wanted him to know I was here, present and listening.

"Anyway, when you're in an elite military group that you can't talk about with other people, you kind of begin to look at the team as your family. There were six of us, and two war dogs. One was Akio." The dog in question was currently peeing on every fence post along the tree line. "My commander was a career Marine. Had come up through the ranks. He was an amazing tactician, marksman, and could kick my ass in hand-to-hand combat.

"Sometimes they keep themselves apart from the rest of us, making it easier for them to send us into situations where we might not come out. But not Matt. He was there with us every step of the way. When we were wounded, he was at our bedside. When we cried, he cried with us. In a firefight, he was right there, beside you, shoulder to shoulder. He might have been twelve years older than me, but he was like a big brother and best friend all rolled into one. He was that to all of us.

"We were a group for years, longer than most. They tend to split you up after a while, because it starts to become 'men before the mission.' But we had such a good success rate, with such low casualties, that they kept us together. We did some terrible shit, and the ones who had lives, wives and families, they didn't stay long. It was just us."

His voice was shaky. I hugged him tighter, and this time, he wrapped both arms around me and held me close. He needed me; I could feel it in my bones. This was the start of something.

"Our last mission went to shit. We got pinned down in a minefield—it was dark, and we couldn't see the signs. It's how I got half my face blown off, but I was still better off than the rest. They put us down as we lay there bleeding. I thought I was a goner. Everyone else was dead. I couldn't see. The only reason I got out of there was Akio, who led me out. Akio was Matt's partner. His MWD."

My heart broke for the man in my arms. He'd lost his whole family in one terrible night. One failed mission, and his world was gone.

He cleared his throat, and I gave into the urge to climb further up his body, so I could rub my cheek on his and be even closer. He put his hands under my thighs and rested me on the top rail of the fence, leaning into my body, burying his face in my neck so that the next part was muffled against my skin.

"I was discharged, and I fought to keep Akio with me. Wasn't too hard—we were both damaged tools of war. Someone who knew Matt had him reclassified as a service dog, then had him assigned to me. But a lawyer found me soon after, said Matt had rewritten his will a few years ago, and listed all the men in our team as beneficiaries to his estate. If he died on assignment, this property was to go to us all in equal portions. Except there was no one left but me and Akio. So I got the whole lot. That's why I came to Rock Hill."

He let out a shaky breath. "But when I got here, I couldn't go in. Matt was everywhere, even outside. His bike in the garage. His pictures on the wall in the living room. I slept in the stables for a bit, but even that got too much. It was like a giant testament to my failure to keep them alive. A reminder that I was here, while they're all buried in a military graveyard up north. That I had to attend five military funerals for the only family I had. That I had nothing left. Just their ghosts, Akio, this house, and survivor guilt."

Not for the first time in my life, I didn't know what to do or say to make it better. So I just held him. "Thank you for telling me. And thank you for bringing us here." I stroked my fingers through his hair. I didn't want to tell him what a man I didn't know would have wanted; that was presumptuous. But if Matt had left this to his men in his will, then I didn't think he'd be the type who'd want them to carry around guilt at his death. I couldn't tell Lance that, though. I could only offer him one thing.

"You aren't alone anymore, Lance. You have me—us—for as long as it makes you content." I chewed my lip, not sure it was the right time for this. "Even if that means forever." I tried to keep the hope out of my voice, but doubted I was successful. His arms tightened around me slightly, but he didn't reply, just held me silently.

I couldn't see the guys, though I knew they'd be here somewhere. I wasn't sure how long I spent carding my fingers through his hair, soothing him in the only way I knew how, before he pulled back a little. His hands stayed on my hips so I didn't fall backwards off the fence rail, and he picked me up easily, setting me on my feet.

"Matt would've liked you. Liked that this place was going to be used as a refuge for creatures no one else wanted." He grabbed my hand, still not meeting my eyes, and pulled me gently toward the house, pulling keys from his pocket as we walked. Truett and Sonny appeared, standing a few feet back, giving silent support to us both.

It was hard, but it was healing, and that was the only thing I wanted for my Lancelot. My white knight.

TWENTY-FOUR
STRAT

Apparently, moving the animals to Lance's place was an "all hands on deck" kind of deal. Even I'd been roped in, and honestly, I was happy to be included, even if I knew nothing about animals. My parents hadn't been pet people. Hell, they hadn't even been kid people.

But I was happy to follow orders and haul boxes. Otillie-James's vet friends had also come along, bringing a large horse trailer to load goats and crates into. I imagined this was how Noah had felt when it started to rain.

I stood holding the leash of a truly obese dog, though you wouldn't know that from the athleticness of his tail. He was very sweet, even if walking looked painful for him. I scratched behind his ears while we waited for our turn to be loaded onto Otillie's Ark.

We hadn't talked about what had happened during

her heat. We hadn't spoken about where we all went from here. We were just continuing as if it had never happened and she wasn't an Omega, and we were back to the getting-to-know-you portion of our friendship, pretending like I didn't know how she tasted when she came all over my tongue.

One of Otillie-James's friends wandered toward me. From what I could tell, they were a large Pack, and the woman walking toward me was their Beta, Anakie. She and Rex were both vets, while their other Alpha was a mechanic, and their Omega was their heart.

Anakie dipped her head as she approached me, bending down to pet the obese Lab. "Omega. How are you doing over here?"

I shrugged. "He's a very good boy," I said softly, making the dog look up at me adoringly. He really was cute. I wondered if Otillie would keep him.

"That he is. He just needs a little extra care. He's got a really big heart, and some people would abuse that."

I looked at the Beta. She was pretty, in an earthy way. Light brown hair, freckles from being in the sun, rough hands and laugh lines—she was a beauty in her own unique way. But she didn't make me feel anything like what Otillie made me feel. Well before she'd been an Omega, even.

I met her eyes. "She's tougher than she looks. She doesn't need us to fight her battles for her. But I promise that I'll protect her, heart and body, for as long as she'll let me. Those Alphas over there? They adore her. I'm also fairly sure Lance would jump in front of a bullet for her, and they're still at some weird emotional impasse." I shook my head. "We haven't got it all figured out yet, but Otillie-James is our focus."

If I'd thought that would be the end of it, I was sorely mistaken. These people obviously loved Otillie, so when the other Omega popped up beside me, I wasn't even surprised. Anakie's Omega was the opposite of her; Sophie was soft, curvy with dark hair and a wide smile that stretched across her face. She looked nice, but her Omega didn't call to me the way Otillie-James's did. My connection to my Omega defied logic.

Sophie tilted her head at me. "You're okay that she's another Omega? That you'd be sharing Alphas? Because I love Tills, but the idea of her joining my Pack makes my Omega hiss like a wildcat."

I shrugged. It was hard to explain to anyone outside of myself. "Not only does my Omega not care about her designation, he wants her. I don't want her Alphas—" I cut myself off. "Okay, no, I *do* want her Alphas. There's a connection there. But if I had to choose, I'd choose her."

Sophie looked at me appraisingly, then grinned. "In that case, welcome to the family, Strat!" She hugged me tight and bounced off toward her Packmates. Rex, her giant Alpha, was carrying one of the crates, but leaned down, picked up his Omega one-armed, and kissed her. Honestly, it was impressive as hell.

Anakie snorted. "I better go save Gert before she ends

up sitting in that cage for ages, because they're making out like teenagers again." The Beta headed over there, but I watched as Rex broke off the kiss with his Omega to kiss her too. Man, they were the picture of perfect Pack bliss.

"Are you checking out other Alphas there, Omega?" someone whispered in my ear, and the scent of browned vanilla and sweet tobacco flooding my nose told me it was Truett.

A smirk curled my lips. "You have to admit, he's kind of hot, in that giant tank kind of way."

Truett grunted, pulling me back toward his chest. "Is that so? Is that what you like, Strat? Do you want a giant to pick you up and throw you around?"

Well, I wouldn't say no to that, but I wasn't interested in Rex. Not in the way I was interested in the man behind me. "Mmm, no. I prefer my Alphas with smart mouths and stacked bodies."

He nuzzled the back of my neck, making me want to pant. "Hmm, that sounds like someone I know." He nipped my shoulder, and I barely bit back a moan.

"Sonny?" I teased.

"Cheeky," he growled. "We still have to talk. I know that, but I can't stop fucking thinking about you. You'll let us court you, won't you, Omega?"

My heart stilled in my chest. "Do you all agree? Is this something everyone wants?" I hadn't felt so uncertain in my life. So nervous.

"We all agree. I think OJ might even like you more

than she likes us." He spun me around, so I was looking up into his face. He was only a few inches taller, but it was enough to make me tilt my head back. "Do you know, before she designated, OJ was trying to convince me that you were the perfect Omega for us? At that point, she meant for just me and Sonny, but I told her that if there was going to be an us, she was included in that. She didn't know it yet, but there was only ever going to be a future for our Pack with OJ in it.

"The fact she's an Omega is a curveball, but it doesn't change what we want." He kissed my cheek, just to the left of my lips. "We want you too, and we're happy to work hard to show you that."

They already had me. But it wouldn't hurt for them to make grand gestures, to show Otillie-James what she deserved. "Okay, but you have to court us both. Me and her."

Truett grinned, that smile with those dimples making my stomach do swoops. *Unfair bastard.*

"This is how I know you're perfect, Strat. You're a stubborn fucker, just like in the courtroom, but you are still looking out for our girl's best interest. We'll woo you both. Just you wait." He kissed my lips quickly, then bounded off to help herd Kevin the pig into the truck.

Our girl. I loved the sound of that.

Seven hours later, animals had been placed in stalls, kitten cages had been set up, birds had been placed in temporary aviaries, and the Remorne Pack had all gone home. We'd had a bit of a cookout in Lance's backyard, and I still couldn't believe this place. Or that he'd been living under a bridge when he could've been here.

But I didn't pretend to understand people's trauma, or what led them to the decisions they made. I might have made a different choice in their position, or maybe I wouldn't have. It was hard to know without living someone else's life experiences.

The Beta in question was haunting the house like a ghost, trapped somewhere between the past and present. I didn't know much about Lance, only what Otillie-James had told me. I didn't know where he fit into the Pack they were building. However, I thought he'd be staying around, which meant if I wanted to be part of her life, it would be pertinent for me to get to know him.

He was standing out in the backyard, throwing a rope toy for the dogs, including Akio, who was kindly letting Doodles the zombie dog get to it first. Doodles, however, had trouble holding onto the toy with his messed-up mouth, so Akio would pick it up and carry it back to Lance.

Honkers the Labrador was lying on his side, doing his best impression of a speed hump, exhausted after a big day of moving house. I reached down to scratch his ears, his tail thumping twice the only indication that he was alive.

Akio gave me the side-eye, but sidled up to me so I could scratch his ears too. "He seems to be enjoying the company," I said lightly as Doodles jumped all over the bigger dog.

Lance nodded. "He was lonely." He threw the rope again, both dogs running after it. Even Honkers attempted to sit up to chase the rope, but immediately decided it was too hard and flopped back down. Doodles leapt over him on three legs, like he was an Olympic long jumper.

"He doesn't seem so lonely now. He seems content, even. I know the group has accepted him, and he seems to have accepted them in return." I grinned as Doodles and Akio played tug of war with the rope, though Akio only had to lightly shake it, and the scrappy little dog went flying. "I wish it was that easy for us. Without the conjecture, the overthinking, the what-ifs and buts. Just pure acceptance. Then no one would have to be lonely anymore."

Lance looked at me from the corner of his eye. His face was a mess of scars, but somehow, they just made him interesting. One pulled up the corner of his mouth, tugging at in a way that must've been almost painful, even now. "I don't think you'll be lonely for much longer," he murmured, and I wanted to shake this big, stupid brute.

Okay. So subtle allegories aren't going to work.

I stepped in front of him, looking him in the eyes, startling him for a moment. Maybe making sudden movements toward a former Marine with PTSD wasn't my smartest idea, but I was all in now. "Neither of us has to be lonely anymore, Lance. She has enough to give us both. They have a place for us all. She looks at you like you're the last piece of candy in the bowl; she wants to eat you up in one bite." I shrugged and stepped back. "No one needs a martyr when they can have a hero, Lance."

Leaving it at that, I went back inside his house and found a collapsed Otillie lying on the couch, watching some reality TV show about an animal rescue—probably getting ideas. Ideas I'd help her achieve, if it made her happy. Sliding onto the spot beside her, I crawled between her thighs and rested my head on her lower stomach. Immediately, she scraped her fingers through my hair, making me purr.

Laughing, she smiled down at me, and I wondered if you could fall in love with someone in a week. I hadn't seen it; my parents hated each other. My grandparents had too, before they died. My friends' parents were either divorced or both working full-time careers, barely seeing each other.

From what I'd seen, love was a fantasy. And this love at first sight stuff? A fairytale.

But when she looked down at me, her eyes sparkling, that feeling in my chest felt a lot like love.

She stroked my cheeks. "Thank you for today."

I turned my face to kiss her fingers. "Anytime, sweetheart. Tomorrow, next year, forty years from now."

Her laughter told me she didn't think I was serious, but that was okay. I'd have time to prove to her I was dead serious. We lay there in silence for a bit, her fingers stroking through my hair, and my hand wrapped around her thigh.

I started to wonder if I could turn this moment into me eating her out on the couch.

She stiffened. At first, I thought I'd fucked up and said the inside words on the outside, but when I looked up at her face, she wasn't looking at me at all. She was staring at the TV.

"Pass me the remote."

I grabbed it from down beside the couch and passed it to her. She scrolled back the video, then paused the screen. I couldn't see what had her rattled at all. The host of the show sat with one of the owners beside a barn. The man's smiling face was warm, and whatever anecdote he was saying was making the owner laugh.

"Does that guy seem familiar?" Otillie asked, frowning.

I stared at the screen again. I mean, of course he looked familiar. The guy was basically a celebrity in South Carolina, with the reality TV program, and a vlog before that. His whole Pack were celebrities now, from their Omega, Allegra, to their other Alpha, John, who was a retired college professor.

I tried to see what I was missing, but came up with nothing. "Anthony Smalls? I mean, yeah?"

She shook her head, sitting up. "No, behind him, carrying that bucket."

I looked behind the interview, at all the workers

bustling around, trying to make such a large rescue run smoothly. When I spotted it, I sucked in a breath.

The guy from the lineup. The one she hadn't been able to place, with the red hair.

What were the chances that a worker from an animal rescue would also be at a cockfight?

Twenty-Five
Otillie-James

Two days later, I was still shaken by what I'd seen on *All Creatures Great and Smalls*. The Smalls Pack were my idols; they took in all the animals that no one else wanted, from guinea pigs to draft horses.

I tried to tell myself it was a coincidence, and Strat had said he'd look into it, but still, I was off balance. It played on my mind constantly.

At least it was distracting me from the fact that my parents were coming back tomorrow, and I'd have to face them and their inevitable disapproval.

Lance was back at his house, and I missed him. Missed him being here, with Akio, a steady presence. Even though I was there every single day caring for the animals, it wasn't the same as when he'd been here, listening to me blather on about the dogs at work, my dreams, the animals and all their damn problems.

I'd been selfish; I hadn't asked what *his* dreams were. I'd been so intent on his survival that I hadn't taken care of his hopes.

Everything was so up in the air, and it was making my skin itch. I hated that we were so spread out, that I could go days without seeing Strat or Truett as they caught up on their caseload. My Omega wanted them close by. She wanted more.

Sonny appeared in the doorway of my room. "Hey, Tillie. You okay? You smell... distressed."

Waving him in, I held out my arms. I was so glad he'd taken time off from the fire department, but eventually, he'd have to go back too. My Omega whined at the thought.

He held me closer, kissing the top of my head. "What's wrong, baby?"

Shaking my head, embarrassed, I just buried my face in his chest. I couldn't believe that my emotions were so out of control now. No, not out of control, just close to the surface. Apparently, there was no bottling up your emotions when you were an Omega—they were just out there on display for any designation with scent sympathy.

"My Omega is just being a whiny little bitch. I'm fine."

He looked down at me. "She just doesn't like being apart from her Pack, hey?"

My cheeks flushed. "No, she doesn't, but that's a little presumptuous of her, you know?"

Sonny pulled me across his lap, spreading my thighs

over either side of his until we were nose to nose. "Not presumptuous at all, sweetheart. Have no doubt—you're going to be mine. I'll claim you right now, this very minute, if that's what you want. You're ours, Otillie-James Baler. We're trying to be respectful. You've only been an Omega a week. What if there are other Alphas out there you want more?"

Snorting a laugh, I stared up at him, then realized he was serious. "There's never been anyone else for me, you big idiot." Then I thought of Strat. Of Lance. "You guys are mine too. I'm never going to change my mind about that. You and Truett are a part of my soul, and have been for so long. Will there ever be any other Alphas? I don't know. But Strat..."

How did I tell him I wanted Strat too? What if Strat wanted other Alphas? Why did I have so many questions and no answers?

Sonny leaned forward and kissed me, a soft kiss full of promise and heat. I pushed against his body, kissing him back, as he palmed my ass. He tasted like heaven, and I wanted to lick every inch of his skin. His tongue pushed into my mouth, tangling with mine, and I gripped his hair, holding his face to mine. Sixteen-year-old me would be giddy at this moment, a kiss I'd imagined so many times in my life.

I felt him grow hard in his sweats as I rode his lap, only the soft fabric of them and my sleep shorts between us. I needed him.

"Sonny, please," I breathed against his lips, and he

growled low in his throat. The sound made me moan. *Fuck, that was sexy.*

He rolled us onto my bed—well, my new bed. The old one had been so coated in bodily fluids that it needed to be thrown out, but I'd missed their scents immediately. Not enough to sleep on crusted cum, but still, I wanted their scents to pad out my room.

Sonny tugged off my clothes with gentle hands, his eyes taking in every piece of exposed skin like it was a revelation, and not at all like he'd just spent nearly five days fucking me in every position known to man.

He leaned down and kissed across my collarbone, down between my breasts as he tugged off my shorts. He kissed down my stomach, his teeth scraping over my hip bone, before he buried his face at the apex of my thighs. His tongue, which had just fucked my mouth, swirled and pressed, flicked and licked, until I was writhing against him. He pushed my thighs wider, settling himself deeper, and he moaned happily against my thighs, like eating me out was the only thing he wanted to do today.

And fuck, he did it well.

"Sonny," I panted. I wasn't even sure what I was trying to tell him. I didn't want him to stop, or go faster, or do *anything* but keep doing what he was doing. "*Yes,*" was all that came out.

Quicker than I would've thought possible, I was arching up into his face, coming on his tongue. He lapped me up, making pornographic noises.

Once he'd wrung out every last ounce of pleasure

from me, he climbed up my body and kissed me. I could taste myself on his tongue, undeniably sweet. So freaking weird. As he kissed me deeply, I pushed him onto his back.

I wanted him inside me. I clawed at his sweats, releasing his cock, stroking the hard length as he strained beneath my body. I wrapped my hand around the swollen knot at the base, and he basically whimpered. This was right. So right.

"If you keep doing that, sweetheart, I'm going to embarrass myself and have to spend the rest of my life making up for this moment."

I ran my hand down his chest and purred my satisfaction, sliding my slick-coated pussy down his length, making us both groan. I wanted to make him come. I wanted to come again. I wanted him inside me *right now.*

So I notched him at my entrance, then slid down slowly, aggravatingly slow. I was torturing us both, but what was a little torture between lovers? The stretch was unlike anything I'd ever felt, especially not as an Unshown. It was like he was splitting me in half in the most delicious way possible.

When he was seated up to his knot, he finally lost control. He gripped my hips and moved me up and down his cock. I clawed at his arms, rolling my hips and feeling him everywhere as I came once more.

"Are you going to take my knot, Tillie? Are you going to stretch for your Alpha?"

God, I would have promised him anything at that moment, but the idea of taking a knot outside of the heat was actually kind of terrifying.

"We'll go slow?" I asked, and as if he sensed my hesitation, he stilled.

Pulling me close so our lips were touching, he held me still, though his cock was hitting all the different places and making me see stars. "I would never hurt you, Otillie-James. You don't have to take my knot now, or ever." He kissed down along my jaw. "But I promise you can take it; your body was made to take mine. And when you do, I promise it'll feel amazing. But there's no rush. You feel like heaven, just like this."

I trusted Sonny. Of all the people in my life, I trusted that Sonny would have my back most of all. He always had, and if I had my way, he always would. So I captured his lips again and kissed him with a fervor that told him he was it for me.

"I'd like to try. But take it slow."

"Always." He flipped us over, still deep inside me, and I squealed, wrapping my arms around his waist. "Slow, baby. If you need to stop, say the word. Promise?"

Once I nodded, he thrust in and out shallowly a few more times, making me writhe. He was hitting all my good spots, and I was so *close*. My newly emerged fib was flexing; my pussy wanted his knot, and it didn't give a shit what the rest of me wanted.

He dropped his head to my shoulder. "Fuck, I can

feel you fluttering against me. It's driving me mad." He breathed out through his teeth, then slowly pushed in more. I could feel his knot spreading me wider, almost painfully so, but he'd been right. My body was different. It had adjusted so I could take his knot.

Soon enough, he popped past my fib, then began to swell, pressing on all the good spots until I was whimpering with pleasure beneath him. He muffled his groan against my breast, taking my nipple between his lips and sucking hard. It was like a lightning bolt between my clit and my nipple, and I screamed as I came, clamping down hard.

"Jesus Christ!" he grunted, shifting his body in small motions until he was rubbing his knot inside me. The pleasure was unimaginable, and white spots began to dance in my vision as I came again. "I'm going to fill you up until your little belly swells with my cum, Omega."

Yeah, he was more Alpha than man right now, and I *loved* it. I whined, my whole body arching as I chased the pleasure. Finally, he came, grunting my name like a damn prayer, his seed painting the insides of me in hot spurts. The sensation made me come once more, before I flopped all my limbs to the bed, panting.

He was still locked inside me as he rolled us to the side. He kissed me softly, and a contented sigh brushed across my lips. Our skin was damp, sticking in places, like we were two halves of one soul. I wanted to stay like this forever.

"Tillie?"

I snuggled into his chest contentedly. "Mmhm?"

"Would you like to go on a picnic?"

Looking up at him beneath my lashes, with his gentle breath fanning my cheek, I couldn't help but smile. "I'd love that."

Twenty-Six

LANCE

I tried not to wait at the door for Otillie-James like a lovesick hound every day, but so far, I was failing. Even though I'd said I could take care of the rescues for now, she still came out every day. Not because she was obligated, but because she wanted to. And I liked having her here.

I wasn't sure why I'd offered this place up when I'd been trying to extract myself from Otillie-James, but there was something about her that just made me want to solve all her problems.

And honestly, Matt would have loved her. She was everything an Alpha dreamed about. Everything a man could ever want, Alpha or not. And Matt had never wanted us to feel alone.

I heard a car coming down the drive, and Akio's ears perked up. He was such a smart dog; he knew the difference between cars he knew, and those of strangers. So when I stuck my head out and saw Sonny's Range Rover coming down the driveway, I tried not to feel irritated. I liked Sonny—he seemed to genuinely care about Otillie-James, and despite our minimal interactions, me. It wasn't the self-important kind of caring that was for show, or to make himself feel good, like I'd seen so often after returning from active duty. No, much like Otillie-James, he saw a creature in need and he wanted to help it.

It would be interesting to meet their parents. They'd both raised kids with very similar values, considering that they hadn't met until Otillie-James was sixteen, according to Sonny. Maybe it was fate?

Sonny climbed out of the driver's seat, walking around to open the door for Otillie-James. Old-school Alpha chivalry wasn't dead. Then he walked to the back and pulled out a cooler. Setting it on the ground, he bounded up the front steps and knocked on the door.

I waited a few seconds so they didn't realize I was watching them out the window like a weirdo, then walked toward the front door.

Smiling brightly at me, Sonny was leaning against the porch railing. "We're having a picnic, and we'd like it if you joined us." He looked down at Akio. "You too, buddy." He stepped closer, blocking my view of Otillie-James. "I'd be honored if you'd assist me in courting our Omega. If joining my Pack is something you'd want. No pressure." His eyes were serious, despite the smile on his face.

He was telling me, very gently, to shit or get off the

pot. I couldn't have this half-life with her, and I knew it. I did. But could I risk letting anyone else in? The idea of losing Otillie-James—of letting myself care for and even love the rest of the Pack—filled me with dread, and I wasn't sure I could survive that pain again.

But was I even living now? What would my team have wanted?

That was easy. They'd want me to get the girl.

Swallowing hard, I nodded. "I'd like that. I..." Fuck, how did I tell this man that I was all sorts of messed up? That the Lance he knew was just the tip of the iceberg when it came to baggage?

Sonny reached up and clapped a hand to my bicep. "Welcome to the Pack, man. We've got your back now." Stepping away, he tilted his head toward our Omega. "I saw a pond toward the back of the property. She's always loved being outside."

I knew the spot. I also knew something else she'd like. "Meet me at the garage."

Four-wheeling hadn't much interested me, but listening to Otillie-James squeal her joy made it a whole new experience. Sonny had let her ride with me, and honestly, the guy deserved a sainthood. I wasn't sure that in his position, I would have handed over her safety to anyone else. I guess he was serious about being a Pack, and including me in it. He was driving along at a slower pace behind us, with Akio on the back and the cooler strapped down.

It definitely wasn't Akio's first time on the four-wheeler, and I wondered how often Matt must've brought him out for him to be so comfortable. I wondered if the dog missed him as much as I did. I also wondered if Otillie-James's ragtag bunch of animals was filling the hole in his heart the way they were with mine.

We cleared the small wooded area between the big house and the barn, and traveled along the bike path to the pond. Otillie-James pointed to the water, and sure enough, there was Gert, with a bunch of stolen baby wood ducks. There was probably a pissed-off mama duck around here somewhere.

I pulled up a little away from the water, so I didn't scare the mean old goose or her new stolen progeny. Otillie-James climbed from the ATV and walked straight over to the pond. "Gertrude Rita Baler, they are not your babies! Take them back this instant."

Gert hissed in her direction, defiantly leading the babies to the middle of the pond. I saw Spartacus the rooster sitting on the edge of the pond in the sun, pecking at bugs around him. That chicken was smitten.

Laughing, I led Otillie-James back to where Sonny was setting up the picnic rug. It was really nice out here.

It was even nicer when she was here too.

Sonny pulled out containers filled with all sorts of food. Chopped fruit, fried chicken, finger sandwiches, potato salad. He must have been cooking for hours to make this spread. He was making an effort to court her, even though she was basically his now. I was glad he was still doing things the right way, because Otillie-James deserved to be fussed over. She deserved for the whole world to know how perfect she was.

The rug was huge enough to fit a whole Pack, so there was plenty of room for the three of us, and Otillie-James lowered herself regally before flopping onto her stomach and kicking up her legs. Sometimes it was really obvious that despite the big house she lived in, and the trust fund allowance, she definitely hadn't been raised in high society. Me either.

"This looks amazing, Sonny. I'm not going to lie—I'm kind of glad your apartment was getting 'exterminated.'" That really had been the worst lie ever. "I'd forgotten how good you were in the kitchen."

He leaned forward and rolled her onto her back, so he could nuzzle her throat with a mock growl. "I'm good in every room, baby."

"I mean, I guess you're okay in the laundry too," she teased, and he launched himself at her playfully. She laughed and slapped at his back, and while it should feel like I was interrupting a moment, it didn't. When his hands came up to tickle her, she squealed. "Help me, Lancelot!" she giggled, reaching out a hand to me.

I took her fingers. "Sorry, Tills, you poked the dragon, and now you have to pay your dues."

"Traitor!" But she still wiggled out from underneath him and crawled over to my lap, hiding herself beneath my arms.

Sonny leaned back on his elbows. "Oh I see, you

brought in a knight to save you. Well played, little Omega."

She snuggled firmly into my arms, nestled between my thighs, with her body pressed right along mine. I'd never felt anything more perfect in my entire life.

As she laid her head on my chest, the warm afternoon wind picked up pieces of her hair and blew it across her face. "Thank you for saving me again," she murmured, her big eyes looking up at me. "Do you want me to move?"

God no. I never wanted her to move again. I wanted to stay in this moment forever, with her resting between my thighs, a smile on her face and mine. This was the most picture-perfect moment I'd ever experienced.

So I shook my head. "I like you right there," I told her softly, and was rewarded with a smile so brilliant, it threatened to steal my breath.

Her face was still tilted up to mine. "I like it too."

God, I wanted to kiss her. Just a little. My eyes flicked to Sonny, and there was no jealousy on his face. If anything, his face was encouraging me. His expression screamed *do it!* I still couldn't believe he was so open to letting me touch the girl of his dreams.

But when I leaned down and brushed my lips across hers, barely a whisper of a kiss, it changed my whole world. She sighed happily, her eyes closing briefly, and I knew she was it for me. I could fight it as much as I liked, but there would be no other girl for me, no other person on this planet who could make me feel what Otillie-James did in that moment.

She didn't deepen the kiss, or push for more than I wanted to give. She just rested her head back against my chest.

I loved Otillie-James Baler.

And it scared me down to my very core.

Sonny passed me a bottle of Coke and one for Tills, and the day went on, like that one moment hadn't changed my entire life. She stayed in my arms, with Sonny feeding her pieces of food as they talked about things and people. Most of them, I didn't know, but a few I did.

She told us her theory about the guy she saw in the police lineup being in the back of an episode of that animal rescue show she watched, and I had to admit, it was kind of hinky. It could be a coincidence, but my gut said that there was more to it, and I *always* trusted my gut. Strat had told the cops, but I knew that look in Otillie-James's eye. She wasn't going to let it drop.

It was the same determined look she'd had in her eye when she was just going to "run surveillance" on the garage where she thought they were having cockfights.

I still had nightmares about how wrong that could have gone. I'd been out at a VA group therapy session that night, but I definitely would have gone with her, if I'd known she was going to break in and steal the damn chickens. I hadn't known her plans until she'd appeared with a half-dead rooster and a police escort.

Shuddering, I bundled her closer. She was a handful, but I wouldn't have her any other way. Who wanted a boring, docile Omega when you could have someone like Otillie-James? You didn't know if you were going to have to hand-rear a baby lizard or bail her out from the police station. Maybe it was handy that she now had two lawyers in her Pack.

Her and Sonny were softly talking about their parents arriving tomorrow, and what that would mean for them.

For the Pack.

Our Pack.

"I'm going to have to move out," she said, her sigh brushing across the skin of my bicep. "I can't imagine going through my heat in that house, and I'm not sure Citrine would appreciate another Omega there either, despite the fact she loves me."

Sonny had her foot in his lap, massaging the arch. "You can always move in with me. Or Truett has a spare room that's just housing his gym equipment."

She frowned. "Won't your Alpha get upset if I was spending more time with him?"

That was the thing about the designations. It made the disparity between your head and your heart even more pronounced. Because while Sonny might see the logic of her moving in with Truett, his Alpha would be riled by the fact that she smelled more like him. Spent more time with him. Slept in his bed every night. Not that she had to create a roster and follow it religiously, but jealousy could spring up from the smallest of slights. Not to mention Strat, and how it would go with another Omega.

No, I wasn't sure that was a solution at all.

"You could move in here," I told her casually. She glanced up at me, surprised, though I wasn't sure why. It wasn't like all her animals weren't already here. "You could all move in here, if you wanted. It could be, like, a Packhouse." I said the words lightly, like it wasn't a turning point in our relationship, in our lives, to move in together. One step closer to being a bonded Pack.

I could feel both of their gazes running over my face, probably appraising whether I felt obligated to do this out of some weird sense of gratitude. I could have told them I didn't—this house had come to me for a reason, and the more I thought about it, the more I wondered if maybe Matt had been taking care of me from beyond the grave, nudging Otillie-James my way.

It made me feel less guilty when I thought about it like that. When I was happy and not drowning in survivor guilt, it made me feel like I was just following orders once more.

So I gave them an encouraging look. "I mean it."

Sonny still seemed hesitant. "Are you sure?"

I nodded, and Otillie-James let out a joyous peal of laughter. "Then yes, I would love to move in with you, Lance Alcott." She gripped either side of my face and leaned forward to kiss me, but stopped just shy of my lips. "You know I want you to be part of my Pack, right?

That you're mine, if you want to be? That you're part of this Pack we're building?"

Bobbing my head as much as I could in her tight hold, I gave her a soft smile. "Yes."

Then she kissed me, and there was nothing soft or delicate about it. She claimed me as hers, and I claimed her right back.

A frantic splashing had me dragging my lips from hers. Spartacus the rooster was trying to swim out to Gert and the baby ducklings, but chickens *still* couldn't swim.

Pulling back, Otillie-James groaned. "For Christ's sake, Spartacus, you're a damn chicken!"

"Rock, paper, scissors for who has to go out and save the drowning rooster?" Sonny asked me, and I nodded.

That was how I finished the most perfect afternoon, swimming into the middle of a dirty pond to fish out a former fighting cock, who was in love with a goose.

TWENTY-SEVEN
TRUETT

Buck Baler was a big guy. He stood at least four inches taller than me, and about three more than Sonny. It didn't sound like much, until he was standing nose-to-nose with you while you told him that you'd always loved his daughter and wanted to make her your Omega.

"What age did you say you fell in 'love' with my daughter?"

You didn't have to be a lawyer to know that one was a trap. However, it probably also helped if you weren't an honest fool, because Sonny actually answered. "Since the first moment I saw her."

Buck ground his teeth. "You fell in love immediately with your sixteen-year-old stepsister?"

Abort, Sonny. Abort.

"He doesn't mean it like that. It wasn't like we were lusting after her. But we could tell immediately that she was something special. Obviously, she was far too young to think of like that." I widened my eyes at Sonny and hoped he got the subtext of *shut the fuck up* in there.

Otillie-James rolled her eyes at her dad. "Stop, Dad. I was sixteen, not six. I was dating Alex Whitcomb six months after we moved here, and lost my virginity to him in the back of his mom's Tesla. Let's not pretend teenagers don't have sex, and that the guys weren't teenagers too. You're blowing it out of proportion. Besides, it doesn't matter now."

Frowning at his daughter, Buck grunted and turned to pace away. Citrine was sitting on her favorite armchair, perched on the edge, raising a single eyebrow at us. That expression always made me feel two inches tall, ever since I was ten, when she'd busted Sonny and me having a food fight in the formal living room.

Sonny obviously saw her as the more sympathetic party, but I wasn't so sure. "Mom, you know it wasn't anything nefarious."

She smiled at us all. "Of course I do, sweetheart. I'm an Omega; the ridiculous teenage pining basically stunk up the house for years. I thought I might have to step in eventually. But when you never made any move to court her, I thought perhaps you'd moved on. That you'd decided she wasn't good enough for you when she didn't designate and instead became Unshown."

I frowned at Citrine. She wasn't one to care about people's designations. What was she getting at?

I didn't have to wait long to find out.

"And I decided if you didn't think she was worthy of your Pack as Unshown, then you didn't deserve her anyway. Otillie-James deserves someone who can appreciate just how special she is, as a human being, heart and soul." She reached over and held OJ's hand tightly. "If this is what you want, you have my support. But just know that being an Omega is only a small part of what makes you special. You make sure they treat you how you deserve to be treated, Sugar."

Buck huffed, his arms still crossed over his chest, but he didn't contradict his wife. I mean, I didn't blame him. His wife was scary as hell. People tended to think Alphas were the ones in control of their Packs, but if they had an Omega? We were basically just there to make them happy.

Okay. This is good. Now for phase two. "I'm glad that we have your support, guys, because now we've consolidated our Pack, we actually have more exciting news."

"She's pregnant?" Citrine gasped.

Sonny went pale. "No! I mean, I don't think so." He looked at OJ, who glared back at him, like he was a dumbass.

"Uh, no. We're too young for babies just yet. Sorry?" she added, clearly unsure if Citrine was happy or sad about the idea.

Buck harrumphed. "Good."

Well, this should make the next bit easier then. "But we have added two more people to the Pack—kind of—

and we'd love to introduce them to you. Lance is a former Marine and a Beta. And he adores OJ," I added. I conveniently left out the PTSD. And the fact that he'd already been living in their house for the last month.

OJ smiled at the mere thought of the Beta. If I was a more jealous man, I'd want to track him down and beat the shit out of him for making her smile like that. But soon, he'd be Pack, and I'd be proud he made her smile. "And I adore him," she said, her eyes wistful. "He has a cute dog too, Akio."

Citrine laughed. "Well, loving animals is definitely a point in his favor."

Sucking in a deep breath, I was about to launch into an explanation about Strat, but OJ beat me to it. "We also plan on claiming a second Omega. Strat Wilmington."

"Eloise Wilmington's son, Strat?" Citrine gasped, like it was some kind of surprise that Strat was an Omega. It wasn't; he'd been quite big news on the gossip grapevine when he'd designated.

OJ nodded. "Yeah. I met him through Truett." I mean, I guess we could leave out that he'd been the district attorney prosecuting her case. Being an Omega and part of our Pack seemed to have made them forget she'd been in a jail cell less than a month ago.

Citrine looked thoughtful. "Two Omegas is a lot." She paused, tilting her head at OJ. "By now, you'll know that being an Omega means everything and nothing all at once. It means that your emotions are closer to the surface. That you'll want to be beside them all the time. And you'll feel quite territorial. All of these things are on top of your normal, human emotions. You're a woman first, and an Omega second. Don't let anyone convince you otherwise." Buck was nodding along with his wife. "But when it comes to heats and, uh, other matters of biology, sometimes the Omega shoves her way to the front. Are you going to be okay in those moments?"

Flushing, OJ cleared her throat. "Uh, yeah. Should be fine. Strat, uh, helped me through my last heat. We went through sympathetic heats together."

Buck's cheeks went red. It definitely wasn't something a father wanted to know about his daughter, but Citrine just nodded. "Good. That's good." She screwed up her nose. "Does that mean I'll have to be in-laws with the Wilmingtons? Eloise is such a nosey bitch."

Throwing back my head, I laughed. She wasn't wrong. "Sorry, Citrine. But Strat's really nothing like his parents."

The Omega, who was more like a mother to me than my own, gave me an understanding smile. "I'm sure. We aren't merely reflections of our parents." She hesitated. "Have you informed yours?"

I shrugged, because it didn't really matter to me. I hadn't seen my parents in ten years. Not because we'd fallen out or fought, or anything like that. They'd just packed up one day while I was at school, moved to Majorca, and left me with the nanny. They never came back, not for birthdays or holidays, and that was when Citrine had stepped up to become my family, along with her son.

I didn't need my parents back then; I'd barely known them when they'd lived in the same house. It was a testament to their shitty parenting that I hadn't even noticed they were gone, until my nanny Colleen had asked how I felt about them moving overseas, telling me that it was okay to feel sad and miss them. Obviously, she'd been new, because any of the old nannies would've told her that my parents had hated having a kid.

So I certainly didn't need them now.

"I emailed the lawyer. He'll probably let them know."

Citrine nodded, and I ignored the looks I got from Sonny and OJ. We could pat my hand and lament about my shitty childhood another day. I mean, they both knew how it was—especially Sonny, who'd been my friend when they'd left. Who'd taken me home with him after school when I'd told him they were gone, who'd given me a taste of what family was supposed to be like as we sat around the small kitchen table with his mom that night, having the first family dinner of my life.

It had been a long time in the past by the time Buck and OJ had turned up, though, and maybe I'd glossed over how fucking useless they were as parents. We could dive into my parental issues another time. Maybe me and Lance could get a two-for-one offer at my therapist's office.

Okay, enough focus on me. Time for phase three.

I lifted my chin at Sonny, and he cleared his throat. "As we're a Pack now, we're moving into a Packhouse about thirty minutes out of town. You're welcome to come and visit anytime, of course."

Buck frowned at OJ. "You're moving out? Isn't this all a little fast? You only designated a couple of weeks ago. You haven't even had a claiming ceremony yet."

OJ stood up, moving to hug her dad. "I know this all seems like too much, too quickly, but I promise that it isn't. I just know it's right. Do you remember when you told me we were moving to South Carolina after you met a woman for one weekend at a conference in Montana? I said you barely knew Citrine. Do you remember what you told me?"

Squeezing his daughter tighter, he sighed heavily. "I told you that sometimes your soul just knows its other half, and that when you know they're the one for you, there's no fighting it."

She patted him on the back. "My soul has known for a long time that Sonny and Truett are pieces of its puzzle. Strat and Lance are newer, but I feel it right here in my chest. They're mine. Together, we create a beautiful picture. We mightn't be perfect, but we're right."

Sighing once more, he kissed the top of her head. "Okay, Peaches. It's just hard to think of you as someone grown up enough to have a life and a Pack, who doesn't need me anymore."

She shook her head at him, amusement curling her lips into a smile. "I'll always need you."

Citrine was looking glassy-eyed. "Well, that's settled. We'll miss you both, but you better believe we're coming to visit as soon as you invite us." She took a long sip of wine. "Now, does anyone want to tell me what happened to my azaleas?"

TWENTY-EIGHT
OTILLIE-JAMES

Strat hadn't committed to moving into the Packhouse yet, and we were all respecting his decision. However, he spent more time here than at his own apartment, and more time in my bed than anywhere but his office.

Stretching, I hooked my leg over his, leaning over to turn off his alarm. Then I kissed my way over his shoulder and across his chest. "Strat, it's time to get up."

He grunted, gripping my hips and grinding his morning wood against my core. "Sweetheart, I'm already up."

I flicked my tongue across his nipple, lazily rolling my hips over his. "So you are. Wouldn't want to waste it, though, would we?"

He chuckled deep in his chest, and I felt the vibration through my lips. "Babe, I'm an Omega. I'll get hard in my coffin as they lower me into my grave."

Sitting up, I gave him an incredulous look. "Ew, Strat."

Still laughing softly, he dragged me up so he could kiss me. The man could kiss—slow and thorough, like his lips were memorizing mine, fucking me slowly until I was panting with need. His cock rubbed against my clit as we dry humped. Well, wet humped, because there was nothing dry about what was going on down there.

"Well, looks like I was sleeping through the best kind of dirty dream," Truett murmured from where he was spooned behind me, his voice pitched low, and it made goosebumps break out over my skin with pleasure. "Don't let me interrupt."

I wasn't sure what time he'd crawled into my bed, but they were normally pretty good about giving me and Strat time to bond. Seemed like my big Alpha was getting impatient.

Rolling up so I was straddling Strat's lap, I grinned down at the two sexy men in my bed. I reached out and ran my fingers over Truett's abs, the coarse hair that trailed down his stomach tickling my fingers. "Well, now that you mention fantasies, I have one that has regularly featured in my pleasure sessions."

Strat ground up, making my eyes roll back in my head. "Are you having pleasure sessions without us, Omega? Are we not satisfying you?"

I pinched his nipple, making him grunt and moan at the same time. It was an odd noise. "Shh, I was telling you guys what my fantasy was." I leaned down and kissed

Strat again. "What I really want is to fuck you between Truett and me." I curled my body until his cock slid against my entrance, notching easily. On a moan, I slid down his length, the stretch making my eyes close of their own volition.

When I felt fingers at the base of his cock instead of his lock knot, I realized Truett had helpfully held his dick for me. *Such a good Alpha.*

I leaned forward until my chest was pressed against Strat's, our lips once again devouring each other. I moaned softly as he moved in short, shallow strokes inside me. "Is that something you want too?" I breathed, though each exhale came out as a gasp. I'd almost forgotten that I'd asked him a question.

The small muscle at the base of his cock was hitting my G-spot with every thrust, and unlike the Alpha knot that stretched me wide, it was like the male Omega's lock knot was just there for my pleasure. To make me come over and over again.

Gripping my hair close to the roots, Strat pulled my face away from his. "More than I want to breathe."

Rolling us to the side, he moved my leg up over his hip, switching the angle and making me gasp with pleasure. I looked over his shoulder at Truett, who was watching us with enough heat, it was a wonder we didn't have third-degree burns.

Hands moved over my body as I captured Strat's lips once more, tongue-fucking him in the most obscene way. He groaned into my mouth, a filthy whimper that I knew meant Truett had just slid inside him. I wanted to both be part of this moment and watch it from the corner.

A strong hand—that I knew was Truetts's by feel—grabbed a handful of my ass, then he was thrusting, fucking us both. Strat whined, and I wondered how amazing it must feel, to be getting pleasure from all sides.

Then there were no more thoughts, because Truett fucked us both in a way that left no doubt who we belonged to now. He owned our body and our pleasure, whispering sweetly filthy things to us until Strat was whimpering with the need to come. I'd already come twice and was gasping my way to a third.

"I'm going to lock myself inside you, Omega. I'm going to fill you right up until I'm dripping out this tight little hole. Then you're going to do the same to our girl. I want you both coated before you get out of this bed."

Holy shit. Holy shit.

Strat pulled my thigh higher and slammed into me over and over in time with Truett's thrusts. I came once more, and that was all I could take, my pussy clasping onto Strat's cock, holding him still and immobile as Truett used him in the dirtiest way possible. The combination seemed to tip Strat over the edge, as he released inside me with a stifled yell. All I could do was hold on and enjoy the ride.

Truett wasn't far behind, his teeth clamping down on Strat's shoulder but not breaking skin, making our Omega come once more.

As we lay there, a connected, sweaty bunch, I giggled.

Truett lifted his head and looked at me over Strat's shoulder. "What are you laughing at over there? Because if you're laughing, instead of panting with overwhelming desire, I'm going to have to up my game, and spank you for every giggle."

My pussy clenched, which set off a chain reaction of pleasure. Gripping Truett's hand in mine, I squeezed tightly. "It's just... I'm so happy. This is more than I could have hoped for."

Strat nuzzled my cheek. "It's everything you deserve. Everything *we* deserve." He nipped my earlobe, and I hissed with pleasure. "But if you don't stop strangling my cock like that, none of us are going anywhere, and I have a big preliminary hearing today."

I sighed. Strat didn't seem positive that he'd be able to indict some of the people picked up by the cops at the cockfight raid, other than the owner of the garage and one of the bookies, who'd been there taking bets. Everyone else had lawyered up or refused to speak to the cops, so it was the state's word against theirs that they'd been there conducting illegal activities, not just there chilling out with friends, unknowingly stumbling onto the cockfighting. Unless it could be proven they took bets, they hadn't really been doing anything bad.

Bullshit, if you asked me, but I knew Strat would do what he could.

I sighed. "Fine, but stop doing that thing with your mouth."

"What thing?" Strat asked. "You mean this?" He

sucked a spot on my shoulder, and I groaned. Laughing, he thrust up into me once more, making us all groan. "Screw it, I have time."

Lance and I headed into the city once Strat left for the day. I had to do a supply run for both human food and animal supplies. I introduced the guys at the tractor supply store to Lance, my Beta, and appreciated the look of surprise on their faces.

While we were in the city, we planned on going to lunch with Strat, because I really couldn't wait until he got home to know how it had gone. Plus, it was part of the Pack's courting process. We all took it in turns taking him to lunch, or dinner. Last week, we'd gone to the movies, which was nice.

I fidgeted with the interior compartments of my Fiat as we waited for Strat in the court's parking lot. Akio had stayed home, and I didn't know if that was a step forward in Lance's healing or not. Did it mean he no longer needed a support animal? Had I become his support animal?

"Stop thinking so hard over there, Tills," he murmured, reading a book he'd picked out of the giant library in his house. Granted, it was mostly autobiographies and action adventure novels, but at least I'd have a place to store all my smutty romances once I'd finished them.

I flopped back in the seat. "What if they all get away with it, then go back and do it again?"

He dog-eared his book—I'd have to break him of that habit, because what the actual fuck?—and put it in the back seat. "One thing I learned overseas was that shitty things happen. All the time. Every minute of the day, something terrible is happening to someone, somewhere."

I screwed up my nose. "If this is your version of a motivational speech, we might have to work on it."

He grinned, and my god, he was handsome. "It gets more motivational. As I was saying, you'll never be enough to blot out all the bad in the world. Neither will Strat, nor the cops, nor any one person. What you *can* do is work on making the lives of those you touch better. Those animals at the farm know nothing but love now, because you give it to them so freely. The people at the rescues, your friends, me—our lives are all better with you in them. And that's all you can do. Change the lives you *can* touch for the better, and hope the universe fucks the bad guys with a cactus."

Laughing, I leaned over the console between our seats and kissed him softly. "I take it back. You give a damn fine motivational speech."

He cupped my cheek, and I had no idea how a man who'd been steeped in such violence in his life could kiss me the way he did, but it made me breathless every time. By the time he pulled back, there was loud chatter around the front doors of the courthouse. I realized the court reporters had roused themselves. Court must be out.

My heart sank as people I'd pointed out in the lineup left smiling, and I knew it hadn't gone well for Strat. *Damn.*

One guy had his head covered as he walked toward the car opposite us. A flash of red hair told me it was the guy I'd recognized in the *All Creatures Great and Smalls* show, and I watched him climb into the back of an expensive SUV.

I also recognized the guy in the back seat with him. Anthony Smalls.

Lance followed my gaze, his eyes narrowing. "That doesn't seem like he's oblivious to the extracurricular activities of his employee, does it?"

Lifting my phone, I snapped a quick photo. As their driver pulled out of the parking spot in front of us, I dragged Lance's face to mine and kissed him again. Let them think we were just two business people making out in a car on our lunch break, and not that we now knew that a mega-rescue—one I'd looked up to as an example of what I wanted to be one day—was up to something dodgy.

Lance threaded his fingers through my hair, further obscuring my face, until the car left the parking lot. Focused on the lawyers at the front of the courthouse, the media were none the wiser of the story that was just there, just out of reach.

I pulled back and stared at Lance. "Holy shit.

Anthony Smalls is complicit in his employee going to cockfights? Drive, I don't want to lose them."

Lance started the car and followed the SUV out of the parking lot. "You're right. Something about this feels off. Put your seatbelt on."

Strapping myself in, I blinked at the brake lights of the SUV in front of us as we pulled out into traffic. *What the hell do we do now?*

TWENTY-NINE
STRAT

The judge hated my guts. He was of the old school, where the only thing that would be worse than me being an Omega ADA, would be if I was a *female* Omega ADA.

According to him, and the other old-school judges with this way of thinking, women and Omegas belonged in the home, making sure it was perfect for their Alphas.

Gag.

With his name on the docket, I knew I'd have a tough time selling to him that the state had enough evidence to at least fine the men found at the event, if not give them jail time.

But Judge Chastain—the people in the office called him Judge Shitstain, though never to his face—already had it out for me. In the shortest pretrial of my career as a prosecutor, he found the evidence for everyone, except the garage owner and the bookie, to be too circumstantial to warrant a trial.

Half a dozen people had walked away with zero consequences for their cruelty. Otillie-James was going to be so angry. I strode out of the courtroom, stopping to talk to my associate and give him instructions, before making my way to the parking lot.

My heart sank, seeing no one there. Maybe she was angry at me? This was the first thing she'd asked of me, and I'd failed miserably.

I sighed heavily, turning back toward the courthouse. This was why I hadn't moved into the Packhouse yet; maybe they'd wake up one day and find me defective, and then where would I be? Back home with my parents?

Fuck no.

My phone rang, and I was both relieved and terrified to see that it was her. "Hello?"

"Strat! I'm so sorry we aren't there, but you're never going to guess what happened!" Lance was muttering something in the background, which I didn't think was a good sign. "That guy from the show? He walked out and got in the back of an SUV, and you'll *never guess* who else was in it... Anthony Smalls."

I frowned. That was surprising. "Okay..." I said suspiciously. "And where are you now?"

Deep down, I already knew. If I'd learned anything about Otillie-James, it was that she was impulsive as hell, and I doubted Lance would be able to temper that impulsiveness much. He would give in.

"We're trailing their car—"

"Otillie!" I interrupted, and she hushed me. That damn Omega who'd crawled her way under my skin *hushed* me.

"Stop being a worrywart, Strat. I have Lance with me. He can kill a man with a spork and a rubber band." She said something to our Beta, but it was muffled, like she'd covered the microphone of the phone. "Not that he'll need to do anything like that. We are just surveilling them. I want to see where they go."

I sighed, pinching the bridge of my nose. This girl was going to give me gray hairs. "Need I remind you that the last time you surveilled anything, you ended up *in a holding cell?*"

Otillie-James just laughed at me, and I was beginning to see why she made Truett so stressed. Honestly, though, this was something I loved about her. I wouldn't change her for the world.

Sighing, I stepped back inside the foyer of the courthouse. "Okay, but only looking. Do *not* do anything rash. Lance, do not *let* her do anything rash. Observe, then we'll go from there. And you better call me as soon as you're on your way back. I'll be at the office. You two owe me lunch."

She promised and hung up the phone, and I tried not to worry. Lance wouldn't let anything happen to her. He might have no care for himself, but he would protect her with his dying breath.

Not for the first time, I impulsively wished we were

bonded, so that I could feel her emotions down a soul-deep connection between us. So that I would always know she was okay.

Wherever they'd gone, they didn't arrive home until late in the afternoon. By then, I was going insane. I'd left work early, unable to concentrate, and headed back to the Packhouse. My energy definitely wasn't helping the two Alphas in the house either, and it was only the message from Otillie-James saying they were on their way home that stopped Sonny and Truett from jumping in the car and going to retrieve her from wherever the hell she was.

I should've been soothing them, or they should've been soothing me, but Otillie-James was our core. It was wild how much she'd come to mean to me in this last month.

I sat by the dog on the porch, Akio watching the setting sun right along with me. I buried my hands in his fur, and he leaned against my legs as we watched a car come down the drive. Recognizing Otillie-James's Fiat, I breathed a sigh of relief. *Thank fuck.*

Sonny was out the door first, but Truett was close behind him, and they bounded down the steps. They were at the passenger door before the car had even rolled to a stop. Sonny pulled the door open, and Truett had her out of the car and into his arms before the ignition was off.

"OJ, you can't fucking do this anymore! Do you

know how much you stressed out our Omega?" Truett indicated where I sat on the front porch, and I frowned. He'd been stressed too.

Guilt washed over her face, but then I took in her posture, her eyes.

She'd found something.

I was down the steps immediately, tugging her from their arms and into mine. "What happened?"

She shook her head and burst into tears. Her wracking sobs were like bullets to my chest. I held her closer, lifting her into my arms, and walking into the house. Lance would debrief the guys. He would find the words that seemed to be escaping Otillie.

I sat gently down on the couch, just holding her to me as she cried. I rubbed her back and murmured reassuring things that were probably nonsense.

Eventually, she stopped crying, just rubbing her face over my chest and clothes. She was marking me. Did she even know what she was doing?

My heart swelled, and I marked her back. I rubbed my face over her hair, stroking her scent gland at the back of her neck. I touched every part of her I could, my Omega becoming more and more frenzied with each touch, until I was almost tearing at her clothes. Sonny appeared in front of us, his hands gripping Otillie-James, like he was trying to take her from me.

No. No one can take her from me.

I growled at him, and he squatted down until we were face-to-face. "Easy, Omega. I'm just going to clean her up and give you a moment to calm. It's okay. She's safe with me." His voice was soft, soothing. Almost a purr.

It took every one of my higher reasoning skills to talk myself into loosening my hold on her. With one last kiss across her lips, I let her go. I watched him carry her toward the bathroom, her arms around his neck, and his huge body dwarfing hers.

Truett slid into the seat beside me. He gripped my thigh, his thumb rubbing in circles on my skin, until it was all I could focus on. Once my heartbeat had calmed, he leaned over and kissed me. "It's okay, Strat. She's fine, safe. I need you to come back to me, because we need to talk about what they found."

He handed me Otillie-James's phone. There were pictures on the screen: dogs in cages, battered and scarred, cats that looked half dead. Other animals that I couldn't discern from the pictures, but I would bet there were at least a few roosters.

I flicked through more and more pictures, and I understood why Otillie-James was so distressed. Some of these were awful. If I hadn't seen the worst humanity had to offer on a daily business, I would've been distressed too.

Swallowing down the last of my Omega hysteria, I looked past Truett to Lance. His face was shut down almost completely, his gaze running over my face. Whatever had happened today had hurt him too. Probably her turmoil. An Omega's distress was a powerful thing.

"Tell me everything. But first, tell me you didn't let Otillie close enough to take these herself."

Lance shook his head, and it didn't surprise me that he was standing in an at-ease position. Defaulting back to his military training in a time of crisis was textbook PTSD. "No. I took the pictures."

"Obviously, because one of you is highly trained in reconnaissance by the finest military in the world, and the other got caught with a cock up her shirt by arguably the shittest cop known to man," Truett pointed out, clearly trying to lighten the mood.

I huffed an almost-laugh. Even Lance's lips twitched—at least, until he continued. "We followed the redhead and Anthony Smalls to a warehouse on the south side. They both got out and went inside. The buildings around it were empty, but there was a shitty little deli that we parked in front of, like we wanted salmonella and a hot dog, hold the hot dog." Shaking his head, he added the part we all knew was coming. "Otillie-James wanted to go check the warehouse out, but I thought that was a bad idea."

No shit.

"So I told her to stay, while I went around the back. I scaled the side of the building to the skylights and looked inside. Needless to say, I was pretty sure they weren't there rescuing the animals in those cages. I couldn't hear what they were saying from the outside, but they looked comfortable. Not like they were there freeing those animals."

Rubbing my temples, I pushed down my rage. "So we think Anthony Smalls is using his rescue as a front?"

Truett nodded. "It's the perfect front, if you think about it. They get a free, steady supply of animals, and no one pays any attention if those animals disappear again quickly. They can just say they were adopted by people who didn't want to be filmed. If they manage to actually adopt a couple out, they'd film it as success stories. Who would even know?"

"And what do we think he's doing with the rest of the animals?"

Lance looked over his shoulder to ensure that Otillie-James was nowhere in hearing distance. "I think he's using them in dogfighting rings, or as bait animals. Cockfights are an obvious one now too. Do you know that over a quarter of dogs in shelters and on the euthanasia list are pitbulls or similar breeds? He'd be taking them from kill shelters with the promise of adopting them out, then just shove them in dogfights."

My stomach turned. It really was the perfect front. *That son of a bitch.* "I'll talk to some detectives I trust. His days are numbered; he just doesn't know it yet."

THIRTY
EDISON

"I'm sorry," she hiccuped at me once again as I washed her face gently with a washcloth.

Shaking my head, I replaced the cloth with my lips, kissing her puffy eyes. "Don't be sorry for caring, Tillie. It's one of the things I love about you." I sighed heavily. "You worried me today, though. I hated not knowing if you were okay."

I really did. My Alpha still felt riled. I didn't like feeling helpless, like if something went wrong, I'd never know. Honestly, I briefly considered chaining her to my wrist forever. I had to go back to work next week, and even the idea was making me break out in a cold sweat. I wondered if I could become a good-for-nothing trust-fund baby, just so I could stay at home with Tillie for the rest of my days.

Oblivious to my inner thoughts, Tillie gripped my hands. "That's easy to fix, Sonny. Claim me."

I blinked at her dumbly for a long moment, my brain trying to catch up to what I'd just heard. "Tillie..." God, what did I say to that? I wanted to claim her more than anything. But she was distraught right now, and that would make me the worst kind of Alpha. "You're not—"

Covering my mouth with her hand, she shook her head. "No, Sonny. I mean it. Why are we drawing it out? I have no doubt in my mind that you guys are it for me. I feel it in my soul. And today, I wanted to reach out to our bond, to find comfort in you guys, and I couldn't. We're waiting, but for what?" She reached out and pulled me closer to her body. "Claim me."

"But what about the ceremony? A big wedding? You deserve perfection, OJ."

She gripped the sides of my face. "We're already perfect, Edison. You and me, Truett, Strat and Lance. We *are* perfect. Bite me. *Claim* me."

I groaned, burying my face in her neck, right over her scent gland, and breathed in her pretty floral scent. It was addictive, and I wanted to roll around in it all day. My lips dropped further down to her shoulder. This was where I'd claim her eventually.

Shuddering against me, she held my head to her throat, encouraging me. *Jesus.* I was only a man; I didn't have a will of steel. Still, I summoned some kind of sanity and pulled back.

"I'm not going to claim you in a bathroom right now, Tillie." She whined, and I stroked her face. "But if you want to be claimed, I want nothing more than to do it. I want to claim you, claim this Pack as mine. We have to do it right. Together."

I picked her up and kissed her hard, before carrying her back into the living room, where everyone sat around with solemn expressions. I assumed Lance had debriefed Strat on what they'd seen. Even the thought of those pictures made my stomach turn. My poor, soft-hearted Otillie-James would have hated it.

They looked at me, still holding her. "It's time."

Truett's gaze sharpened as he took in the way Tillie was nuzzling my cheek, her body wrapped around mine like a koala. "By time, you mean...?" Obviously, he wanted me to spell it out, but I didn't blame him, because I'd want to be sure before I got my hopes up too.

"Otillie-James wishes to be claimed. So it's time. If you're in this Pack, tonight, we make us one. You aren't obligated to bite into the Pack yet"—I looked at Strat, giving him a reassuring smile—"but it's an integral moment in our story, and I'd—*we'd*—like you to be there to witness it."

Strat nodded, and I looked over at Lance. I knew Truett was already in; his teeth had been waiting to sink into Tillie for years. However, for Lance, this must've all been pretty quick. He'd only had a month to come to terms with his feelings for Otillie, and then her heat and the Pack stuff. This was a lot.

My eyes met his, which held more emotions than I'd ever seen on his face. The overwhelming one, though, was sheer determination, and maybe a little love. He nodded too.

I grinned. Today, two became three, or even five. "Do you hear that, baby? Everyone's going to be there, watching you become ours." I looked over my shoulder at Lance. "Is it done?"

Our surprise for our Omegas. I'd had time off, and Lance was a guy who had fidgety demons that needed to be blocked out by hard work, so when he'd approached me for help with his project, I'd been totally on board. He'd started before we'd even officially moved out here, when there were just long days without anyone else to talk to. We'd done it together while everyone had been out of the house, so I was hoping it was a surprise, anyway.

Up the stairs we went, until we hit the door at the end of the hall. Behind it were more stairs that led to what had once been an attic storage space, though unlike most old houses, it was blissfully free of junk. Lance's former CO hadn't been the type to keep sentimental things, obviously. So the transformation from bare bones room to dual nests had been easy enough.

Each side of the room had a little alcove, a small nook that could fit an Omega and a couple of Alphas, which could be closed off from the rest of the nest, as well as the rest of the house. In the middle of the floor was a nest bed. The soft furnishings had been really my only contribution to the room; the rest had been Lance. But the bed was made for Omega nests, with a huge mattress that was almost pillowy, and sharply raised edges. It looked almost like a pond made of pillows and blankets, and I knew those ramped sides would be perfect for bending my Omega over.

Groaning, I willed my dick to behave. There was plenty of time to be inside her.

Tillie's eyes were wide as she walked around the nest. "Is this for me?" she asked me, and I shook my head.

"Ask Lance. He did all this."

She turned to the Beta, whose face was flushed in a way that was kind of adorable on the large, scarred, former Marine. "You made this for me?"

He nodded. "For you and Strat. There's a place for each of you, in case you need some alone time. You'll have to make it yours, of course, but it's a start."

She ran and launched herself at him, kissing him furiously. He kissed her back, his hands cupping her ass to hold her tight against him. Watching them together made my Alpha happy. He was still anxious to claim her, but he could wait, if it meant the two of them could heal each other a little more.

Finally, Strat walked over to run a hand over Lance's shoulder, and the Beta pulled his mouth away from Tillie. I didn't get the vibe from Lance that he was anything but one hundred percent in this for her, but he respected Strat—that much was obvious.

"Thank you, Lance."

Lance stared at the Omega with a warm expression. The two men were around the same height, though

Lance was twice as wide across the shoulders. "I mightn't want to have sex with you, but you're my Omega too, Strat. You deserve the best as well."

If I'd had any doubt that Lance belonged in our Pack, it evaporated in that moment. Strat leaned his face against Lance's shoulder, scent marking him a little, a huge smile on his face.

The combined scent of Strat and Otillie was enough to make my teeth hurt with the need to claim them. Or fuck them. Or both. I didn't think Strat was ready for that yet; he still doubted us a little. He just needed time, and we'd give him that.

Lance walked her backwards to the bed, stepping into the nest and lowering her gently onto the heaped blankets and pillows. Next time she went through her heat, she could arrange this how she liked, nesting heavily. I couldn't wait.

I also couldn't wait to watch her nest when she was big and round with our babies. When her and Strat went into combined heats. I couldn't wait to spend my entire life with her.

Our Beta was still kissing her, and Truett went over to Strat, sitting with him on the side of the nest. I climbed onto the pillows with my girl, as Lance continued to kiss her. I dragged her into a sitting position on my lap, facing him. I didn't want to interrupt, but if I didn't get inside her soon, my knot would explode.

Luckily, despite being on my lap, Tillie wasn't done yet with Lance. To my knowledge, they'd never made it past second base, and I didn't think today would be the day that changed, but watching them frantically kiss each other was hot as hell.

I stripped her out of her clothes, and she lifted her ass to help me. When she was finally naked, I dragged my sweats down my thighs, my cock springing free and rubbing against her dripping pussy. I settled her back on my lap, and we both groaned as I slipped the tip of myself inside her.

"Kiss your Beta, sweetheart. Fuck his mouth while I fuck this tight little hole. Show him how much you love him, while I claim you with my teeth."

There wasn't any more time for talking after that, because as I buried myself inside her, pleasure stole the air from my lungs. I moved her up and down my length, and Lance chased her lips with his. His hands came up to grab her tits, rubbing her nipples, making her grind down harder on me.

In the back of my mind, there was the thrum that was telling me that this was it—I was going to claim my Omega. It was making my knot inflate already. I was going to blow like an amateur, because the idea of having Otillie-James with me for life was making me horny as hell.

Dragging my mouth from the skin of her shoulder, I looked over at Lance. "Play with her clit, Beta," I growled, almost all Alpha now. "Make her come as I make her ours."

Bless his fucking order-following heart, because he

dipped his fingers down, stroking her clit, and she began fluttering around me almost immediately. I shoved her down on my knot, stretching her wide, and her fib flexed around it, locking me to her.

I sank my teeth into the back of her shoulder, marking her as mine, claiming her. She turned her head to my bicep and bit me right back, right there over the muscle, on an arm that will hold no other woman ever again.

Contentment made me purr as the bond settled into place. She was mine now, and no one could ever take her from me. Love pulsed down the bond between us, followed by impatience down my bond with Truett. He wanted his turn, but I wasn't ready to give her up yet.

THIRTY-ONE
OTILLIE-JAMES

The bond between Sonny and me pulsed with so much emotion, it threatened to make me cry again. Love. Desire. Admiration. It was all there. It was all the more special, because Lance was right here with me, making me feel good, working with my Alphas.

"I want you to claim me. I want to be yours too," Lance murmured against my hair as I lay down in the nest he'd made for me, Sonny still locked in behind me, tending to his bite. His tongue on my mating mark was making my fib pulse, which then made his knot re-expand. At this rate, we might be locked together all night.

Leaning up to brush my lips over Lance's, I smiled softly at him. "Don't feel obligated. We'll get there when you're ready. We'll have our moment."

He shook his head. "If I'm honest with myself, I'm

worried I won't be able to keep all the fucked-up feelings from you. That where the other guys give you love and security, all I'll give you is the burden of my darkness. I don't deserve you." The painful longing on his face made my heart hurt.

I blamed what happened next on several things: the emotion-fuelled day, the excess endorphins in my body, and the fact that he looked so sad. I knew, in my soul, that he'd struggle to take that next step, no matter how much he wanted the bond. He'd try and protect me from himself for as long as possible, until we drifted apart. So I did what any insane person would do.

I snapped forward and bit him. I sunk my little Omega teeth into his chest, right beside the war wounds of his past.

Everyone in the room hissed out a shocked breath. "Oh fuck," someone murmured. I could feel Sonny's shock in our bond.

Worse than that, I could feel Lance's fear down the fledgling claim. He'd have to bond me back for it to be a two-way street, but he made no move to do it. I licked his bond mark, tending to it the way Sonny had just done mine, and I felt the desire briefly overshadow the worry and panic.

Lance hadn't been wrong; in comparison to Sonny's bright bond thread, it was darker. More somber. But I wasn't swamped by terrible thoughts or emotions, like he'd worried.

"I don't need protection, Lance. I need you. Forever." I lifted my wrist to his lips. "Claim me back. I want you to feel what I feel when I look at you."

Tentatively, he bit my wrist, and the bond locked into place. I flooded him with the love I felt. The happiness he brought me. The feeling of safety. The desire I felt in his presence.

"Oh," he breathed, and I smiled, leaning forward to kiss him. I'd hold his darkness with him. We'd drag him back into the light together.

Surrounded by my bondmates, my Omega settled more than she had in a long time. But we still weren't done.

Sonny's knot had deflated enough that he could slide out of me, making his seed drip down my thighs. Moving up onto my hands and knees, I crawled over to where Truett and Strat sat on the edge of the nest. I ignored the pulse of pleasure down the bonds from Sonny and Lance, probably because the view from behind was straight-up pornographic.

Truett watched me crawl toward him, before leaning down and taking my chin in his hand, tilting my face up to his. "I know Lance wanted the bond, but... you can't just bond people without their express consent. You're new to the whole Omega thing, and it's all a little overwhelming, trying to control the Omega's urges, however you can't do that with Strat. He gets to make the choice."

Lance went to protest on my behalf, but Truett shook his head. Shame washed through me as I nodded. I wanted to deny that I would ever steal Strat's choice, but

I guess the last few minutes had made everyone a little less sure. It had worked out this time, because I could feel the love down Lance's bond, and I pushed mine back to him. But still, I looked between them all. "I'm sorry."

Shaking his head, Truett bent down and kissed me. "Naughty little Omega. I'll spank you for it later. But right now, I want to feel my teeth in your flesh. I want to make you mine." Shifting onto his knees behind me, Truett ran his fingers through Sonny's cum leaking down my thighs, pushing it back up and stuffing it inside me. "Can't let this go to waste, baby." He stroked his fingers inside me, and I groaned.

"One day, I'm going to stuff you full of my babies," he growled. "You're going to be big and round and give me so many tiny, blond-haired terrors that I won't know anything but happiness. *You* won't know anything but complete happiness. I promise you, Otillie-James, that I'll take care of your heart and soul forever." He ran a hand down my spine. "Now, present for your Alpha."

It was a promise and a command, and I bent over the edge of the nest, my chest supported by the sloped edge. A collective groan echoed around the room.

"Holy shit," Strat breathed.

Truett chuckled low in his chest. "You're so clever, OJ, that I think perhaps you can suck down our Omega while I take you. What do you think? Want to take him down that pretty throat as I mark you as mine?"

Hell yeah, I did, but I didn't voice my agreement. I just scrambled to grab Strat's cock, which was already hard and out of his pants, swallowing it down until it hit the back of my throat. Strat groaned, gripping my hair on the back of my head close to my scalp. He didn't try and move my mouth up and down, or fuck my face. He just kept his hand there, a subtle reminder that I was his too, despite the lack of claiming mark.

Truett slid inside me, his thick cock spreading me, and I moaned around Strat's dick. His fist tightened in my hair, a pleasurable burn that swirled around the pleasure coursing through my body. Hands ran over my body—probably Truett's, I thought—and they played my body like an instrument.

An orgasm washed over me, though I wasn't fool enough to think that would be it. No, Truett was going to wring every ounce of pleasure from me before he was done, before he gave me his bite. Fingers plucked at my nipples, then moved down to strum my clit, every one of my nerve endings feeling like they were on fire.

Reaching up, I rolled Strat's balls in my palm, and he cursed, coming down my throat in such large amounts, I had to pull off or drown. Cum ran down my chin, and I was tugged up, until I was pressed back against Truett's chest. He turned my face to kiss me, licking inside my mouth like he was sharing Strat's taste with me.

"Fuck..." someone else murmured, and I couldn't agree more. I felt Truett's knot start to swell, and I knew this was it. This was the moment I bonded my other Alpha. I reached behind me, gripping the back of his head as he rutted up inside me, spreading me over his knot until I was trapped, our bodies clinging to each other.

He moved his lips along my shoulder, briefly stopping to run his tongue over Sonny's claiming mark, making both me and his Packmate groan in unison. It was like flicking his tongue over my clit. He chuckled darkly, and I knew he was going to take every opportunity he could to do that.

Sexy asshole.

When he reached the opposite shoulder, almost completely parallel to Sonny's, he stopped. Against my skin, he made whisper-soft promises. "I love you so much. I'm going to make you so happy, going to protect your body and your heart. I'm yours *forever*, and you're mine." With that, his teeth sank into my skin, and once again, I turned my head and bit into my Alpha's bicep. My matching Alphas, who had both haunted my most hopeful dreams and wildest fantasies for so long.

The bond flickered to life, and with it, came an intense male satisfaction, coated in pleasure and happiness. The other bonds flared briefly too, and I felt like a power board running someone's Christmas lights—like I was the center of something beautiful, and without me, it wouldn't quite be the same.

It was a heady feeling, and tears of happiness ran down my cheeks. Strat reached down, scooping up the fat tears with his fingertips. Looking up at him, I worried I might see envy, or sadness, but I didn't need to stress.

The look of absolute adoration reflected back at me made something loosen in my chest.

"Congratulations, sweetheart," he said softly, dipping forward to take my lips. "Soon, it'll be me taking a bite from you, making you mine." He ran a finger across my lower lip. "I've dreamed of putting my claim on that pretty, heart-shaped ass since the moment I watched it walk into my office. But one of us has to hold out, so these Alphas make honest Omegas of us," he whispered to me conspiratorially. "I can't wait to spend the rest of my life with you."

Truett dragged us all down into the nest, and I wrapped myself up in the bodies of my Packmates. As my eyes fluttered closed, exhausted from the strain of the bonds and the insane number of orgasms, there was nothing outside this moment of happiness.

No good. No bad. Just my Pack.

THIRTY-TWO
LANCE

I met Tillie's eyes across the yard, and our new bond pulsed with warm feelings. Desire. Affection. Amusement, which was fitting, since I was currently trying to take photos of the kittens, now that they were old enough to go off to forever homes.

Trying to get a bunch of kittens to sit still long enough to have their photo taken was an impossible task. It should be one of the entrance exams into the police force or something—can you herd cats into cute positions without them attacking each other, or you, or the camera, or a random bug, or even your giant, scary dog?

If the answer is yes, then congrats, here's a badge.

We had to name them all for their photos, because studies showed that named kittens had a better chance of getting adopted than unnamed ones. However, naming six kittens was difficult.

Unfortunately for them, we'd been eating Italian

food when we'd decided on their monikers, so I was currently attempting to photograph Linguine. Carbonara was trying to climb from the basket they were waiting in, but he wasn't the brightest, so I had at least a few more seconds before he absconded. I snapped a bunch of pictures of Linguine, looking up just in time to see Pancetta take off across the lawn.

"Akio, fetch," I instructed the dog. "Gentle."

I didn't even need to tell him to be gentle, because he loved these damn kittens. He picked Pancetta up gently, though he seemed to grab the whole kitten in his mouth. Some of the more boisterous kittens were already getting a little slobbery. He dropped Pancetta back at my feet, the kitten's fur now looking a little crazy with all the dog drool.

Scooping up the outraged kitten, I raised an eyebrow at him. "You brought that on yourself, you little escape artist." I brushed down his fur and stuck him in another, more decorative basket that was being used to photograph them. As I snapped pictures, I knew that Otillie-James was now behind me by the strength of her bond and the way her scent washed over me. Pointing the camera up at her, I took a quick picture of her smiling down at me, her face shadowed by the sun that was like a halo behind her.

She grabbed Carbonara, who'd finally made it out of the basket, and snuggled him close to her chest. "Are you guys being naughty for Lance?"

I took another quick picture. *God, she's beautiful.* I was so fucking lucky.

She sat down beside me, the kitten still in her arms. "You're doing a great job," she praised me softly, which was a lie, but I appreciated it all the same. Most of the pictures were just a blur of fur, because they were incredibly quick for creatures with two-inch legs.

She gently put Carbonara back in the basket and snuggled into my side. I put my arms around her shoulders, holding her close. I didn't need to ask her if she was happy; I could feel it down the bond.

I hadn't bonded with the Alphas yet. There'd be plenty of time for that, and we'd decided it might be less overwhelming if I did one bond at a time. I didn't argue, because having someone else in your head, in your chest, was wild. It wasn't like we could talk through ESP, or anything like that. It was just that I could tell how she felt at all times, unless she actively tried to block it. When Truett had knotted her after claiming her, I'd thought I might pass out from the pleasure that came down the bond.

But it also meant I could feel her simmering worry about that fucker Anthony Smalls, and all those animals that had been at the warehouse. That whole situation was stressing her out, and I *hated* that. It was an oozing wound on our happiness.

Which was why I planned to do something risky and stupid. Because if I knew one thing about Otillie-James in the short time we'd been together, it was that she wouldn't be able to ignore the suffering of those animals for long, and that was when she usually came up with crazy schemes, like rescuing fighting cocks in backwater garages.

Better I carry out the crazy schemes instead.

Strat had talked to some detectives he knew, but he'd said that the warehouse's title wasn't under the rescue foundation's name, or even any personal name we could trace back to Anthony Smalls or his Pack. It was an umbrella company, under a second umbrella company, which told me everything I needed to know about their setup. It was sophisticated, and I wondered what else they were running through there.

I'd reached out to some friends, so we could go and have a slightly closer look. I had pictures of Anthony Smalls there already. If it came down to it, maybe they could find a way to prosecute the Smalls Pack, without all those animals dying while we waited for due process.

Otillie was eyeing me. "What are you up to?"

Wiping my thoughts clear, I looked at her. Man, that was going to take some getting used to. *Distraction time.* "I think I should meet your parents. I bonded with you, and I still haven't met your dad."

Of all the distractions, why did I have to open my big mouth and mention that one? I mean, it was true, but I was nervous as fuck. What if they thought I wasn't worthy of their daughter? I wasn't, but it was too late for that now. Would they think I was trying to ingratiate myself into their Pack for the money?

Otillie's fingers wrapped around mine. "Stop it. They'll love you. I'll invite them around for dinner this week. We'll do it here, on our own turf." She climbed over my lap, her lips brushing mine. "They'll love you, because I love you, Lance Alcott."

I was helpless to resist kissing her back. I kissed her and kissed her until Akio whined, and we drew apart in time to see all the kittens making a break for it across the lawn. Laughing, she climbed off me and chased them down, her sundress fluttering around her thighs.

I hadn't ever thought I was capable of feeling this way; my heart had long ago turned hard and rotten in my chest. But she was out here, proving me wrong yet again.

"I love you too, Otille-James Baler," I called after her, and she looked over her shoulder and smiled at me.

My heart stopped at that moment, and when it restarted, it beat only for her.

I'd been attending my VA group therapy sessions pretty regularly since I'd been discharged. Sometimes, back at the beginning, they'd been the only thing that had kept me going. Kept me from sinking completely into the darkness. I'd made friends—well, acquaintances, at least —and I knew back then that my death would hurt their own recovery processes.

I'd already let enough of my brothers down.

As I walked into the church hall we used for meetings, Rio was already there, standing beside the coffee machine. He was the guy I was the closest to at these things, because his experience had been a lot like mine. Different branches of the military, but the same spec-ops training. Same tragic outcome. His whole team had been taken by the enemy, and he was the only one who'd survived the torture until he'd been extracted.

I was physically fucked, but Rio was mentally scarred in ways I couldn't even understand. How he was still walking around was amazing, and it probably had more than a little to do with Max, his Beta Pack-mate. Max was also fucked up, but neither of them wanted to do anything that would cause the other to spiral. It was a delicate balance that eventually had to tip, and then they'd both be gone. They needed an Omega, and I felt kind of bad hoarding two, but fuck it. They were *mine*.

Besides, there wasn't a realm of reality in which Rio and Max could take care of an Omega yet. If my darkness sat heavy in my bond with Otillie-James, then Rio and Max's would drown an Omega in their pain. They needed to heal a lot more first.

Walking over, I shook Rio's hand, and he reached down to ruffle Akio's fur behind his ears. "How are things?"

I felt the smile on my face, and as much as I tried to wipe it away, I couldn't. Instead, I pulled my shirt down and showed him Otillie-James's claim on my pec.

His eyebrows rose so high, they almost touched his hairline. "The Omega you've been living with bonded you? I thought you didn't want that. Didn't want your pain to affect her."

I hadn't been wrong, but I *had* underestimated the sheer amount of love that Otillie gave me. It chased away the darkness, and when it couldn't disappear anymore, she held the broken parts of me close to her heart and soothed them.

I shrugged at Rio. "She didn't give me much of a choice."

"She claimed you against your will?" Rio's frown was a dark and ominous thing. Everyone wanted an Omega, but consent was still key.

Shaking my head, I instantly defended the woman who was everything to me. "It wasn't against my will. Fuck, I wanted her to bond me more than anything. But I guess she knew I would never get past my own demons, so she barged past them herself."

"So you're happy?" he asked, his eyes still narrowed, like he was convinced I was being body-snatched or coerced or something.

"Happier than I've been in a long time." Or maybe ever. Someone *loved* me. I couldn't remember the last time someone had loved me. But that wasn't the kind of thing you said to another guy at a meeting for people with war-induced PTSD.

He ran his tongue over his teeth. "Good. That's good."

Deciding a subject change was the right idea, I asked,

"Where's Max?" I needed them both here, so I could pitch some illegal activities to them as a team.

Rio lifted his chin at the door, just as Max bustled in. Where Rio was hardened to the point that there was no way you could look at him and think that he was anything but a killer, Max looked like he'd just stepped out of the computer lab and had forgotten his retainer on the school bus. He was in his late twenties, but somehow, he looked sixteen. Like he'd never even seen boobs, let alone bloodshed.

But you'd be wrong. He was a highly qualified naval intelligence officer. He was a fucking spy. Well, a retired spy. He came to these things for Rio, but I sensed he got just as much out of it as his Packmate.

He cooed at Akio as my service dog wandered toward him, wagging his tail like mad at the tall Beta. "How is the most handsome boy here today?"

"I'm fine," I joked. Rolling his eyes, he straightened and fist-bumped me. Dorky, but kinda endearing.

"Now that you aren't pretending to be a yeti, you might almost have a chance against Rio, but Akio has you both beat, sorry."

More people trickled in, and it looked like it was going to be a busy night. I cleared my throat. "I'm glad I caught you both. I was wondering if you might, uh, like to do a little mission with me. Nothing dangerous"—*I hope*—"and you'd be getting a lot of good karma. And I can probably pay you."

Rio narrowed his eyes. "What kind of mission?"

Max raised an eyebrow. "The illegal kind?" he asked in a quiet voice that couldn't be heard outside the three of us.

"Of course it is, or he wouldn't be asking us," Rio muttered with a snort.

I pulled out my phone, showed them the photos, and told them the whole situation. We might be all bathed in blood and suffering, but I knew these guys had joined the military because they wanted to do what was right. And you couldn't look at the miserable faces on those animals and not *know* that what we'd be doing was right, even if it was a legal gray area.

In the end, I knew I had them. But Rio gave me a hard look. "I want to meet her."

I frowned. "Who?"

"Your Omega."

The Beta who lived inside me growled at the Alpha in front of me, making Max chuckle and Akio come to stand in front of my feet. Swallowing down the instant jealousy, I tried to reason with the instincts that wanted to keep Otillie-James locked away and safe forever. I knew these guys; I trusted them.

So I beat back my more primal denial and nodded. "Come around tomorrow for a cookout. I'll introduce you."

Max laughed at me, then he frowned. "Wait, what Omega?"

THIRTY-THREE
OTILLIE-JAMES

When Lance had said he wanted to bring around some VA buddies for a cookout, not going to lie, I went into panic mode. What if they hated me?

I knew most of Truett and Sonny's friends. We'd either grown up together, or they'd come around for Thanksgiving or New Year's parties.

What did I know about army guys? Nothing.

So I experienced what I liked to call an Omega frenzy. I cleaned the house until it sparkled, though Lance followed me around, cleaning as I cleaned. He didn't question why we needed to rewash the windows and the floors. He didn't ask why we were vacuuming in rooms they'd never go in. He just lifted things when I asked, scrubbed things when I scrubbed.

Sonny had finally gone back to work, and the days

were kind of lonely without him. I didn't like another one of my mates being gone all day, but that was just how the world worked, I guess. Being a firefighter was what made him happy, and he couldn't just walk around adoring me all day. I wasn't that high maintenance.

Though, right now, Lance might have argued my low-maintenance claims. The grocery store was quiet, thankfully, as the lunch rush started to die down. I put a sixth type of meat in the cart, along with some carrots.

Lance raised an eyebrow. "You do know we're feeding two men, not the entire United States Army, right?"

"What if they don't like steak?" I put veggie patties in the cart too. *Just in case.*

"Everyone likes steak," he answered.

"Not vegetarians," I shot back, and he sighed.

Wrapping a hand around my arm, he pulled me back until I was against his body. "They aren't vegetarian, Angel. What's really wrong?"

I sighed, wishing I knew. "What if they don't think I'm good enough for you?"

There, right in the middle of the grocery store, the man I'd rarely seen smile before this week, broke out into near-hysterical giggles. He drew stares from people around us, laughing until his cheeks turned pink, his scars pulling tight.

Still chuckling, he hugged me to his chest. "Angel, no one in their right mind is going to think you aren't good enough for me. They might think you're too good for me, but not the other way around, I promise. You're perfect in every way. A shiny beacon of goodness in a world that's full of shitty things and people. The guys will love you." He sighed against my hair. "I'm more worried they'll try and steal you away. Or worse, join the Pack," he mock-growled.

"No way. I'm at capacity for partners, I promise." Kissing his cheek, I squared my shoulders and gripped the cart. "Come on, we better hurry this along." I headed to the charcuterie section, where Lance shook his head at the bougie cheeses I grabbed.

"You know they made us eat mush in the military, right?"

I was in a light blue dress, and the night was warm. I'd done the animal bedtime routine a little early, so no one would be rushing off to do the night feeds, and we could just relax and be casual. Like normal people.

Truett had seemed a little put out about another Alpha coming onto what he considered his territory, which was making him a little grumpier. I kissed him—a lot—and eventually, he chilled out.

Strat came out to the farm too, and it was always nice to spend time with my Omega. Having him here calmed me, and I found myself leaning into him more and more throughout the night.

Sonny turned up to help me cook, and he looked so

fucking sexy in his uniform, I almost undid all my hard work taming my hair to go upstairs and fuck him senseless.

Like the perfect house alarm he was, Doodles began barking like mad, and I went over, redirecting him to the treats I kept on the kitchen counter. "Thank you for the alert, buddy, but no more, okay?"

I had a feeling that Doodles would be a foster fail. He had way too many medical conditions for the average household, and despite being ugly-cute, he did not photograph well. He was old, which meant that if people did adopt him, they'd have him for a few years at most. None of that made him particularly adoptable. It was better that he stayed here, with me, where he could be loved forever.

Trying not to look as nervous as I felt, I breathed out a long sigh as Lance came over and wrapped an arm around my waist. "I love you. That's all that matters. There's nothing anyone could say that'd make me change my mind. You could be a crazy serial killer, and I might still love you anyway," he murmured against my cheek.

I huffed a laugh. That was oddly reassuring.

Giving me one last kiss, he bounded out the door to meet his friends. Truett came up beside me, wrapping his fingers in mine. "Nervous OJ is kind of an anomaly, like seeing the Aurora Borealis from Queens or something."

Nudging his arm with mine, I leaned my head on his shoulder. "I didn't think I'd have this."

"A cookout?"

"No, a Pack. I thought I'd meet a nice Unshown guy, bring him around on the holidays, and try to convince myself that you guys were shit and I wasn't missing out on anything."

Chuckling softly, he kissed me, tilting my chin up so I felt properly claimed. When he eventually drew back, my cheeks felt flushed. "We would've been the ones missing out. And we *definitely* would have run the guy off." He didn't even look remotely remorseful about chasing away my imaginary boyfriend. "Now let's go and greet our guests, yeah?"

We stepped up to the front door just as Lance reappeared. The two men with him weren't what I'd imagined. I'd thought they'd be huge and burly, but the one on the left looked about seventeen, tall but lithe, like he'd never quite grown into his body. The other guy was much more how I pictured a military Alpha: broad shoulders, close-cropped hair, and straight, dark brows that made his expression seem severe. He was still maybe an inch shorter than Lance.

But all three moved with the kind of grace that told me they'd been trained to walk quietly. Stealthy or dead.

I stepped forward, putting my hand out. "Hi, I'm Otillie-James. I'm excited to meet some of Lance's friends."

The Beta smelled like cookies, which matched with his completely innocuous appearance. He was the first one to take my hand. "Hi, I'm Max. Man, Lance didn't tell us how pretty you are." Lance glared, and the guy just grinned, clearly ribbing his friend.

The Alpha put out his hand, shaking mine delicately. "I'm Rio."

I looked up into his eyes, and was immediately swamped by his sadness. I'd thought Lance was traumatized by his time in the military, but whatever had happened to this guy must've been bad. It was tingeing his scent, turning the edges of his citrus scent into something bitter. I couldn't pinpoint how I knew that the darkness inside his soul was eating him alive, but I did.

My face softened, and I gave him a warm smile. "Hello, Rio. Welcome." I drew my hand away as Truett introduced himself, then I waved them inside, through the house and out the back.

Lance caught me around the waist, and I looked up at my wounded Beta mate. "What's wrong?" he asked quietly.

"He's so sad, Lance." It was breaking my heart.

He kissed the top of my head. "I know, Angel. But he's healing. One day, he'll get lucky, and his own angel will appear, but he isn't ready for that yet."

Nodding, I grabbed some appetizers, and Lance carried them outside. Sonny was already grilling, but he'd stopped to introduce himself and Strat to the newcomers. Strat was looking at them with what I liked to call his lawyer gaze, like he was trying to find weaknesses in their facade.

As Lance placed the food down in the middle of the large picnic table, the smell of food dragged over Doodles and Honkers, who stared up at us with big, sad eyes, like they were being starved. No one who ever saw the fat Lab would think he'd been starved a day in his life.

Kevin the Pig had his own stall down in the barn now, so at least that was one less creature watching us eat. He'd been pissed, but he could go out into the run and roll in the mud all day, and that made him happier.

"You fucking cocksucker, give me my money!"

I flushed as Rufio screamed at us through the newly converted screened porch. I'd turned it into an aviary with parrot-proof mesh, and the birds had all been much happier.

Our guests looked around, startled, and I winced. "Sorry, that's one of the rescue parrots. He was found in a crack den."

Laughing, Max walked over to the new aviary. "Holy shit, that's the best thing ever. What kind of parrot?"

"Uh, an African Gray. He has quite the repertoire."

As if he knew we were talking about him, Rufio went off on a tangent. "Who ate the last of the fucking Cheerios? Bitch, shut up. God, you're a noisy fucker. Where's my *money?*"

By the end, Max was laughing so hard, he could hardly breathe. "We had parrots growing up. Mainly cockatoos and macaws, though. Never had an African Gray. And none with his conversational prowess."

I perked up. "Oh, so you know how hard they are to care for, then?"

He nodded. "Yeah. They need a lot of enrichment. Especially the bigger parrots."

I grinned, a plan forming as I led Max back to the picnic table. "Lance said you and Rio are Pack?" Opening the cooler, I offered him a drink. He took a Coke, not a beer. Thank goodness, because he didn't look old enough to drink.

"We do. We have a house on the east side."

I smiled widely. *Perfect.*

Truett chuckled beside us, his lips near my ear. "I know that look."

Kicking him under the table, I continued to ask Max about his life, with Rio adding bits and pieces. By the time the meat was finished being grilled, I realized I knew only a little about Max and Rio, but had somehow told Max everything there was to know about me, from what my mom died of when I was six, to which mechanic I used.

I blinked, pulling back, and stared at the man in front of me. "Holy shit, you're a spy. Or some sort of interrogator." Whistling low, I shook my head. "You're *good*. I'm glad you're on our side."

Lance just laughed, picking me up and setting me on his lap. He nuzzled into the back of my neck, and I relaxed against him.

"He's really good, Lance," I told him, like Max had just performed a magic trick.

"The best."

We sat and ate, the guys reminiscing about boot camp, arguing about which branch had the worst basic training, food, missions, etc. Even Rio finally relaxed, and when Truett and Strat took the plates away, and Lance took Max over to look at the ATVs, it was just Sonny, Rio and I.

Rio looked at me appraisingly. "I was worried, you know."

Sonny tensed slightly beside me, and I rubbed his thigh. "Why is that?"

Rio shrugged. "Lance told me you claimed him without his express permission." I flushed. It was true, and I opened my mouth to apologize, but he lifted his hand to stop me. "But I also know that if you hadn't, he never would've taken that step. He's pretty self-sacrificing like that. I just wanted to make sure you guys weren't using him as some kind of hired help. It happens to Betas a lot more than people think. Some people think that Betas aren't quite as worthy as Alphas and Omegas."

I shook my head vigorously. That wasn't me.

But it was Sonny who came to my defense. "Even if Otillie-James put any credence in the designation system of society—which she doesn't—she fell in love with Lance when she still thought she was Unshown and would never have a Pack. We all love and respect Lance for the man he is."

Rio gave me a small smile. "I know that now. You truly love that surly bastard. Gives me hope that maybe one day an Omega..." He trailed off, like even saying the words would tempt the universe.

I reached over to squeeze his hand. "Definitely one day. When you're ready." I grinned at him. "But first, you need to take care of something else, before you can take care of an Omega. On that note, how do you feel about parrots?"

THIRTY-FOUR

TRUETT

Watching Strat work had always been exciting. Even before we were qualified, watching him do mock trials had been annoyingly riveting. He had presence, and spoke so eloquently, it was hard not to be pulled under his spell.

I could watch him for hours. Unsurprisingly, the jury came back with a guilty verdict within fifteen minutes, because the case had been pretty open and shut.

But that was enough of a reason to take my Omega out to dinner to celebrate. Sonny and OJ were going to meet us at the club afterwards. Lance had opted to stay home; clubs and crowds still weren't his thing, which I could understand.

I was excited to take my Omega out for dinner, just the two of us. We'd all been so caught up in our new bonds with OJ and Lance that Strat hadn't been getting the attention he deserved, but tonight, we'd change that.

We'd all agreed that he'd been working hard, and he deserved to be celebrated.

I stood and walked out of the courtroom, waiting in the halls for him. I saw the defense come out, their faces sour from the loss. *Too bad, too sad.* I'd been on the receiving end of Strat's skills, so I could sympathize a little, but they just needed to be better.

Plus, their client was a scumbag who'd robbed the elderly at knifepoint, causing one to have a heart attack and die. How sad could you be that you lost your case, meaning that trash had to go to jail? The quandary of being a defense attorney, I guess. It was why I'd gone into corporate law.

"I fucking hate going against Wilmington. He shouldn't even be a lawyer," grumbled the defense lead, who I'd never met. "Being a fucking Omega is an unfair advantage. He had the jury eating out of his hands—using his pheromones, probably."

The other defense attorney huffed. "They shouldn't let them into positions of power where they can sway outcomes. Better suited to the kitchen or the nest. Leave the law to the Alphas," he chuckled.

I growled low in my chest. I was going to beat the *shit* out of these fuckers. Especially once I saw Strat behind him, overhearing that toxic bullshit spewing from their mouths. The Alpha lawyers didn't know he was there, as the courthouse was pumped full of de-scenter, but that didn't make it okay. I was going to pound some sense into their heads.

Still growling, I stepped forward, ready to defend the smartest man I'd ever met. I looked past them, and Strat must have predicted what I was about to do, because he was vigorously shaking his head.

For a moment, my Alpha didn't care. This was a man I loved. No one spoke about the person I cared for like that. But logic told me that fighting in a courthouse was a sure way to get reprimanded, maybe even have my license suspended.

So I took in a couple of deep breaths and moved into the path of the defense lawyers. They looked up, and I knew they recognized me. If people didn't know me from the court circuit, they probably knew me from the society pages back when I was younger. I was rich as hell, and Sonny and I had partied pretty hard once upon a time.

"Heathstone, good to see you," Asshole Alpha Number One said, putting his hand out for me to shake. It physically hurt me to take that guy's hand and not rip it off.

"Have we met?"

The guy didn't even look offended by the dismissal in my tone. "August Hilt. I was a year below you in high school. I went into law, because my parents wanted me to be you so bad."

I curled my lip. "I'm sorry. I don't remember you." I raised an eyebrow. "I hope your parents aren't too disappointed. I watched your case in there, and it was lacking at best, and grounds for a professional misconduct case at worst. I hope your client appeals, because he's going to get thirty years due to your incompetence."

I leaned down toward him. "I wouldn't *ever* blame my own failures on someone else's designation. Strat Wilmington is a hundred times the lawyer you are, and I hope you go home, cry yourself to sleep, and pray you develop half of his talent. He didn't win that case because he's an Omega; he won it because he's damn good. It didn't help that you are dangerously useless."

Stepping back, I looked at them like they were both worse than shit on my shoe. I moved around them and over to Strat, who was watching me with an amused expression. Placing a hand on his lower back, I escorted him out of the courthouse and to my car.

As soon as we were inside the vehicle, Strat leaned over and kissed me hard, the embrace filled with a fervent need until I was panting and my cock was straining. When he pulled away, I felt drunk with lust.

He grabbed the front of my shirt. "That wasn't necessary, but you defending me was hot as fuck. Thank you, Truett."

I shrugged like it was nothing, which it was. It was the bare minimum I should do as a human being, let alone his Alpha. "All I told them was the truth."

He flopped back into his own seat, his cheeks a shade of pink that made me want to take him back to my apartment and strip him down. Shaking his head, he gave me a resigned expression. "Their words don't affect me, Truett. I've heard hundreds of versions of the same speech since I was a freshman in college, from my peers, judges, clients. It doesn't bother me anymore."

I hated that. I hated that he just had to grin and bear the disrespect. "I never thought you were using your Omega-ness to win during college. You were fucking good—anyone with half a brain could see that." I started the car. "You kicked my ass fair and square more than half the time."

Pulling out into the traffic, I drove us to the restaurant. It was a little hole-in-the-wall Turkish place that was a hidden gem. The chef was a seventy-year-old Turkish matriarch, who ran that kitchen like a drill sergeant. It helped that most of the other chefs were her sons and grandchildren.

Laughing, Strat put his hand on my thigh. "That's why I had the hugest crush on you. I jerked off to the thought of you more times than was probably healthy. Every time my heat came around, I thought about asking you to see me through it. But you were one of the few who saw me as just another student and not an Omega. I wasn't about to change that just because of my heat."

The idea of anyone else seeing Strat through his heat made my stomach curdle with jealousy. *Never again. Just me and my Pack from now on.*

How different would life have turned out if we'd taken Strat as an Omega back then? "I would've been honored. It wouldn't have altered my respect for you." I laid my hand over his where it rested on my thigh, entwining our fingers. "I can't help but feel like everything worked out how it was supposed to, though. I would've been a shitty Alpha back then, too filled with cocky bravado and absolutely zero skill," I teased. "Now, you can have everything your heart desires, Strat Wilmington, and I'll be right there in the wings, giving you what I can and supporting you to achieve what I can't."

He squeezed my thigh as I pulled up to the parking space out the front of the restaurant. "Everyone says Sonny's the sweet one, but I think deep down, you're a bit of a marshmallow, Truett Heathstone." He lifted my hand to his lips, kissing and then scent marking it. "I can't wait to be your Omega."

We made it to the club before Sonny and OJ, and we were led straight to our table. I was so full from dinner that you wouldn't know I had abs underneath the food baby straining against my shirt buttons. Strat had lost his suit jacket and tie, and had unbuttoned the top three buttons of his dress shirt. How he'd gone from highly paid lawyer to wet dream in the space of a car ride was nothing short of a miracle.

As we walked through the club, people eyed him like they wanted to mount him right there, Alphas and Betas alike, and I had to swallow down my growls. But I did put a possessive arm around his waist.

I was tempted to drag him to the bathrooms, to show him just how much I wanted him, to prove to him that he was mine, to cover him in my scent. We could maybe pretend we'd just arrived once the others got here.

Strat raised an eyebrow. "Stop looking at me like you want to fuck me on this table, or I might take you up on it."

Growling, I lunged across the booth. I'd claim him here, in this writhing mass of people, for everyone to see. *My Omega.* He was laughing, but when I reached over and grabbed his cock, it turned into a moan. Let him see I was serious.

The scent of orange blossoms and gardenias suddenly washed over me. "Stop groping my Omega," OJ whispered in my ear from behind me, saving me from claiming Strat right here in the club. Strat was now looking wide-eyed, his lips parted. Looking over my shoulder to see why, I sucked in a breath.

She looked fucking *beautiful.* She was in a dress I'd certainly never seen before, and if I'd seen her in it before leaving the house, it would have been straight on my bedroom floor. It was a short black bodycon dress that clung to her curves, with long sleeves and a high, straight neckline that brushed her collarbone. It had mesh cutouts, hinting at the curve of her breasts. Her hair was up, so you could see the long curve of her throat.

Glancing down, I realized she was wearing sparkling black Converse, and I smiled. She'd never mastered stilettos. God, I loved her. As she leaned in to kiss me softly, I put my hand on her waist and realized that the dress had absolutely no back.

Just acres of exposed skin.

God, I was going to murder someone tonight. At least her claiming marks were visible, sitting above her shoulder blades like tiny wings.

As she leaned across me to kiss Strat, Sonny slipped in behind her, so she didn't flash the whole damn club her underwear. I gave him a *what the fuck were you thinking?* look.

Years of friendship and a Packbond let me interpret his return expression as *she looked so beautiful, I couldn't say no.*

That was fair. There was very little I'd deny OJ. But man, tonight was going to give me a heart attack. We should have brought Lance. He could have put some Alphas into a sleeper hold or something.

Strat had tugged her over my lap and was nuzzling his face into her neck. Scent marking her, I realized. *Man, why didn't I think of that?*

"Otillie-James, you take my breath away," he growled, his hands running up and down her spine. "I vote we grab a bottle of something top shelf and just go back to my apartment."

She threw her head back with a laugh. "No way. I got all dressed up and did my makeup and everything. We're going to dance."

As Sonny slipped in on the other side of the booth, I groaned. "We're going to need alcohol, and a lot of it." I signaled the bottle girl, who quickly returned with a bottle of tequila and an assortment of mixers. Sonny poured a couple of fingers of straight tequila into our glasses, and I raised mine in toast. "To our brilliant and talented Packmate on winning his case."

"Cheers," everyone chimed, clinking glasses and downing the smooth liquor, all except Sonny, who was on call for work. He was drinking pineapple juice. Poor bastard was going to have to watch our Omegas grind on the dancefloor sober.

OJ looked down at Strat. "Want to dance?"

I was far too full to dance, and my horror at the thought must have shown on my face. Sonny laughed, slapping my shoulder. "Don't worry, True. I've got it." Because there was no way in hell we were going to let our two sexy-as-fuck Omegas go onto the dancefloor by themselves. I didn't trust any other fuckers.

Rightly so, because as soon as they started dancing, moving against each other sinuously, I got hard as a fucking rock, and I'd bet my fortune so did half of the club. The amount of eyes on my Omegas, watching them hungrily, made my skin itch.

I hated that I didn't have my claim on Strat. To anyone who was looking, he was still fair game. They couldn't know he was mine. They were both mine.

I growled low in my chest. *Fuck it.* Standing, I grabbed the bottle of tequila and walked out onto the dancefloor. Didn't want the bottle rats to swipe it from the booth. Stepping up behind Strat, I buried my face in his neck as we moved to the fast-paced beat.

Just like everything he did, Strat was an excellent

dancer. I passed him the bottle, and he took a mouthful, leaning forward and spitting the shot into OJ's mouth.

Fuckkkkkk. I wasn't going to survive.

We continued to dance as one song turned to another and then another. I'd undone my shirt halfway down my chest, and strands of OJ's hair were sticking to her face. The white of Strat's shirt was going see-through in some places.

I couldn't see Strat's face, but OJ's pupils were blown wide, and I could scent her over the de-scenter they pumped into the clubs, so Alphas didn't get frenzied while drinking. I looked up at Sonny and saw we were in agreement. We needed out of this club, and into somewhere that had a big bed.

He suddenly stilled, pulling out his phone and frowning. He flashed it to me, showing the text calling him into work. That sucked, but I guess that meant I got two Omegas all to myself.

Leaning into Strat's body, I whispered in his ear, "Let's get out of here."

THIRTY-FIVE
LANCE

The problem with being a mastermind was that you expected a certain level of intelligence from your underlings. Even if they said all the right things, followed orders, didn't think and just *did*, they were still kind of stupid. You'd have to be kind of stupid to take all the risks for a fraction of the reward.

It was how Rio and I had ended up in a shitty bar, watching Max talk to that redheaded fucker, Joseph Powell, who'd somehow dodged getting charged for the cockfighting incident. Max was plying him with decent liquor, and the guy was gobbling it down greedily.

Unfortunately for him—or maybe unfortunately for Anthony Smalls—he had a loose tongue when he was drunk, and Max was really fucking good at interrogation techniques. I was of the school of thought that we should just take him out the back and beat the truth out of him, but Max had insisted that perhaps that would make the evidence inadmissible.

I wasn't sure what he said while hammered would help either. I sipped at my beer, making enough small talk with Rio that we didn't look suspicious. I kept looking at my phone; Otillie was going clubbing with the rest of the Pack tonight, and she thought I was at my VA meeting. She kept sending me picture updates, and fuck me, she was *gorgeous*.

I'd told her that I was going from the VA meeting back home, because I didn't really like clubbing, but really, I was going to do something a little risky. I mean, it was true that I didn't like clubbing. A mass of people, loud music, flashing lights and smoke machines all fucked with my PTSD more than I'd like to admit to anyone outside of a therapist.

"The fucker can talk," Rio grunted, turning away from glaring at the back of Joseph Powell, who was really getting quite animated. He hadn't realized that Max was wearing a recording device. I assumed it wouldn't even have occurred to Joseph Powell that a random guy at the bar could be anything but that.

I lifted my beer. "Let him talk himself right into a jail cell." Or a shallow grave, depending on what he was spilling over there.

Rio tapped the neck of his beer against mine. "Cheers to that, man."

We both took a deep sip, and I leaned back in my chair, watching everyone else in this bar. It was definitely a dive, and the clientele showed it. But it was out of the main part of town, the beer was cheap, and the music was still from the eighties. I could see the appeal for the old barflies.

Rio's eyes slid to me. "I liked your Omega. She's sweet. I can see why you're smiling so hard these days, and would go to these lengths for her."

I gave him a crooked smile. "She's perfect."

Frowning at me, he pointed a finger in my direction. "I still don't know how we ended up with that fucking parrot, though. Today, he called me a cuntwaffle. Where the *hell* would a bird learn the word cuntwaffle?" I snorted a laugh, and Rio shook his head, looking amused. "But Max loves that damn thing already. Your girl definitely knows how to match her pets. I doubt there are many people who could stand that language outside of former military men. If only she could match me to an Omega that easily."

Otillie had been really subtle about it too. She'd laid the seeds of the idea in Max's mind. Then, she'd equated the care of an Omega with the care of a pet. Before you knew it, when she pitched the idea of the parrot to Max, he was down, and so was Rio, because it was one step closer to his dream of an Omega.

Clever little Omega.

I must have been smiling goofily because Rio snorted an incredulous noise. "So whipped." But then Joseph Powell began wobbling his way to the bathrooms, and

Max was following him down the hall. "I'll go around the back," Rio murmured.

"I'll grab the car."

We both left the bar through the front door, Rio cutting down the alley like a normal man going to take a piss in an inappropriate location. My car was just across the street, and I started it quickly, driving down the alley in time to see Rio and Max rolling Joseph out the emergency exit. Slowing the car enough that they could bundle in the inebriated fall guy, I waited until they were in too, then pulled out of there and back onto a main arterial road as quickly as possible.

Joseph must have sobered up pretty rapidly, because he was beginning to shout, "Who the fuck are you guys? Where are you taking me? You're going to regret this…"

Blah, blah, blah.

I tuned him out, looking over at Max. "Did you get everything?"

He nodded. "It's as bad as you think, maybe worse, but he spilled it all like he had verbal diarrhea. The misappropriated funding grants. The animal fighting rings. Selling them for scientific testing. Every inhumane purpose you can think of, this guy has been providing it. And people were giving him the money and animals to do it."

That son of a bitch. "Is it enough to put him away?"

Max nodded. "Unless the cops bungle it, the Smalls Pack is going away for a long time."

Nodding, I allowed myself a small moment of satisfaction. *Onto phase two of the mission.*

We drove through the darkened streets, and out this way, there were hardly any people. The ones who were here turned the other cheek, because they didn't want to be up in anyone's business. It was perfect, really.

Joseph was getting more and more vocal, and Rio finally snapped, putting him in a sleeper hold and shoving him unceremoniously toward the car window. Max huffed, and Rio shrugged. "What? He was annoying."

Seemed entirely reasonable to me. We pulled around the back of one of the warehouses a few doors up from the Smalls warehouse, and found the truck Rio had stashed there earlier. It was empty, so no one paid much attention to it. Inside were as many animal crates as I'd been able to source on short notice. I was hoping we could appropriate some from inside the warehouse too, but this would have to do for now. We'd figure the rest out later.

Jumping out, Max drove the truck up to the back of the Smalls warehouse. Killing the power to the building, we scanned the place for security cameras, but obviously, no one wanted video evidence of their illegal activities. We dragged Joseph out, stuffing him inside one of the empty crates. One that was still coated in shit and piss, from whatever terrified creature had been in there before.

There must have been a hundred animals in this

place, and Rio whistled. "Fuck. This is worse than I thought."

Max looked downright feral. "Let's get to work. Then I vote we burn this shithole to the ground."

I nodded my agreement. This place didn't deserve to stand after we were done.

We did the dogs first, some of which were so beaten that they were basically shut down. They didn't even look at me as I picked them up and carried them out to the truck. They just trembled as I put them in the cages.

I wanted to kick Joseph around a little, then track down Anthony Smalls and beat the shit out of him too.

There were cats with kittens, battered-looking dogs covered in scars, and dogs so aggressive I wasn't sure they'd even be able to be rehabbed. But at least they wouldn't die in pain, scared and alone. Rabbits, guinea pigs, and even a fucking monkey were in a side room. Plus a whole wall of battered-looking roosters.

By the time we had everything loaded in the back of the truck, and even more in the cargo area of the SUV, I was emotionally battered. There was something about people doing this to innocent creatures for entertainment that made me irrationally angry. I really needed to go home and hug Akio. Then cuddle with my Omega and let her soothe the hurt in my heart right now. I'd killed more people than I could count, and even some animals, during my time in the Marines. But this was fucked, even by my standards.

Rio was holding two puppies with huge paws and

blocky heads, who whimpered and shook, and I could sense the same rage in him. We might have blood on our hands, but at least I was fairly certain we were the good guys. Not whatever fucking evil this was.

"Is that the last of them?" I asked softly, and he nodded. "Good. Get them loaded up. Max and I will finish taking out the trash." I walked over to where Joseph was still in the cage, unable to get out, and I smirked at him. The expression must have been as scary as intended, because he pissed himself. I squatted down in front of him. "I'm going to burn this place down now, Joseph. You'll spend your last moments in fear and pain, just like you wanted for these helpless creatures. I hope God grants you forgiveness, because you'll get none from me."

Nodding at Max, I watched as he got out a can of gas and started to pour it around the building, where the floor met the walls, and over the now-empty cages. He poured a great big puddle right in front of Joseph, who watched it spread underneath his cage.

I looked at Max. "Do you think he'll die from the smoke and flames before he's cooked alive?"

Max shrugged. "I hope not."

Joseph was shaking his bars now. "No, please! *Please!*"

I turned away and walked toward the doors. I wasn't actually going to burn this little weasel alive, but I wanted him to feel real terror before we let him go.

"There's an Omega here! Anthony was getting into

human cattle," Joseph shouted, and my feet stopped dead.

Maybe I'd changed my mind. Maybe I *would* let him cook.

Turning on my heel, I strode back to the cage. "What did you just say?"

He was shaking now. "There's an Omega here in the warehouse. If you let me go, I'll tell you where she is. I'll tell you everything. Please." Joseph was crying now, snot running down his face.

Max growled. "You better start fucking talking, asswipe, or I'm going to beat the truth out of you."

Joseph shook his head. "I didn't want to. I mean, animals are one thing, but Omegas are something else. I like money, but I'm not a psycho, you know? But Anthony got into business with some cult, and they agreed to sell him their Omegas. He was going to farm them out to feral Alphas."

"How many?" Max ground out.

"Just one. She's the prototype." Joseph looked desperate. "I swear, I didn't want to do it."

God, this piece of shit. "Where is she?"

Joseph shook his head. "Let me out first. I promise, I'll leave. I've never seen you guys before. I'll leave the state. The country. The fucking *planet.* Just please, let me go."

I opened the cage, hauling him out and holding the cocksucker high in the air. "You have until I count to five before I snap your neck and search this place myself."

He was now panting, and it smelled like he'd shit himself. "In the main office, under the rug is a trapdoor. She's below us."

I looked at Max. "Go." But he was already running before I'd even finished the syllable.

Joseph was still stammering out excuses and pleas, and I tuned him out. I was tempted to still snap his neck. If I didn't think that it would undo all the hard work I'd done to make myself stable, that it wouldn't affect my bond with Otillie-James, I just might've.

Max reappeared, a girl in his arms. She was wrapped in a blanket, and he nodded at me, striding straight out of the warehouse. His face was a cold mask of fury, and I knew if I didn't let this fucker go right now, Rio would be back in here and would kill him personally. I didn't want that on my friend's conscience either.

I dropped Joseph to the ground. "Leave this city tonight. If I find out you contacted your former boss, I will track you down, cut out your tongue, and then set you on fucking fire. Do I make myself clear?" I leaned forward until I was in his face. "I can and *will* find you if you fuck me over, Joseph. There isn't a rat hole on this fucking planet that I won't trace you to. Do you believe me?" I whispered the threat, and he shook harder.

"Yes."

"Then go, before I decide the world is better off without you in it." He didn't need to be told twice, sprinting out the door and into the night.

I found Rio striding back into the warehouse, incandescent rage on his face, as I'd predicted. "Omegas?" he hissed, and I nodded. Pulling out a Zippo from my pocket, I lit it and threw it behind me. Silently, we watched as the place went up in flames.

Then I climbed back into the truck, Rio and Max climbing into the SUV. As we drove away, that hellhole was lighting up the darkened Rock Hill skyline.

Let the fucker burn.

THIRTY-SIX
EDISON

My whole station had been called in to deal with a fire, and when I arrived and suited up, I heard it was a warehouse fire. The exact address made ice freeze in my veins. It was the same one that Tillie and Lance had scoped out the other day.

Had Anthony Smalls got wind that he was being investigated and decided to burn the evidence? The whole way there in the truck, I steeled myself for what we might find. Charred and injured animals? Fuck, that would devastate Tillie.

But when we arrived, the commander directed us around back. "The warehouse is empty. However, there appears to be cages all along the walls. The first truck on the scene said they were all empty, though, so it's possible that this fire was deliberately lit. I need you to stop it spreading to the other warehouses on the east side of the building."

Then he was gone, and I just stood around, stunned. Someone called my name, and muscle memory kicked in as I treated this as any other fire.

Whatever they'd lit the fire with, it had gotten into the roof and burned across to the empty warehouse beside it. The old wooden structures didn't stand a chance of surviving.

Hours passed as we worked to get it under control, and the sun was lighting the sky by the time we had it smoldering. There was hardly anything left of the original warehouse. The cages that had been in the pictures taken by Lance were melted pools of metal on the concrete floors. Any evidence the cops would find was gone.

Tillie was going to be inconsolable. I wasn't sure how I was going to break this to her, but I needed a shower, and to hug my Omega as soon as possible.

Dez, one of the guys from my station, shook his head as he climbed into the truck beside me. "One of the guys from Station 16 said that when they arrived, the place was filled with cages. What do you think they were keeping in them?"

I shrugged, playing dumb, though I knew exactly what had been in them. "Did the cops find the owners? Maybe they'd be able to shed some light on it."

Shortie up the front made a rude noise. "In a warehouse in the middle of that shithole? No way it was anything legitimate. Puppy mill, maybe?"

I swallowed the growl that wanted to bubble from my lips. I was silent the rest of the way back to the station. A callout this late meant I got the rest of the day off as the day shift came on, and I showered the soot and smoke from my skin, then climbed back into my club clothes. I ignored the wolf whistles from the guys, flipping them the bird as I left.

Looking at my phone, I saw a message from Truett. It was just a head explosion emoji that was our version of a 911 emergency. Shit, had they found out about the warehouse already?

I drove a little faster than necessary, making it home a full fifteen minutes quicker than I should have. And when I walked into the house, I realized that I didn't have to tell them the warehouse had burned.

Instead, I found out why all the cages had been empty.

A wide-eyed Otillie-James appeared, a grimace on her face, like I was going to be disappointed in her or something. "It wasn't me this time, I swear." She was holding a black-and-white rabbit in her arms while puppies ran around her feet.

Stepping toward her, I cuddled her tightly to my chest. "Somehow, this shit always finds you, Otillie-James Baler, and today, I couldn't be happier."

My nose twitched as I picked up a foreign scent.
Was that another Omega?

· · ·

We all sat around the big table, except Tillie and the broken Omega. Her scent was all wrong, almost like spoiled fruit or something. I couldn't explain it, but it upset my Alpha senses. Tillie had taken her to the spare bedroom to get her cleaned up, talking to her quietly, though the strange Omega hadn't said a word to anyone apparently. Not to Max, who'd carried her out of that warehouse, or Lance, or Rio.

The only time she'd looked anything but completely comatose had been when Doodles climbed on her lap and licked at her face. She'd buried her fingers in the weird little dog's wiry fur and kept them there.

Strat looked stressed. We had him wedged between Truett and I, and I placed my hand on his thigh, anchoring him. He needed to be ours, so I could flood our bond with my strength, shoring him up.

"This is a mess, Lance. The animals were one thing, but the girl..."

Yeah, she was a human-sized wrench. She was a victim—that much was clear. But a victim that no one knew what to do with. Did we tell the authorities, so they could shut down her cult? Or would they send her back? Would they investigate the arson more, if there was human trafficking involved, and would it lead back to us? Would being interrogated by the cops make the girl even more comatose? So many fucking questions, with no good answers.

"We handle it in-house," Rio grunted. "We give the girl the choice, wait until she's in a better headspace to give us more intel, and then I'm going to put down the fuckers who think they can sell Omegas like cattle." He stared at us, and I could see the trained killer in his demeanor. "Sometimes justice doesn't involve lawyers and courtrooms and police reports. Sometimes it needs to be a lot more final."

Strat shook his head, lifting his hands. "I don't want to know any more. Do whatever you like, but unless there's a complaint made by the girl, or any evidence that it happened, then as far as the law is concerned, Anthony Smalls was only peddling live animals." He looked at Lance. "Send the recording to the news outlets. To the gossip rags. Social media influencers. I want that bastard's face on the front of every damn paper, and his name on every newsreader's lips by the end of the day. The cops will be *forced* to investigate. If nothing else comes of it, he'll be ruined."

Max pulled out a laptop and went to work. Twenty-four hours would bring that man to his knees, by forces he'd never even met. I hoped he lay in his jail cell at night and wondered where he'd gone wrong.

He'd never know that it was one girl trying to rescue a half-dead rooster who'd brought him down.

"What do we do about all the animals? And the Omega?" Truett asked, and I blew out a breath. That was the real question. There was no way we could hide it from the neighbors. That many animals made a lot of noise.

Strat flicked through his phone. "I took the liberty of

registering this address as a rescue when you first moved out here. I called it 'Matthew's Haven,'" he told Lance, whose face blanched. "I didn't know Otillie-James would be staying at that point, or that you would bond, so feel free to change the name. But I figured that your CO had given you this place as a refuge, and you'd done the same for Otillie." He swallowed hard. "Sorry if I overstepped."

Lance stood, coming around the table to Strat and pulling him from between us. Dragging our Omega to his feet, Lance hugged him tightly to his chest. He clung to him, and when Strat lifted his arms and wrapped them around our Beta, I knew they both needed it.

Pulling back, Lance scrubbed at his face. "Thank you. It's perfect. Matt would have loved it." I could see his eyes were shiny, though he was blinking back the moisture. "So we have a legal reason to have this influx of animals. If anyone asks, we've had them for a while."

We'd have to add some more cages, some temporary housing, maybe a few dog runs, but it was doable. "And the girl?"

Silence sat heavily in the room, until finally, Max stood. "She can come home with us. We have the space."

Lance gave him an incredulous look. "I'm not sending her home with two unknown Alphas. She stays here."

Rio growled. "What are you insinuating?"

They all started arguing, but I saw Otillie-James reentering the room, the girl in question behind her. She wore one of Tillie's knitted caps pulled down low over her head. When I'd arrived, she'd been wearing a lace covering over her head, almost like a wedding veil, but in black. Now, I realized that her head was completely bald.

Tillie cleared her throat. "How about we let Paloma decide for herself? I think she's probably had enough of Alphas telling her what to do to last her a lifetime."

Paloma's eyes darted around the room. She didn't look like a mannequin now, less frozen and afraid. No, that was a lie. She still looked terrified, but like a rabbit surrounded by wolves.

She leaned close to Tillie and whispered something in her ear. Both of Tillie's eyebrows went up, but she nodded. "She insinuated that her Omega doesn't like being around two other Omegas, and she wishes to go home with Max and Rio." Paloma leaned in and whispered something else. "Also, she'd like it if Doodles could come too."

Max nodded. "Of course."

Lance glared between the two outsiders in the room. "She's treated with the utmost respect. Her wishes are final. Or I will fuck you both up; I don't care how well trained you are," he growled, doing a pretty good imitation of an Alpha. In a different world, he would definitely have been one.

As Rio and Max left, Paloma in the back seat of Sonny's borrowed SUV with some of Tillie's clothes and Doodles on her lap, we were back to square one with all the animals. It was going to be a long day before I could fall into the nest with my Omega.

"How many?"

Tillie winced. "Sixty-three."

Truett sighed. "Let's get to it."

THIRTY-SEVEN
OTILLIE-JAMES

Exhaustion pulled at my eyelids, dragging them down. It felt like almost too much effort to lift them again. It had been hard work, but we'd managed to build temporary housing for all sixty-odd animals.

Truett had gone into the city to get an insane amount of dog beds, cat igloos, rodent hides, and anything else I could think of. Sonny had gone to get fencing and food from the tractor supply store. We were a well-oiled machine, and it would have been amazing, if it hadn't been so fucking sad.

Rex and Anakie were here now, casting me worried looks, and I didn't know how much to tell them. I didn't think they'd out us to the cops, but I also didn't want to have to put them in the position where they'd have to lie to the authorities.

Some of the animals had been too far gone, even for

me. There were animals who were angry and in pain from broken bones that hadn't healed properly, and who were so brutalized that they snapped at any human contact.

It had been so hard to watch those ones be humanely put to sleep, their short lives knowing nothing but anger and pain, but prolonging their fear would have been selfish of me. Anakie said as much as she rubbed my back, and I knew she was right. Didn't make it hurt any less.

Of the twenty-seven dogs we'd rescued, four had to be put down. Seven would need intensive work to make them adoptable. The rest were just scared and sad, and abundant food and water cheered them up in a way that made me cry, yet again.

The cats were much the same, though I found that if I housed some of them together, they found comfort in each other. Only two had injuries too severe for rehabilitation. Lance had dug a burial hole in the woods behind the house for those poor souls. I'd cried as we buried them all and hoped their next life was filled with peace.

That just left the roosters, who were happy roaming around the farm itself. With plenty of space and food, there hadn't even been that many fights.

The monkey was a fucking trip, though. A little capuchin, I had no freaking idea what to do with a monkey, so Rex and Anakie were going to take that one home with them to be sent to a primate rescue over in Virginia.

Everything was settled, but the work still to be done was astronomical. First, I had to get through today. Anakie and I finished splitting the rabbits and guinea pigs into boy enclosures and girl enclosures, so we didn't end up with significantly more rodents.

"Are you okay, Otillie?"

I shook my head. No, I definitely wasn't okay. "Nope."

"Where did these all come from? I swear on my Pack, I won't tell a soul."

I looked at my longtime friend. I believed her. "Watch the news tonight. But don't ask *how* I ended up with the animals. Just know that I did."

Shaking her head, she scratched a rabbit behind its floppy ears before putting it in the appropriate pen. "Okay, Omega of Mystery. Just know we're here if you need anything. You've never rescued on this scale before, and it's hard work. Give it a few days, but you might need to try and get a few of these fostered out. There's no shame in needing help; I know you know that." Her voice was stern, but I nodded. I knew my limitations, and we were nearly at capacity.

Finally, after we'd done health checks on all the animals, Rex and Anakie left, with a monkey in tow. *A freaking monkey.* That shit was wild.

Akio nudged at my legs, and I reached down to pat his head. "This is a lot, hey buddy? I'm going to need your help over the next few weeks." I stretched and yawned, and then Lance was there, wrapping his arms around my ribs, breathing me in like I was the only thing keeping him going.

"Are you mad at me, Angel?" he whispered against my hair.

I was shaking my head before he'd even finished. "No. Rescuing sixty animals without the infrastructure to house them is like the front page of the Otillie-James Baler playbook. I'm almost proud," I teased. Turning in his arms, I tilted my head back to kiss him, a tingling kiss that I felt to my toes. "You did the right thing. I'm a little pissed you didn't tell me you were planning to do it—and kind of worried that something might go wrong, and you'll be in trouble—but I can't be mad that you saved all these lives."

He didn't make excuses, or give me false platitudes, and that's what I loved about Lance. My Lancelot. My White Knight. He didn't treat me with kid gloves just because I was a woman, or an Omega, or younger than him.

Gripping his hand, I dragged him back toward the house. "I'm about to fall asleep. You need a shower and then we all need to climb into my nest and sleep. I need you all with me tonight."

"All day," he corrected. He was right. It was like midday. I'd been awake way too long.

Stumbling into the house, I could smell that someone was cooking, and my mouth watered. Strat was there in sweats and no shirt, freshly showered, sliding grilled cheese from the frying pan and onto a plate. Lance kissed my temple, then wandered into the downstairs bathroom to shower.

I walked over, kissing Strat's shoulder. It was the place where I was going to claim him as mine one day. He leaned his head back against mine. "Baby, you must be exhausted. Have some grilled cheese and soup, then I'll take you to bed."

Pressing my nose between his shoulder blades, I breathed in his calming champagne scent and sighed with happiness. "Thank you for taking care of me."

Turning off the stove, he spun in my arms, wrapping his own around my shoulders. "Always. Until the end of time, Otillie-James Baler." Grabbing me around the waist, he lifted me onto the countertop and stood between my thighs. "Now, eat some grilled cheese so you can go to bed, because you look like you're about to drop."

He lifted it to my mouth, and I dutifully took a bite. God, he was so beautiful. He stole my breath, and I didn't think I wanted him to give it back. I wanted to stay gasping for air until he filled me back up with his lips.

I chewed, my eyes still wandering all over his face. "I love you. You know that, right?" I told him after I swallowed. "You mean so much to me. None of this would have been possible without you."

He pressed closer between my thighs. "I love you too." He nuzzled his cheek against mine.

"Be mine?" I breathed. I slid my lips down the long

column of his throat. The urge to bite him, to claim him, was strong.

He chuckled. "I already am. I don't need a claiming bite to promise you that." I pouted, and he caught my jutting lower lip with his teeth. "Soon, baby. When you aren't bone tired. Once everything is settled, we'll make it official, I promise."

When he lifted me from the countertop, I wrapped my legs around his waist and clung on tight as he carried me upstairs to our nest. And when he laid me down in the blankets, my eyes were closed, and I was asleep before my head even hit the pillow.

My phone was blowing up. The rescue world was small, but the reality TV world was huge. When news outlets played clips of Anthony Smalls and the audio recordings of Joseph Powell confessing, it was pretty damning.

We were all sitting around the television, watching cops raid the Smalls Packhouse, the ASPCA removing all the animals from his care, the members of the Smalls Pack being put in the back of police cars. The network that ran his reality show dropped him immediately in a scathing press release, distancing themselves from the scandal, and I felt content.

This was the justice Spartacus deserved.

Former employees were coming out of the woodwork to discuss the unethical processes of the Smalls farm, breaking NDAs everywhere. The downfall of *All Crea-*

tures Great and Smalls was quick and brutal and just what I wanted.

The message from Anakie only said two words. "Holy. Fuck." But she didn't ask any more questions than that. That was what I loved about Anakie.

I'd checked on Paloma earlier, though Max had to hold the phone, because Polly—that's what she wanted to be called now—hadn't ever seen a cellphone before. She wasn't convinced it wouldn't explode. Max had said that she felt that way about a lot of technology, and whatever cult she'd come from had been extremely secular, but not anti-tech. She'd never seen a television before, but had seen a Keurig. She couldn't point to where she was from on a map, but could name every country in the world alphabetically, and rank them by their crime rate.

Whatever her cult was, they'd purposefully kept them blind to the world around them and the idea of what normal was supposed to look like. They'd also kept them terrified of the outside world. Max said she spent most of her days in her bedroom with Doodles the dog, and if she had to go anywhere with a crowd, she would have a panic attack. Especially without the veil that covered her shaved head.

Whatever else her elders in that cult had taught her, it was that her hair was only for her Alpha's enjoyment. Until she was bonded, she had to keep it shaved smooth.

I hoped those bastards got what was coming to them. Lance had told me not to worry about it, that Rio and

Max would take care of it. I had a feeling he meant in the most bloody way possible.

I laid back against Truett's chest and breathed a sigh of relief. It was done. I wasn't stupid enough to think that someone else wouldn't pop up in their place, but I'd done *something*.

"So that's that." Sonny said, Strat's head on his lap as he stroked his hair. "Any other evil empires we need to bring down, or is it just back to normal from now on?"

I raised an eyebrow at him. "Have you met me?"

Laughing, Truett leaned down and kissed my temple. "Yep. It was the best day of my life."

Epilogue
Strat

Six Months Later

Ottilie-James looked beautiful. Dressed in a long white gown, trimmed in Irish lace, she looked like a vision. We stood inside the house, with her clinging to my hand. Her face was lit up with happiness, and I wasn't sure she'd ever looked more beautiful.

She smiled at me, squeezing my palm softly. "Are you ready for this?" she whispered.

I nodded. "I've waited my whole life for this moment. I'm more than ready."

She grinned. "Have I said you look gorgeous?" she asked, softly, waiting for our cue to go.

"Only like twenty times in the last hour," I teased, and she leaned over and kissed me. She was wearing high heels, which could have been part of the reason she was clinging to me so tightly.

"Consider this the twenty-first. You're the most beautiful man I've ever met, Strat Wilmington. Both inside and out. I'm so glad you're here beside me today."

"Today, tomorrow, and every day after," I promised, our own secret vows right here in the living room of the Packhouse.

My sister, Elizabeth, poked her head in. "Okay, lovebirds, it's time. I'm going to take my seat, so give it thirty seconds."

Elizabeth had been a lifesaver when it came to our commitment ceremony planning. She'd flown over from California a week ago to do the last-minute organizing, and I loved her for it. I blew her a kiss, and she rolled her eyes, but still grabbed it and stuffed it in her imaginary pocket.

Stepping out onto the back patio, I held Otillie-James tightly to my side. On the back lawn were all our friends and family, spread out to see our claiming ceremony. There were animals everywhere, rabbits chewing on the lawn, and goats with large bows on their necks eating the plants beside the deck. Honkers lay in the sun in the front row, though he was much trimmer than he'd been when I first met him. All the extra dogs to run around with had really made him lose weight.

Akio sat at our feet, the rings tied to a pillow around his neck. Otillie-James squatted down in her dress, uncaring that she was precariously balanced on her heels already. "You ready, boy?" she whispered. "Go to Lance." Akio trotted off down the aisle to the collective *awww* of the crowd.

Helping her back to her feet, I wrapped her arm in mine. We followed Akio down the aisle, between the two groups of people who'd come to help us celebrate our love. No one seemed perturbed by the fact there were two Omegas, except maybe my parents. They had their noses screwed up, either at the outdoor wedding, or the animals, or Otillie-James. I really didn't care. If I never saw them again after today, I wouldn't lose sleep over it.

I had my family now, and they were about to declare their love for me, in sickness and health, for better or for worse.

Truett, Sonny, and Lance stood at the end of the aisle. The officiant was there in the background, under the arbor that Lance had built with his own hands. Our Pack looked at us like we were everything they'd dreamed of and more.

I'd been worried that I might get lost in the shadow of their love for Otillie-James, but I'd been so wrong. Every day, they showed me how much they loved me individually, and how much they loved us together. Sonny and Truett showed me every night how much they desired me, and I'd been late for work many a morning because we'd decided to "be economical with the water usage" and shower together.

Lance and I had a solid friendship, and I knew I could rely on him to be at my back if I needed him. Plus, he was a surprisingly happy snuggler. He said our love was a bromance, and I was happy with that.

Then it came to the woman beside me. She was all of that and more. Worth every moment of doubt, worry, and confusion to make it to this point.

We stopped in front of the guys, our hands still tightly entwined. "Omegas," Truett breathed, a world of reverence in that word. Sonny looked like he was fighting back tears, which made Otillie-James give him a watery grin. Lance just beamed, a smile so wide that it pulled at the scars on his face. He was completely clean-shaven today, and so fucking handsome, I was a little jealous he didn't swing my way even a smidge.

The officiant cleared his throat. "Let's get started, shall we?" he asked softly, and I nodded. I was ready to be part of the Chalmers Pack. "Friends and family, we are here to witness true love in its most purest of forms..."

The party had been going for hours, the drinks flowing as our reception continued late into the night. Elizabeth and her partner had relaxed once our parents left, and they were dancing with my new Omega. Otillie-James was laughing, her hair beginning to come out of the multitude of pins that kept the curls trapped like a halo around her head. Her parents had left an hour ago, citing that they were too old for partying, but they'd been so happy for us, it made up for the disdain of my own folks.

Lance stood beside me, our shoulders touching as

Truett and Sonny did the rounds. "She's beautiful today," he murmured. "I mean, she's beautiful every day, but..."

I patted his back. "I know."

He smirked at me. "You look amazing too. Truett had to adjust himself like crazy as you two walked down the aisle together. We're all counting down the minutes until everyone leaves."

Laughing, I shook my head. The party was winding down, but the day had been so perfect. Though I wasn't going to lie and say I wasn't anxious for my bonding bites.

We would all be claimed today, our Packbonds completed. Lance would get bond marks from the Alphas, and I would get claiming bites from everyone. I was ready, more than ready. My Omega had been grumpy about being on the outside for months, but I wanted it to be perfect for me, for Otillie, for the Alphas.

And it was.

It was another hour before the bulk of people started to leave, and one look at Sonny told me he was ready to forcibly bounce everyone off the property. He strode toward me and kissed me possessively. "My mate, how are you feeling?"

I whimpered at the old-school wording, my Omega's pleasure washing over me. "Ready to be in my nest with my Pack," I whispered against his lips.

He looked over at Truett and Lance. He made a quick hand gesture, then he picked me up. It wasn't an easy feat; I wasn't a tiny Otillie-James. I was built more like a Beta than an Omega. But he carried me into the house and up the stairs like it was nothing. I purred against his chest, letting myself go completely to my Omega instincts.

I could hear the pounding of feet up the stairs, which meant the rest of my Pack wasn't far behind me. I could hear the soft giggle of Otillie-James, followed by the deep rumble of Lance's voice.

Sonny walked into the middle of my perfect nest, laying me down gently. "My handsome Omega. Mine," he growled, and I knew his Alpha was riding him just as hard as my Omega was riding me. "Going to claim you tonight. Make you mine, body and soul."

"Yes," I breathed and pushed myself up to kiss him. He tugged off my bowtie, before moving down to deftly unbutton my shirt as his lips traced over mine.

Someone cleared their throat, and I lifted my head. "Did you two start without us?" Truett demanded lightly, but his eyes were filled with burning heat. "Rude, but that's okay. We have all night to catch up."

He was watching me with an almost predatory gaze. I met his eyes and licked my lips, watching his pupils dilate. Behind him, Lance was slowly unwrapping our Omega with the kind of reverence that people reserved for their idols.

We all stopped, watching as her ceremony gown slipped down her body and pooled at her feet, leaving her in an ice-blue lace underwear set that matched my suit pants. *Sexy little Omega.*

The pheromones in the room ratcheted up to ten, making my dick hard and begin to leak precum. Fuck, if we weren't careful, the amount of lust in this room would push me into preheat.

Sonny continued undressing me. "Do you see our Omega? Isn't she beautiful?" I breathed my agreement, but he was tracing his lips over the skin he was exposing with deft hands. "When you walked down the aisle together..." He grunted with pleasure. "It took everything in me not to pick you both up and drag you up here, claim you. You were so fucking handsome." He unzipped my suit pants, dragging them down my thighs. "Just mine."

He kissed my hip bone, then dragged my boxer shorts down my thighs too, letting my cock spring free. I kicked my pants free, and when he wrapped his lips around my dick, I thought I'd die of pleasure.

Holy shit. He hummed around my cock, and my eyes rolled back in my head.

Someone knelt beside my head. "Open your eyes, Omega," Truett purred, though the authority in his voice was almost undeniable. I pried them open, and he was there, leaning over my face. He kissed me softly, filled with love, and I wondered what freshman, newly designated Omega me would've thought about us Packing up with the hot Alpha we saw across the room. "I love you, Strat Chalmers."

"I love you too," I panted back as Sonny seemed to try and suck my soul out through my cock.

"Good boy. Now eat out your Omega, before she cracks and claims you right now."

I looked past him to Otillie-James who was now entirely naked, her slick dripping down her thighs. I groaned with pleasure, bucking up into Sonny's mouth. I made grabby hands, and she stepped close enough that I could grab her and drag her to her knees.

"Ride my face, baby," I murmured. She must've also been caught up in the pheromones, because she didn't hesitate for a single moment, throwing her leg over my face and sliding that hot little cleft over my face.

"Fuck me," someone breathed, but it was muffled by her thighs over my ears. This was heaven. It was almost too much, and when Otillie came all over my cheeks, someone plucked her from my face so I could breathe. Honestly, I would have been so happy to die in that moment, happiness like I'd never known surrounding me.

I was so close when Sonny pulled off my cock, dragging me to my knees. "You almost ready, Omega? Ready to be ours?" Our dicks rubbed against each other, and I felt Truett come up behind me, lining his lubed cock up with my slick hole.

"All together?" he asked, and I nodded. I looked around for Otillie, for Lance. Otillie moved in close to Sonny, so they were both in front of me. She leaned close, licking my nipple, making me groan.

I held out a hand to Lance, and he grinned down at me. "Love you, man." He winked at me, and I almost laughed. He placed his wrist to my lips, and I licked the flesh, right next to his pulse point. That was where I would put my claim. In the spot where his claim was on Otillie-James.

And as Truett slid inside me, I moaned, and as one, they all bit down. The snap of four bonds made my thighs go weak, but I was held up by my bondmates. By my Pack.

That's how it would be forever now, my soul tied to theirs. I wouldn't want it any other way.

My life was perfect, and it was all because of a wild Unshown girl with a cock in her hoodie, on the bad side of town, who couldn't outrun the cops. I made a mental note to give Spartacus a slice of wedding cake. I owed that damn rooster my life.

ABOUT THE AUTHOR

Grace McGinty is eclectic. She has worked as a chocolatier, a librarian, a forensic accountant, and finally, a writer. Like her professional career, the genres she writes are chaotic and out of control. From contemporary new adult to smutty reverse harem novels of every sub-genre, if you like it, she's probably written it.

Except dark romance. She's a marshmallow, and somehow the mean guys always end up cinnamon rolls.

Grace lives in rural Australia with her crazy family, an entire menagerie of pets, and will one day be crushed by the giant piles of books that litter every room.

Head over to www.gracemcginty.com and join the mailing list for sneak previews into what she is working on and to stay up-to-date with new releases and giveaways!

Like your omegaverse a little wilder? Check out a preview of Manix over the page.

Manix
Chapter One

Gatlin

This parking lot smelled overwhelmingly of vomit and dried bodily fluids. How the outdoors, with all this fresh mountain air, could have such overwhelming scents was truly a miracle of nature. The crumbling building, lit only with flashing neon signs, sat in the center of a lot filled with pickup trucks. To the left of my group, a couple were fucking down a side alley and the male sounded like a boar with a hot poker up its ass.

I realized why it smelled so much like puke when I stepped into a small puddle of it, and it splashed up onto the laces of my boots. Humans were fucking disgusting sometimes. I lifted my hand to motion us forward and we walked into the club, which was devoid of security at the front door.

The establishment vibrated with too much bass, like

a tribal drumbeat, and it had whipped the crowd into a frenzy. The smell of sweat and lust permeated every corner, and we tightened our formation around Raiden.

The distressed scent of an unfamiliar Omega had me growling low under my breath, and the humans who lingered too close quickly moved away. Not because they could hear the growl, but because they could feel the coiled violence that rolled off my Pack.

Finlo stepped closer to me, leaning in to be heard over the ear-shattering noise of the music. "Are we sure this is the place? Perhaps Seven's nose is broken?" the other Alpha asked.

Seven scowled, baring his teeth at Finlo. Seven was a Beta, but he was a strong Beta. Too strong. It was a generally held belief that a strong Beta would resist orders and cause problems. And it was true, Seven did cause issues at times, especially when given orders. But our Pack weren't hardcore traditionalists when it came to hierarchies. I treated Seven the way I'd treat any other Alpha—hell, any other Manix—with respect and understanding. In return, Seven was grateful to even have a Pack, even if it was one filled with misfits. He was loyal and loved, and that was worth something too.

"My nose didn't lie. There is an Omega here, one that is close to heat."

Ellar hovered over Raiden, practically glued to his side. "I trust Seven's tracking. His nose is his best trait. Goddess knows, it isn't his winning personality," he joked, making Raiden chuckle. Unlike Seven, the family's other Beta was like me. A half-blood Manix. He'd had no other choice than to join us, because no one else would muddy their bloodlines with a half-caste.

This was us. A tiny, ill-formed Pack, except for our one crowning jewel—our Omega.

One of the last male Omegas left, he'd chosen us to be his mates. When an Omega comes of age, he is allowed to choose which Pack he joins. No one had been more shocked than us when he'd chosen ours. Until Raiden, we'd been a rag-tag bunch of mutts on the outskirts of Manix society.

I looked over my shoulder at Raiden, whose soft expression met mine. Just a look from him shored up my resolve. Although our natural instincts wanted to protect and coddle Raiden, he was a warrior in his own right. Maybe that's why he picked us. He didn't want to be pampered and adored. He wanted to fight and fuck, which was wildly un-Omega like. Despite the fact that I *knew* he could defend himself against humans, my Alpha instincts insisted that he be protected at all times. He was the heart of our Pack after all.

I scanned the crowd, but the overwhelming conflicting scents muddled everything. "We'll split up. Raiden will come with me. Trust Seven's nose," I warned Finlo.

Finlo was my childhood best friend, and had chosen to build a Pack with me rather than join one of the more prestigious warrior Packs more suited to his bloodlines. I owed him everything.

He nodded and split off, the two Betas following behind him. I tucked Raiden closer to me as we waded further into the club. There were stages dotted around the room, each lit up with a different color. Blue, red, purple. On each stage, a woman danced, spinning around a pole. I'd been born in human society, raised here until I was eleven, and I knew what a strip club was. But Raiden didn't, and his eyes almost bulged out of his head. He shook his head at me as he grinned.

"My sire was right, the only place you could take me is into the gutter," he teased.

Yeah, not everyone had been overjoyed that Raiden had chosen my Pack. I nudged his shoulder with mine, despite the fact that I wanted to reach out and place a kiss on his temple. "Admit it, you like being dirty down here in the gutter with me."

He laughed, reaching down to squeeze my hand as we parted the crowd. "Wouldn't be anywhere else."

We were getting a few weird looks, and that was another reason we needed to split up. Together, we seemed inhuman. Ridiculously tall and broad, we looked like the warrior race we'd once been, before we were killed off and forced to flee to the mountains of Montana, forever separate until we were slowly dying out for other reasons.

Manix. We were the real reason the word manic entered the English language. It was the way early humans described the rut, where we thirsted for blood or sex, and wreaked havoc. But now there were barely two thousand of us left. Of that, there were less than a hundred full-blooded female Manix. Only twenty-five Omegas, but none of those were female.

We were dying out at a rapid rate. Which is why when Seven said he'd scented an Omega female on the wind, we'd come on this wild goose chase. I was happy to chase a wild goose if it gave my Pack a chance at a real future.

I stayed at Raiden's back, my eyes trawling in front of us for threats. "Scent anything?" I asked, despite the fact it galled me. I was half-blood, the result of a Manix male and a human female. Mating with humans was frowned upon, and according to the Manix Legion, little better than lying with a beast. As a result, I was little better than an animal to the upper crust of Manix society.

I pushed down the residual rage I felt toward the Legion and searched the crowd. Raiden tilted his head, his pupils blowing out wide. "That way," he said softly, his feet taking him in the right direction before he'd even lifted his arm. If I'd had any doubt about Seven's nose, it disappeared at that moment. I kept my hand on Raiden's belt as he moved through the crowd with single-minded focus. He might have been the smallest of us, but he was still over six feet in height, tall in comparison to a human.

He stopped in front of a small platform, bathed in blue light so it appeared like it was in the depths of the sea. Raiden's eyes went wide and his knees nearly buckled as he looked up at the girl on the stage. Finally, her scent permeated my duller senses.

And when I scented her? My dick went rock hard.

She danced in heels that had to be six inches high, her movements easy as her body swayed to the music. She kept her eyes closed, like she could block out the world if she just deprived herself of the sight of these salivating humans.

She was small, tiny in comparison to a Manix female. Her body curved sharply though, her figure like an hour-glass of old. Given the overwhelming smell of lust that hung like a cloud around us, she had a body that men would bankrupt themselves to have just a touch.

Wearing basically nothing, her scent was like a caress, followed by a slap to the face. I could feel the Omega presence, scent her oncoming heat cycle. I cast a worried look at Raiden, whose whole body was taut with the urge to rut.

Breeding in Manix society had historically occurred in one of two ways. A female could be impregnated by a single Manix male, and would usually give birth to a solitary offspring. Or, a female and male Omega could mate during a heat cycle, and the male Omega would draw the viable eggs into himself. Afterwards, the pack would lie together during the rut and all the eggs had a chance to be fertilized. It was animalistic, feral sex that would leave the entire Pack drained and weak.

This is why the heat in a female would send us all into an insane rut, but especially Raiden, as our Pack Omega.

I noticed my Packmates on the other side of the stage,

also looking up at her like she was a gift from the Goddess. She was definitely the one, and I would make her ours. Raiden was all but shaking with need, and I moved him toward the back wall so we could watch her and be obscured by the shadows a little more.

Her hips swayed with exaggeration to the music. She hooked her leg around the shiny metal pole in the center of the stage, swinging in a slow loop, her left foot barely scraping along the floor. Her breasts were barely contained in a tiny little bikini which matched the barely-there thong that both covered her intimate flesh and attracted the gaze of the audience to it.

As I searched the crowd, watching the hungry eyes of the humans, smelling their lust and violence, my Beast rose up in my chest. They were looking at what was mine, or at least, what would be mine. I looked at the red lever beside me, secure behind its safety glass from accidental knocks. The fire alarm.

Looking over at Finlo, I lifted my chin toward the girl. Finlo would know what to do. He nodded back, so I pushed through the safety glass and pressed the fire alarm. Within seconds, there was a loud whooping noise that blared across the music, the interior fire sprinklers opening the metaphorical heavens.

Panic ensued, and there was a mass exit for the door, people pushing and shoving as they nearly trampled others to make their escape from nothing. As people turned and fled, the girl jumped off the stage, but Finlo moved incredibly fast. He gathered her up into his arms and walked out the rear exit, the girl over his shoulder, Seven and Ellar at his back.

Raiden whined as he lost sight of the other Omega, and we moved with the tail end of the panicked exodus. The rest of our Pack would get her where we needed her to be. I would just take care of Raiden.

An Omega pair... Could we really be that lucky? Raiden whined low under his breath, his hand gripping mine. "She's close, Gat. So damn close. Maybe a week? It's making my skin itch."

Female Omegas had been the first thing to die out. There were no Omega pairs left. Back when they'd found out the Omega females were dying out, we'd tried the Omegas of different species, but while they might be hierarchically the same, they weren't physiologically similar enough for there to be an Omega bonding. That had led to an uprising against us by shifters, because the Manix of the past didn't exactly ask for the Omegas nicely, which drove us further into the Mountains, isolating us even more.

It had been a bleak time in our history. Because we weren't like shifters, or other supernaturals. We were different completely, an entirely different genus. That was why the girl we'd just pulled off the stage was such a miracle, a true gift from the Goddess.

She was going to save our Pack, and then maybe, our species. But first, we had to get her to like us.